Stalking the Unicorn

"You're drunk," said the elf disgustedly.

"Of course I'm drunk," replied John Justin Mallory, who just noticed the little green elf standing in front of his desk. "That's why I'm seeing little green men. The important question is: Who are you and what, pray tell, are you doing in my office?"

"I have a job for you, Mallory," answered the elf Mürgenstürm. "Please believe me when I tell you I wouldn't be here if it wasn't a matter of life and death. Something that was entrusted to me is missing, and unless I recover it before morning my life is forfeit."

Mallory stared at the elf for a long time. "And what might this treasure be?"

The elf returned Mallory's stare. "I don't think you're ready for this yet, John Justin."

"How the hell can I find something if I don't even know what I'm looking for?" demanded Mallory. The elf Mürgenstürm sighed, and then blurted it out.

"It's a unicorn."

Also in Arrow by Mike Resnick

SANTIAGO

STALKING THE UNICORN

A Fable of Tonight

Mike Resnick

ARROW BOOKS

Arrow Books Limited
62-65 Chandos Place, London WC2N 4NW

An imprint of Century Hutchinson Limited

London Melbourne Sydney Auckland
Johannesburg and agencies throughout
the world

First published 1987

© Mike Resnick 1987

Printed and bound in Great Britain by
Anchor Brendon Limited, Tiptree, Essex

ISBN 0 09 951070 7

To Carol, as always

And to Bill Cavin,
God-Emperor of Midwestern fandom

Chapter
1 ————————————

Mallory walked over to the window and stared out through the dirt.

Six floors below him people were busily scurrying about the street, parcels and briefcases in hand, as an endless row of yellow cabs inched past them.

Christmas decorations were still attached to most of the lampposts, and a couple of Santa Clauses, evidently unaware that it was New Year's Eve—or possibly simply displaying a little individual enterprise—were ringing their bells, laughing their laughs, and asking for money.

He leaned against the window and looked directly down at the sidewalk in front of his building. The two burly men who had been stationed there all day were gone. He grinned; even enforcers got hungry. He made a mental note to look again in half an hour to see if they had returned to continue their vigil.

The phone rang. He looked at it, mildly surprised that it hadn't been disconnected yet, and briefly wondered who could be calling him at this time of night. Finally the

1

ringing stopped, and he walked over to his chair and sat down heavily.

It had been a long day. It had been an even longer week. And it had been an absolutely endless month.

There was a knock at the door and he sat up, startled, then let out a yelp of pain.

The door squeaked open and an ancient, white-fringed head peered in at him.

"You okay, Mr. Mallory?"

"I think I pulled something," muttered Mallory, rubbing his back gingerly with his right hand.

"I can call a doctor," offered the old man.

Mallory shook his head. "We've got all the medicine we need right here."

"We do?"

"If you'll open the closet door, you'll find a bottle on the top shelf," said Mallory. "Pull it down and bring it over."

"Well, now, that's mighty generous of you, Mr. Mallory," said the old man, walking across the worn linoleum to the closet.

"I suppose it is, at that," acknowledged Mallory. He stopped rubbing his back. "So, what can I do for you, Ezekiel?"

"I saw that your light was on," replied the old man, indicating the single overhead light above Mallory's bare wooden desk, "and I thought I'd stop by and wish you a Happy New Year."

"Thanks," replied Mallory. He smiled ruefully. "I don't imagine it can be much worse than the last one."

"Hey, this is expensive stuff!" said the old man, pushing aside a couple of battered hats and pulling out the bottle. He stared at it. "There's a ribbon around it. Did one of your clients give it to you for Christmas?"

"Not exactly. It's from my partner." He paused. "My

ex-partner. Sort of a surprise going-away present. It's been sitting there for almost four weeks."

"It must have cost him, oh, twenty bucks," ventured Ezekiel.

"At least. That's first-class sour-mash bourbon from Kentucky. It was probably fertilized by Secretariat or Seattle Slew in its natural state."

"By the way, I'm sorry about your missus," said Ezekiel. He opened the bottle, took a swig, murmured a contented "Ah!" and carried it over to Mallory.

"No need to be," said Mallory. "She's doing just fine."

"You know where she is, then?" asked Ezekiel, seating himself on the edge of the desk.

"Of course I know where she is," said Mallory irritably. "I'm a detective, remember?" He grabbed the bottle from the old man and filled a dirty New York Mets mug that had a broken handle he had glued back on. "Don't take *my* word for it. Check out my office door."

Ezekiel snapped his fingers. "Son of a bitch! *That's* what I was going to talk to you about."

"What?" asked Mallory.

"Your office door."

"It squeaks a lot. Needs some oil."

"It needs more than oil," replied Ezekiel. "You crossed out Mr. Fallico's name with red nail polish."

Mallory shrugged. "I couldn't find any other color."

"The management wants you to hire a painter to do it properly."

"What makes you think a painter can cross out Fallico's name any better than I can?"

"It don't make any difference to me, Mr. Mallory," said Ezekiel. "But I figured I ought to give you a friendly warning before they start making threats again."

"Again?" repeated Mallory, lighting a cigarette and

tossing the match onto the floor, where it created a tiny burn mark to go with several hundred similar charred brown spots. "They've never made any threats about my door before."

"You know what I mean," answered Ezekiel. "They're always after you about your rent, and throwing paper cups out the window, and the kinds of clients that walk through the lobby."

"I don't choose my clients. They choose me."

"We're getting off the subject," said Ezekiel. "You've always been nice to me, always willing to pass the time of day and share a drink or two, and you're the only one who doesn't call me Zeke even though I ask everyone not to . . . and I'd hate to see them throw you out over something as trivial as the sign on your door."

"Wait until they open the mail next Monday and my check's not there," said Mallory with a grim smile. "I guarantee you they'll forget all about the door."

"I know a guy who could paint it over for twenty bucks," persisted Ezekiel. "Twenty-five if you want gold lettering."

"It's part of the building," said Mallory, staring thoughtfully at the glowing tip of his cigarette. "The management should pay for it."

Ezekiel chuckled. *This* management? You've got to be kidding, Mr. Mallory."

"Why not? What the hell am I paying my rent for?"

"You're not paying your rent," noted the old man.

"Well, if I were, what would I be paying it for?"

Ezekiel shrugged. "Beats me."

"Beats me, too," agreed Mallory. "I guess I won't pay it." He turned to the door. "Besides, I kind of like the way it looks."

"With Mr. Fallico's name all crossed out like that?" asked Ezekiel, scrutinizing the door.

"The son of a bitch ran off to California with my wife, didn't he?"

"I know it's none of my business, Mr. Mallory, but you've been bitching about both of them for the better part of five years. You ought to be glad to be rid of them."

"It's the principle of the thing!" snapped Mallory. "Nick Fallico's off in Hollywood collecting two thousand dollars a week as a consultant for some television detective show, and I'm stuck back here with all his deadbeat clients and a month's worth of laundry!"

"You haven't done any wash since she left?"

"I don't know how to work the machine," said Mallory with an uncomfortable shrug. "Besides, they repossessed it last week." He looked at the old man. "I didn't get this deep into debt on my own, you know," he added sharply. "I had a lot of help." He glared at his cigarette. "And to top it off, the two-timing bastard took my slippers."

"Your slippers, Mr. Mallory?"

Mallory nodded. "Doreen for the bourbon was a fair trade, but I'm going to miss those slippers. I'd had them for fourteen years." He paused. "That's a hell of a lot longer than I had Doreen."

"You can get another pair."

"I'd just gotten these to where they didn't pinch."

Ezekiel frowned. "Let me get this straight. You wore slippers that pinched for fourteen years?"

"Twelve," Mallory corrected him. "They felt just fine the last couple of years."

"Why?"

"Because Doreen never took a broom to a floor in all the time I lived with her."

"I mean, why didn't you go out and get a pair that fit right?"

Mallory stared at the old man for a long moment, then

exhaled heavily and grimaced. "You know, I hate it when you ask questions like that."

Ezekiel laughed. "Well, anyway, I just thought I'd let you know they're going to start complaining about the door."

"Why don't *you* paint it? After all, you're the janitor."

"I'm the sanitary engineer," the old man corrected him.

"What's the difference?"

"Thirty cents an hour, more or less. And I don't paint doors. Hell, I'm getting so old and stiff I can barely push a mop down the hall."

"Ten dollars," said Mallory.

"Twenty."

"For twenty I can get your friend."

"True," admitted Ezekiel. "But he can't spell."

"Then why did you recommend him in the first place?"

"He's neat, and he needs the work."

Mallory smiled ironically. "Yeah, my keen detective's mind tells me that a sign painter who can't spell needs all the work he can get."

"Fifteen," said Ezekiel.

"Twelve, and you can see all the dirty photos I take the next time I'm on a divorce case."

"Deal!" said Ezekiel. "Let's seal it with a drink."

"You'll have to wait until next week for the money," added Mallory, passing the bottle to him.

"Come on, Mr. Mallory," said the old man, taking a swig. "How hard can twelve bucks be to come by?"

"That all depends on whether this damned rain stops in time for Aqueduct to dry out by tomorrow afternoon." He snorted in disgust. "Who ever heard of rain on New Year's Eve?"

"You're not betting on Flyaway again?"

"If the track is fast."

"Doesn't it bother you that he's lost eighteen races in a row?"

"Not a bit. I'd say that statistically he's due to win one."

"Pay me before he runs and I'll do it for ten dollars," said Ezekiel.

Mallory grinned, reached into his pocket, and pulled out a number of crumpled bills. He tossed two of them across the desk to the old man.

"You're a sharp bargainer, Mr. Mallory," said Ezekiel, pocketing the money. "I'll paint it the day after tomorrow." He paused. "What do you want it to say?"

"John Justin Mallory," replied Mallory, arranging the words in the air with his hand. "The World's Greatest Detective. Discretion Assured. No Job Too Small, No Fee Too High. Special Discount to Leather-Clad Ladies with Whips." He shrugged. "You know—that kind of thing."

"Seriously, Mr. Mallory."

"Just my name."

"You don't want me to put 'Private Detective' below it?"

Mallory shook his head. "Let's not discourage any passersby. If someone comes in here with enough money, I'll play point guard for the Knicks."

Ezekiel chuckled and took another sip from the bottle. "This sure is good drinkin' stuff, Mr. Mallory. I'll bet it was aged in oak casks, just like the ads say."

"I agree. If it was a cigar, it would have been rolled on the thighs of beautiful Cuban women."

"A man ought to drink something this good to ring in the New Year."

"Or get rid of the old one," said Mallory.

"By the way, what are you doing up here at this time of night on New Year's Eve?"

Mallory grimaced. "I had a little disagreement with my landlady."

"She threw you out?"

"Not in so many words," replied Mallory. "But when I saw my furniture piled up in the hallway, I applied my razor-sharp deductive powers and decided to spend the night at the office."

"Too bad. You ought to be out celebrating."

"I'll celebrate like hell at midnight. This damned year can't end fast enough to suit me." He looked at the old man. "What about you, Ezekiel?"

Ezekiel looked at his wristwatch. "It's about eight-forty. I'm locking up at nine, and then I'm taking the wife out to Times Square. Check your TV in a couple of hours; you might be able to spot us."

"I'll do that," said Mallory, not bothering to mention the obvious fact that he didn't have a television set in the office.

"Maybe you'll get an assignment yet tonight," said the old man sympathetically. "A couple of guys were looking for you earlier, at about four o'clock. They said they might be back."

"Big guys?" aked Mallory. "Look like they've been munching on steroid pills?"

"That's the ones."

"They're not looking to hire a detective," answered Mallory. "As a matter of fact, they're out to dismember one."

"What did you do to them?" asked Ezekiel.

"Not a damned thing."

"Then why are they after you?"

"They're not," said Mallory. "They just don't know it yet."

"I don't think I follow you."

Mallory sighed. "Nick needed a grubstake to go out

West—Doreen is many things, good and bad, but inexpensive isn't one of them—so he blackmailed some of our clients.''

"And left you to take the heat?"

Mallory nodded. "It appears one of them took exception to Nick's notion of fund-raising.''

"You'd better tell them that it wasn't your fault.''

"I intend to. I just haven't found the right opportunity yet. Something about their faces implies that they're just not in a very conversational mood. I suppose they'll calm down in a couple of days, and we'll work things out.''

"How?" asked Ezekiel.

"Well, if all else fails, I'll give them Nick's address in California.''

"That doesn't sound like you, Mr. Mallory.''

"I got into this business to *catch* blackmailers, not hide them,'' replied Mallory.

"I always wondered about that,'' said Ezekiel.

"About what?''

"Why someone becomes a detective. It's not as exciting as the TV makes it out to be.''

"You ought to see it from *this* side.''

"Then why did you become one?''

Mallory shrugged. "I don't know. I saw too many Bogart movies, I guess.'' He took the bottle back, filled the New York Mets mug again, took a swallow, and made a face. "It sure as hell isn't the way I imagined it, I'll tell you that. Most of the time I feel like a photographer for *Hustler*—and whenever I *do* luck out and bust a thief or a pusher, he's back on the street before I'm back in the office.'' He paused. "The worst part of it is Velma.''

"I don't know any Velma,'' said Ezekiel.

"Neither do I,'' replied Mallory. "But I always wanted a big, soft secretary named Velma. Nothing special: outfitted by Frederick's of Hollywood, slavishly devoted, and maybe a little bit oversexed. Just your typical detective's secretary." He stared at the bottle. "So what I got was Gracie."

"She's a nice lady."

"I suppose so. But she weighs two hundred pounds, she hasn't gotten one message right in close to two years, all she can talk about is her kid's allergies, and I share her with a one-eyed dentist and a tailor who wears gold chains." He paused thoughtfully. "I think maybe I'll move to Denver."

"Why Denver?"

"Why not?"

Ezekiel chuckled. "You're always talking about getting out of the business and moving away, but you never do."

"Maybe this time I will," said Mallory. "There's got to be someplace better than Manhattan." He paused. "I hear that Phoenix is pretty nice."

"I've been there. You can fry an egg on the street at midnight."

"Then one of the Carolinas."

Ezekiel checked his watch. "I've got to go now, Mr. Mallory," he said, getting up and walking to the door. "You have a nice evening."

"You, too," said Mallory.

The old man went out into the corridor and closed the door behind him.

Mallory walked over to his window and peered out through the dirt for a couple of minutes. Finally he pulled some peeling gray paint off one of the walls, wondered how such an empty room could seem so small, and sat back down at his desk. He uncapped the whiskey bottle again and had a drink in loving memory of the Velma who never was. He had four more in honor of four unnatural sexual acts he had never had the courage to suggest to Doreen (and which he was absolutely sure she was gleefully performing with Fallico at that very moment), another one for the last race Flyaway had won (assuming that he actually *had* won a race in the dim and distant past; it was always possible that he had only gone to the post eighteen times, and one more for the year that was finally crawling to a close.

He was about to have a drink to mourn the loss of his slippers when he noticed the little green elf standing in front of his desk.

"You're pretty good," he said admiringly. "But where are the pink elephants?"

"John Justin Mallory?"

"You guys have never talked before," complained Mallory. "Usually you just sit around singing 'Santa Lucia.' " He squinted and looked around the office. "Where are the rest of you?"

"Drunk," said the elf disgustedly. "This won't do at all, John Justin. Not at all."

"The rest of you are drunk?"

"No. *You* are."

"Of course I am. That's why I'm seeing little green men."

"I'm not a man. I'm an elf."

"Whatever," said Mallory, shrugging. "At least you're little and green." He looked around the room again. "Where are the elephants?"

"What elephants?" asked the elf.

"*My* elephants," answered Mallory, as if explaining the obvious to a very slow child. "Who are you, and what are you doing here?"

"Mürgenstürm," said the elf.

"Mürgenstürm?" repeated Mallory, frowning. "I think he's on the next floor."

"No. I *am* Mürgenstürm."

"Have a seat, Mürgenstürm. And you might as well have a

drink before you vanish." He checked the amount of whiskey remaining. "A *short* one."

"I'm not here to drink," said Mürgenstürm.

"Thank heaven for small favors," murmured Mallory, raising the bottle to his lips and draining its contents. "Okay," he said, tossing it into a wastebasket. "I'm all through. Now, sing your song or dance your dance or do whatever you're going to do, and then make way for the elephants."

Mürgenstürm made a face. "We're going to have to get you sobered up, and quickly."

"If you do, you'll disappear," said Mallory, staring at him owlishly.

"Why did it have to be New Year's Eve?" muttered the elf.

"Probably because yesterday was December thirtieth," replied Mallory reasonably.

"And why a drunk?"

"Now, hold your horses!" said Mallory irritably. "I may *be* drunk, but I'm not *a* drunk."

"It makes no difference. I need you now, and you're in no condition to work."

Mallory frowned. "I thought *I* needed *you*," he said, puzzled.

"Maybe a professor of zoology . . ." muttered Mürgenstürm to himself.

"That sounds like the beginning of a limerick."

The elf uttered a sigh of resignation. "There's no time. It's you or no one."

"And that sounds like a bad love song."

Mürgenstürm walked around the desk to where Mallory was sitting and pinched him on the leg.

"*Ouch!* What the hell did you do that for?"

"To prove to you that I'm really here, John Justin. I need you."

Mallory glared at him and rubbed his leg. "Whoever heard of an uppity hallucination?"

"I have a job for you, John Justin Mallory," said the elf.

"Get someone else. I'm mourning my lost youth and other elements of my past, both real and imagined."

"This is not a dream, this is not a joke, and this is not a delirium tremens," said the elf urgently. "I absolutely *must* have the help of a trained detective."

Mallory reached into a drawer, pulled out a dog-eared copy of the Yellow Pages, and tossed it onto the desk.

"There's seven or eight hundred of them in town," he said. "Let your fingers do the walking."

"All the others are already working or are out celebrating," said Mürgenstürm.

"You mean I'm the only goddamned detective in New York City who's in his office?" demanded Mallory unbelievingly.

"It's New Year's Eve."

Mallory stared at the elf for a long moment. "I take it I'm not exactly your first choice?"

"I began with the *A*'s," admitted Mürgenstürm.

"And worked your way all the way down to Mallory and Fallico? You must have been looking since October."

"I'm very fast when I have to be."

"Then why don't you hustle your little green ass out of here very fast?" said Mallory. "You're making me think."

"John Justin, please believe me when I tell you I wouldn't be here if it wasn't a matter of life and death."

"Whose?"

"Mine," answered the elf unhappily.

"Yours?"

The elf nodded.

"Someone's out to kill you?"

"It's not that simple."

"Somehow it never is," said Mallory dryly. "Damn! I'm starting to sober up, and that was my last bottle!"

"Will you help me?" asked the elf.

"Don't be silly. You're going to vanish in another half minute."

"I am *not* going to vanish!" said the elf in desperation. "I am going to die!"

"Right here?" asked Mallory, sliding his chair a few feet back from the desk to make room for a falling body.

"At sunrise, unless you help me."

Mallory stared at Mürgenstürm for a long moment. "How?"

"Something that was entrusted to me is missing, and unless I recover it before morning my life will be forfeit."

"What is it?"

Mürgenstürm returned his stare. "I don't think you're ready for this yet, John Justin."

"How the hell can I find something if I don't even know what I'm looking for?" demanded Mallory.

"True," admitted the elf.

"Well?"

Mürgenstürm looked at Mallory, sighed, and then blurted it out. "It's a unicorn."

"I don't know whether to laugh in your face or throw you out on your ass," said Mallory. "Now, go away and let me enjoy what little remains of my inebriated condition."

"I'm not kidding, John Justin!"

"And I'm not buying, Morganthau."

"Mürgenstürm," corrected the elf.

"I don't care if you're Ronald Reagan. Go away!"

"Name your price," pleaded Mürgenstürm.

"For finding a unicorn in New York City?" said Mallory sarcastically. "Ten thousand dollars a day, plus expenses."

"Done!" cried the elf, plucking a fat wad of bills out of the air and tossing them onto Mallory's desk.

"Why do I feel that this stuff isn't exactly coin of the realm?" said Mallory as he thumbed through the pile of crisp new hundred-dollar bills.

"I assure you that the serial numbers are on file with your Treasury Department, and the signatures are valid."

Mallory cocked a disbelieving eyebrow. "Where did it come from?"

"It came from me," said Mürgenstürm defensively.

"And where did *you* come from?"

"I beg your pardon?"

"You heard me," said Mallory. "I've seen some pretty weird sights in this city, but you sure as hell aren't one of them."

"I live here."

"Where?"

"Manhattan."

"Give me an address."

"I'll do better than that. I'll take you there."

"No, you won't," said Mallory. "I'm going to close my eyes, and when I open them you and the money will be gone, and there will be pink elephants on my desk."

He shut his eyes for the count of ten, then opened them. Mürgenstürm and the money were still there.

He frowned. "This is going on longer than usual," he commented. "I wonder what the hell was in that bottle?"

"Just whiskey," answered the elf. "I am not a figment of your imagination. I am a desperate supplicant who needs your help."

"To find a unicorn."

"That's right."

"Just out of curiosity, how the hell did you manage to lose it? I mean, a unicorn's a pretty big thing to misplace, isn't it?"

"It was stolen," answered Mürgenstürm.

"Then you don't need a detective at all," said Mallory.

"I don't?"

"It takes a virgin to catch a unicorn, right? Well, there can't be two dozen virgins left in the whole of Manhattan. Just pay each of them a visit until you come to the one with the unicorn."

"I wish it was that easy," said Mürgenstürm gloomily.

"Why isn't it?"

"There may be only two dozen virgins in *your* Manhattan, but there are thousands in *mine*—and I've got less than ten hours left."

"Back up a minute," said Mallory, frowning again. "What's this 'yours and mine' stuff? Do you live in Manhattan or don't you?"

Mürgenstürm nodded. "I told you I did."

"Then what are you talking about?"

"I live in the Manhattan you see out of the corner of your eye," explained the elf. "Every once in a while one of you gets a fleeting glimpse of it, but when you turn to face it head-on, it's gone."

Mallory smiled and snapped his fingers. "Just like that?"

"Protective coloration," replied Mürgenstürm.

"And just where is this Manhattan of yours? Second star to the right and straight on until morning—or maybe over the rainbow?"

"It's right here, all around you," answered the elf. "It's not a different Manhattan so much as a part of your own Manhattan that you never see."

"Can *you* see it?"

Mürgenstürm nodded. "You just have to know how to look for it."

"How *do* you look for it?" asked Mallory, curious in spite of himself.

Mürgenstürm gestured toward the money. "Accept the job and I'll show you."

"Not a chance," said Mallory. "But I'm grateful to

you, my little green friend. When I wake up, I'm going to write this whole conversation up and send it off to one of those sex forum magazines and let them analyze it. I think they pay fifty bucks if your letter gets published.''

The elf lowered his head in defeat. ''That's your final word?'' he asked.

''Right.''

Mürgenstürm drew himself up to his full, if limited, height. ''Then I must prepare to meet my death. I'm sorry to have troubled you, John Justin Mallory.''

''No trouble at all,'' said Mallory.

''You still don't believe any of this, do you?''

''Not a word.''

The elf sighed and walked to the door. He opened it and walked out into the hall, then stepped back into the office.

''Are you expecting visitors?'' he asked.

''Pink elephants?'' asked Mallory.

Mürgenstürm shook his head. ''Two very large, mean-looking men with bulges under their arms. One of them has a scar on his left cheek.''

''Shit!'' muttered Mallory, racing unsteadily to the light switch and plunging the room into darkness. ''They were supposed to be waiting downstairs!'' He hurried back to his desk and knelt down behind it.

''Perhaps they got tired of waiting,'' suggested the elf.

''But they don't want *me!*'' complained Mallory. ''It's Nick Fallico they're after!''

''They looked pretty determined,'' said Mürgenstürm. ''I think they want anyone they can find.''

''Well,'' said Mallory, wishing he could have just one more drink, ''it looks like you may not be the only one who doesn't live to a ripe old age.''

''You're going to kill them?'' asked Mürgenstürm.

''I wasn't referring to *them.*''

''Aren't you going to shoot them?''

"With what?" asked Mallory.

"With your gun, of course."

"I don't own a gun."

"A detective without a gun?" said the elf. "I never heard of such a thing!"

"I never needed one," said Mallory.

"Never?"

"Until now," he amended.

"Do you really think they'll kill you?" asked Mürgenstürm.

"Only if they get carried away. They'll probably just break my fingers and see to it that I don't walk without crutches for a couple of years."

Two bulky figures could be seen through the clouded glass of the office door.

"I have a proposition to make to you, John Justin," said Mürgenstürm.

"Why am I not surprised?" replied Mallory with a touch of irony.

"If I make them go away without hurting you, will you help me find the unicorn?"

"If you can make *them* go away, you don't need my help," said Mallory with conviction.

"Do we have a deal?" persisted the elf.

The doorknob slowly turned.

"What about the ten thousand dollars?" whispered Mallory.

"It's yours."

"Deal!" said Mallory just as the door opened and the two men burst into his office.

Chapter
2

Mürgenstürm murmured something in a tongue that was not even remotely familiar to Mallory, and the two figures suddenly froze in mid-stride.

"What the hell did you do to them?" demanded the detective, cautiously getting up from behind his desk.

"I altered their subjectivity *vis-à-vis* Time," replied the elf with a modest shrug. "As far as they're concerned, Time has ground to a halt. The condition should last about five minutes."

"Magic?" asked Mallory.

"Advanced psychology," said Mürgenstürm.

"Bullshit."

"It's the truth, John Justin. I live in the same world you live in. Magic doesn't work here. This is totally in keeping with natural law."

"I heard you chanting a spell," persisted Mallory.

"Ancient Aramaic, nothing more," replied Mürgenstürm. "It appeals to their racial memory." He lowered his voice confidentially. "Jung was very close to it when he died."

"While we're at it, how did you pluck that money out

19

of the air?'' asked Mallory, waving a hand in front of the
nearer gunman and getting no reaction.

"Sleight of hand.''

Mallory stared at him disbelievingly, but said nothing.

"Come along, John Justin,'' said Mürgenstürm, walking to the door. "We have work to do.''

"I don't think this one's breathing,'' said Mallory,
indicating one of the gunmen.

"He will be, as soon as Time starts up for him again—
which will be in less than three minutes. We really should
be going before that happens.''

"First things first,'' said Mallory. He picked the roll of
bills off his desk and shoved it into a pocket.

"Hurry!'' said the elf urgently.

"All right,'' said Mallory, walking around the two men
and stepping out into the corridor.

"This way,'' said Mürgenstürm, racing ahead to the
elevator.

"Let's take the stairs,'' suggested Mallory.

"The stairs?'' repeated the elf. "But you're on the sixth
floor!''

"Yeah. But the stairs don't let us out in the main lobby,
and the elevator does. And whether this is a dream or a DT
or reality, a green elf is just naturally going to look a little
out of place getting out of the elevator and turning right at
the tobacco stand.''

Mürgenstürm smiled. "Not to worry, John Justin. We're
not getting out on the main floor.''

"You think your unicorn is hiding between here and the
lobby?'' asked Mallory. "All we've got below us are two
discount stockbrokers, a drunken one-eyed dentist, a stamp
and coin dealer, a guy who handles hot jewelry, and—let
me think—a tailor who can't speak English and an old
lady who jobs artificial flowers.''

"I know," said Mürgenstürm, stepping into the elevator cab.

"Okay," shrugged Mallory, following him. "What floor?"

"Just press DOWN," said the elf.

"There isn't any DOWN button," said Mallory. "Just floor numbers."

"Right there," said Mürgenstürm, pointing to the panel.

"Well, I'll be damned!" muttered Mallory. "I never noticed it before."

He reached out and pressed the button, and the elevator began descending slowly. A moment later it passed the second floor, and Mallory looked at the elf.

"I'd better press STOP," he said.

"Don't."

"We'll crash."

"No, we won't," said the elf.

"This building hasn't got a basement," said Mallory with a trace of panic in his voice. "If I don't hit the emergency stop button, they're going to spend the next two days scraping us off the ceiling."

"Trust me."

"Trust you? I don't even believe in you!"

"Then believe in the ten thousand dollars."

Mallory felt his pocket to make sure the money hadn't vanished. "If *that's* real, *this* is real. I'd better stop it now." He turned back to the panel.

"Don't bother," said Mürgenstürm. "We passed the main floor ten seconds ago."

Mallory looked up at the lights that denoted which floor the elevator was passing and saw that all of them were dark.

"Great!" he muttered. "We're stuck."

"No, we're not," said Mürgenstürm. "We're still moving. Can't you feel it, John Justin?"

And suddenly Mallory realized that they *were* moving.

"One of the lights must be on the blink," he suggested unsteadily.

"All the lights are working," answered the elf. "They just don't go this far down." He paused. "All right. You can stop us now."

Mallory hit the STOP button, and was about to press OPEN DOOR when the doors slid back on their own.

"Where are we?" he demanded as they stepped out into a plain, unfurnished, dimly lit foyer.

"In your building, of course," said Mürgenstürm. "Elevators don't leave their shafts."

"They also don't go below ground level in buildings that are erected on concrete slabs," said Mallory.

"That's *our* doing," said Mürgenstürm with a smile. "We visited the architect's office one night and made some changes."

"And nobody questioned it?"

"We did it with a very special ink. Let's just say that nobody who could read it questioned it."

"How far beneath the ground are we?" asked Mallory.

"Not very. An inch, a foot, a meter, a fathom, a mile—it all depends on where the ground is, doesn't it?"

"I suppose so." He looked around. "You expect to find your unicorn here?"

"If it were that easy, I wouldn't need a detective," replied Mürgenstürm.

"You brought Time to a standstill and took us to a floor that doesn't exist," said Mallory. "If that's *easy*, I hate to think about what's hard."

"Hard is finding the unicorn." Mürgenstürm sighed. "I suppose I ought to take you to the scene of the crime."

"That's usually a pretty good place to start," agreed Mallory sardonically. "Where is it?"

"This way," said the elf, walking into the shadows.

Mallory fell into step behind him, and a moment later they came to a door that had been invisible from the elevator. They walked through it, proceeded about twenty feet, and came to a concrete staircase. They walked up two flights and stopped at a large landing.

"Where to now?" asked Mallory.

"Down," said Mürgenstürm, crossing the landing and starting down another flight of stairs.

"Hold it," said Mallory. "We just climbed *up* two flights."

"That's right."

"Then why are we going back down?"

"This is a different staircase," said the elf, as if that explained everything.

They climbed down three flights, came to another landing, and then climbed up a flight.

"Give me a second to rest," said Mallory, leaning on a banister and panting heavily. He looked around and saw no other stairs. "By my count, we're right back where we started from."

Mürgenstürm smiled. "Not at all."

"Two minus three plus one," said Mallory, pulling a handkerchief out of his pocket and mopping his face. "We're back at the beginning."

"Look around you," said Mürgenstürm. "Does this look like anyplace we've already been?"

Mallory peered into the gloom and saw an array of lights leading off into the distance, lining what appeared to be a narrow, domed corridor.

"Maybe I'd better not write this up and send it off to one of the magazines after all," he said at last. "They'd probably lock me away."

"Have you rested enough, John Justin?" asked the elf. "We really haven't much time."

Mallory nodded, and Mürgenstürm started off down the long corridor, his footsteps echoing in the stillness.

"This is a hell of a place to keep a unicorn," remarked Mallory. "Don't they need sunlight and grass and things like that?"

"We're just arranging for transportation."

"I *wondered* what we were doing," muttered the detective.

Suddenly the corridor took a hard right, and after another fifty feet they emerged onto a subway platform.

"It's just a subway station," said Mallory. "There were easier ways to get here."

"Not really," replied Mürgenstürm. "Not many trains run on this route."

"What station is this?" asked Mallory.

"Fourth Avenue."

"There *isn't* any Fourth Avenue."

"Don't take *my* word for it," said Mürgenstürm, pointing to a sign above the platform.

"Fourth Avenue," said Mallory, reading the sign. "Come to think of it, it looks different from the other stations."

"In what way?"

"It's cleaner, for one thing." He sniffed the air. "It doesn't stink of urine, either."

"It doesn't get much use," replied Mürgenstürm.

"No graffiti, either," said Mallory, looking around. He paused. "I wish the rest of them looked like this."

"They did once."

"Must have been before my time." Suddenly Mallory tensed. "What was that?"

"What was what?"

He peered into the darkness. "I saw something moving in the shadows."

"It must be your imagination," said Mürgenstürm.

"You're my imagination!" snapped Mallory. *"That* was something moving. Something dark."

"Ah! I see them now!"

"Them?" asked Mallory. "I only saw one thing."

"There are four of them," replied Mürgenstürm. "Have you any subway tokens?"

"Subway tokens?" repeated Mallory.

Mürgenstürm nodded. "Coins will do, but subway tokens really are best."

Mallory fumbled through his pockets and came up with two tokens.

"Toss them over there," said Mürgenstürm, indicating the spot where Mallory had seen the movement.

"Why?"

"Just do it."

Mallory shrugged and flipped the two tokens into the shadows. A moment later he heard a series of shuffling noises, and then two loud crunching sounds.

"Well?" demanded Mallory after a moment's silence.

"Well what?"

"I'm waiting for an explanation."

"Can't you see them?" asked Mürgenstürm.

Mallory peered into the shadows and shook his head. "I can't see a damned thing."

"Cock your head to the right," suggested the elf.

"What for?"

"Like this," said Mürgenstürm, demonstrating. "Maybe it will help."

"It's not going to make the place any brighter."

"Try it anyway."

Mallory shrugged and cocked his head—and suddenly he could see four dark hulking figures, their hairy hands almost dragging the ground, squatting against a tile wall and staring at him with red, unblinking eyes.

"You see?" said Mürgenstürm, watching his reaction. "Nothing to it."

"What the hell are they?" asked Mallory, wishing for the second time that evening that he carried a gun.

"They're the Gnomes of the Subway," replied Mürgenstürm. "Don't worry; they won't bother you."

"They're *already* bothering me," said Mallory.

"They're not used to seeing men down here," explained the elf. "On the other hand, I'm not used to seeing *them* here, either. Usually they spend their time at Times Square or Union Square or down at the Eighth Avenue station in the Village."

"I suppose there's a reason."

Mürgenstürm nodded. "They live on subway tokens, so naturally they tend to congregate in those areas where tokens are most plentiful. They're probably just slumming."

"What kind of creature eats subway tokens?" asked Mallory, staring intently at the Gnomes.

"*That* kind," answered Mürgenstürm. "Didn't you ever wonder why the New York Transit Authority continues to make millions of tokens every year? After all, they don't wear out, and they're absolutely no use anywhere else. Theoretically there should be billions of tokens in circulation, but of course there aren't. You might view the Gnomes of the Subway as ecologists of a sort: they stop Manhattan from sinking under the weight of subway tokens, and provide work for hundreds of people who labor all year to create new ones."

"What do they do when they're not eating?" asked Mallory.

"Oh, they're perfectly harmless, if that's what you mean," replied the elf.

"That was what I meant."

"In fact, they graze for fifteen or twenty hours a day," continued Mürgenstürm. "It takes quite a lot of tokens to fill one of them up." He lowered his voice confidentially. "I heard that a number of them emigrated to Connecticut when they started making look-alike bus tokens up there, but evidently they weren't as nourishing, since most of the Gnomes have come back home."

"What would they have done if I hadn't tossed them the tokens?" asked Mallory, eyeing them warily.

"That all depends. I'm told they can sniff out a token at two hundred yards. If you hadn't had any, they would have left you alone."

"But I had some. What would have happened if I didn't turn them over?"

"I really don't know," admitted Mürgenstürm. "I suppose we could ask them."

He took a step toward the Gnomes, but Mallory placed a restraining hand on his shoulder.

"It's not that important," he said.

"You're sure?" asked Mürgenstürm.

"Some other time."

"Perhaps it's just as well. We're operating on a very tight schedule."

"Maybe you should tell that to the Transit Authority. I haven't seen any sign of a train."

Mürgenstürm leaned over the edge of the platform. "I can't imagine what's delaying it. It should have been here two or three minutes ago."

"I'll bring it here right now, if you'd like," offered Mallory.

"You?" said the elf. "How?"

"*You* can bring Time to a halt," said Mallory. "Well, *I* can make it speed up." He pulled a cigarette out of his pocket and lit it. Just as he took a long puff and exhaled it, the train sounded its horn and pulled up to the platform.

"Never fails," remarked Mallory, tossing the cigarette to the floor and stepping on it.

The doors slid open and they got into the subway car, the first in a line of four. Instead of the usual rows of worn-out and uncomfortable seats that Mallory was used to, the surprisingly clean interior of the car consisted of half a dozen curving leather booths. The floor was covered by a carpet of intricate design, and crushed velvet paper lined the walls.

"We get a better class of service on the Fourth Avenue line," commented Mürgenstürm, observing the detective's reaction.

"You don't seem to get any customers, though," replied Mallory.

"I'm sure the others are in the diner."

"There's a diner car?" asked Mallory, surprised.

Mürgenstürm nodded. "And a cocktail lounge as well."

"Then what are we waiting for?" said Mallory, getting to his feet.

"I need you sober," said the elf.

"If I was sober, you'd vanish into thin air and I'd be back in my office."

"I wish you'd stop saying that," complained Mürgenstürm. "Pretty soon you'll convince yourself it's the truth."

"So what?"

"So when we face certain dangers, you won't believe in them and won't take the proper precautions."

"What dangers?" demanded Mallory.

"If I knew, I'd be more than happy to tell you."

"Take a guess."

The elf shrugged. "I really have no idea. I just have a feeling that when we close in on Larkspur, whoever stole him is not going to be very happy about it."

"Larkspur?"

"That's the unicorn's name."

"What the hell were you doing with a unicorn that wasn't yours in the first place?" asked Mallory.

"Protecting him."

"Against what?"

"Against whoever wanted to steal him."

"Why would anyone want to steal a unicorn?"

"Greed, villainy, an unreasoning hatred of myself—who knows?"

"You're not being very helpful," said Mallory.

"If I knew all the answers, I wouldn't need a detective, would I?" demanded Mürgenstürm irritably.

"All right," said Mallory. "Let's try a different approach. Who owns the unicorn?"

"Very good, John Justin!" said Mürgenstürm enthusiastically. "That's a much better question."

"Then answer it."

"I can't."

"You don't know who owns the unicorn?"

"That's right."

"Then how do you know he'll kill you if you don't get it back by sunrise?"

"Oh, *he* won't kill me," said Mürgenstürm. "He won't get the chance."

"Then who will?"

"My guild."

"Your guild?"

The little elf nodded. "We guard valuable possessions—precious stones, illuminated manuscripts, that sort of thing—and our lives are forfeit if we fail in our duties." He grimaced. "That's why I had to hire you. I couldn't very well go to my guild and tell them what happened. They would have cut me to pieces."

"When was the unicorn stolen?"

"About noon. This was the first unicorn I'd ever been entrusted with. I thought it would be safe to leave it alone for a few minutes."

"Where did you go off to?" asked Mallory.

Mürgenstürm blushed a dark green. "I'd really rather not say."

"So even elves get laid."

"I beg your pardon!" exploded the elf furiously. "It was a beautiful and deeply moving romantic tryst! I won't have you making it sound cheap and tawdry."

"What it mostly was was stupid," commented Mallory wryly. "They wouldn't have paid you to guard the damned animal if they didn't think someone might steal it."

"That thought has occurred to me," said Mürgenstürm unhappily.

"After the fact, no doubt."

"As I was returning to Larkspur," admitted the elf.

"Dumb," said Mallory.

"How was I to know?" demanded Mürgenstürm. "Nothing happened the first six times I went off to answer the siren song of romance."

"Just how long was this unicorn in your charge?" asked Mallory.

"Not quite five hours."

"During which time you went off on *seven* romantic trysts?"

"I may look unapproachable and formidable," said the little elf, "but I have needs just like anybody else."

"You've got needs like *nobody* else," replied Mallory, impressed.

"All right!" exploded Mürgenstürm. "I'm not perfect! Sue me!"

Mallory winced. "Don't yell," he said. "It's been a long day, and I've had a lot to drink."

"Then stop belittling me."

"I can do better than that," said Mallory. "Give me a hard time, and I can stop helping you."

"No!" yelled the elf, causing Mallory to flinch in pain. "Please," he continued, lowering his voice. "I apologize for losing my temper. It's just my passionate nature. It won't happen again.''

''Until the next time.''

''I promise,'' said Mürgenstürm.

Suddenly the train slowed down and came to a stop.

''Are we there?'' asked Mallory as the doors slid open.

''Next station,'' replied the elf.

Mallory turned to the door and watched the passengers enter the car. There were three elves, a ruddy little man with a red handlebar moustache whose long overcoat could not totally conceal his twitching reptilian tail, and a smartly dressed elderly woman who had a small, maned, scaled animal on a leash. A Gnome of the Subway raced into the car just as the doors were closing and, disdaining the leather booths, leaned against the far wall and slid slowly to the floor, staring at Mallory all the while.

''I do wish we wouldn't let them ride first class,'' complained Mürgenstürm softly, nodding his head toward the Gnome. ''They just ruin the ambience.''

''On the other hand,'' remarked Mallory, ''the old lady looks perfectly normal.''

''Why shouldn't she?''

''She looks like she belongs in *my* Manhattan, not yours.''

''That's Mrs. Hayden-Finch,'' whispered Mürgenstürm. ''She used to breed miniature poodles.'' He sighed sadly. ''Twenty-six years and not so much as a blue ribbon.'' His face brightened. ''Now she breeds miniature chimeras, and she's quite a success. In fact, she took Best in Show at the Garden last winter.''

''I don't remember reading about any chimeras at West-minster,'' said Mallory.

''*North*minster,'' corrected the elf. ''It's much older and more prestigious.''

''That brings up an interesting question,'' said Mallory.

''About chimeras?''

"About unicorns. Why was *this* particular one so valuable? Was he a show specimen, or a breeding animal, or what?"

"Another excellent question! Oh, I hired the right man, no doubt about it!"

"I assume that means you don't have an answer."

"I'm afraid not, John Justin," said Mürgenstürm. "If he wasn't valuable, he wouldn't have been placed in my keeping . . . but beyond that, I know as little about him as you do."

"What do you know about unicorns in general?"

"Well," said Mürgenstürm uncomfortably, "they're usually white, and they have horns that I am told are quite valuable. And they mess their stalls with shocking regularity."

"Anything else?"

The little elf shook his head. "Usually I just guard jewels and amulets and things like that. To be perfectly honest, I don't even know what unicorns eat."

"Then has the thought occurred to you that maybe Larkspur just wandered off on his own to grab a little snack?" asked Mallory.

"As a matter of fact, it hadn't," admitted Mürgenstürm. "That would make him much easier to find, wouldn't it? I mean, once we know what unicorns eat."

Mallory nodded. "Yes, I'd have to say that it would." He paused. "You're not much good at your work, are you?"

"No worse than yourself, I daresay," responded the elf. "If I were a detective, the criminals *I* caught would *stay* caught."

"You haven't had much experience with the New York municipal court system, have you?" asked Mallory.

"What has one to do with the other?" demanded Mürgenstürm.

"Not a hell of a lot," replied Mallory with some distaste.

The train began slowing down again, and Mürgenstürm got to his feet and walked over to the door.

"Come on," he said to Mallory.

The detective got up, made a wide semicircle around the miniature chimera, which was hooting at him with an odd expression on its face, and joined the elf just as the train stopped and the doors slid open.

"Where are we now?" asked Mallory, looking around the unmarked platform.

"Unicorn Square."

"New York hasn't got a Unicorn Square."

"I know," replied the elf. "That's my pet name for it." Suddenly he giggled. "That's quite a pun—*pet* name!"

"Hilarious," muttered Mallory, looking around for a staircase. "How do we get out of here?"

"The escalator."

"There isn't one."

"It'll be along any minute," said Mürgenstürm. "Try lighting a cigarette. Oh, and you might step about three paces to your left."

"Why?"

"Because you're in the way."

Mallory moved aside. "In the way of what?"

"The escalator," answered the elf.

No sooner had the words left his mouth than a shining silver ramp was lowered into place, coming to rest exactly where Mallory had been standing. It hummed mechanically as the stairs began moving upward.

"Where does this take us?" asked Mallory, stepping onto a stair just behind Mürgenstürm.

"Up, of course."

They rode in silence for a few minutes.

"How high up?" asked Mallory at last.

"Ground level."

"We've been riding for three or four minutes," said Mallory. "Where did we start from?"

"The subway level."

"Thanks."

They emerged into the open air in another minute. It was chilly and drizzling, and Mallory pulled the lapels of his suit jacket up.

"Looks deserted," he commented. "Where are we?"

"Fifth Avenue and 57th Street."

Mallory looked around him. The buildings seemed vaguely familiar, but somehow the angles were slightly askew. He cocked his head to the right. It didn't help.

"Where are all the cars?" he asked.

"Who'd go driving in this weather?" asked Mürgenstürm, shivering noticeably.

"What about cabs?"

"Here comes one," answered the elf, pointing south on Fifth Avenue, where a large elephant decked out in sparkling finery was walking up the street toward them. It carried a howdah on its broad back, and in it an elf with a megaphone was pointing out the wonders of Manhattan to a number of other elves who listened with rapt attention. The elephant suddenly spotted Mallory and Mürgenstürm, spread its ears out, extended its trunk toward them, and trumpeted.

"I meant like Yellow Cabs," said Mallory, stepping back around the corner and out of the elephant's sight.

"Yellow Cab at your service, sir," cried a voice, and Mallory turned just in time to avoid bumping into a bright yellow elephant, also resplendent in its trappings. "Nonstop to Fifth Avenue and Central Park," continued the elf who perched on its back. "Guaranteed arrival before midnight."

"That's only two blocks from here," said Mallory.

"Not the way old Jumbo goes," replied the cabbie.

"He zigs and zags and backtracks like crazy. Not fast, mind you—it's a perfectly smooth ride, and much better than some of those modern, stripped-down models—but determined. There's a fruit stand at 58th and Broadway that he hasn't missed in twenty years. Great memory!"

"Why don't you train him better?"

"Break his spirit?" said the outraged cabbie. "I wouldn't think of it!"

"It seems to me that there ought to be a happy medium between breaking his spirit and spending two hours to travel a hundred yards."

"We travel *miles!*" protested the cabbie. "Of course, we don't go in a very straight line . . . but then, getting there is half the fun." He glared at Mallory. "It's New Year's Eve and I'm a busy man, a very busy man. Now, do you want a ride or not?"

"We'll walk," replied Mallory.

"Your loss," said the cabbie. He kicked the yellow elephant with a tiny foot. "Come on, Jumbo—mush!"

The elephant squealed, pivoted 180 degrees, and headed off at a trot, ignoring his rider's frantic instructions.

"Does everyone around here make as little sense as you and that elephant driver?" asked Mallory.

"I thought he made perfect sense," replied Mürgenstürm.

"You would," said Mallory. "Let's get going."

"Right," agreed Mürgenstürm, heading off across Fifth Avenue.

As Mallory stepped away from the building he saw that the broad street had suddenly become filled with traffic as elephants, horses, and oversized dogs, all brightly colored and brilliantly harnessed, moved up and down the thoroughfare, either carrying passengers on their backs or pulling them in gaily decorated open-air carriages.

They reached the far side of the street, and then began following a complex and circuitous route between buildings and through alleys, up twisting ramps and down spiraling stairwells, into and out of strange-smelling basements, until Mallory, who was trying to remember which way he had come, was thoroughly confused. Finally they halted at a small, grass-covered, fenced yard.

"Here we are," said the elf.

"What's the address here?" asked Mallory.

"Fifth Avenue and 57th Street."

"Come on!" said Mallory irritably. "We've walked at least a mile since we were there."

"A mile and a quarter, I should imagine," agreed Mürgenstürm.

"Then how can we be back where we started? Where are the streets and the stores?"

"They're here. We just approached from a different direction."

"That's crazy."

"Why must everything look the same from every angle?" asked Mürgenstürm. "Do both sides of a door look the same? Is the interior of a Black Forest torte identical to the exterior? Believe me, John Justin, we're really at the corner of Fifth and 57th. We're simply backstage."

"Where's the front of the stage?"

"Ah," smiled the elf. "To see that, we'd have to retrace our steps."

"I wouldn't know where to begin," said Mallory.

"At the beginning, of course."

"You know," said Mallory, "I'm beginning to dislike you intensely. You've always got a slick answer, and nothing you say makes any sense."

"It will," Mürgenstürm assured him. "Wait until you've been here awhile."

"I don't plan to be here awhile," said Mallory. He turned his attention to the yard, which was about fifty feet on a side and thoroughly overgrown with weeds. "This is where you kept the unicorn?"

"That's right," said the elf, opening the gate. "Watch your step."

"More Subway Gnomes?" asked Mallory.

Mürgenstürm shook his head. "Larkspur wasn't exactly what one would call housebroken." He walked gingerly to a gnarled tree, and the detective followed him. "I had him tethered right here."

Mallory looked at the weathered brownstone house at the far end of the yard. Many of the windows were boarded over, all the lights were out, and a storm door swung noisily back and forth on a single rusty hinge.

"*That* house goes with *this* yard?" asked Mallory.

"Yes."

"Does anyone live there?"

"It's been empty for more than a year," replied Mürgenstürm. "That's why I used the yard; I knew there was nobody around to object."

"*Almost* nobody," Mallory corrected him dryly. He squatted down and examined the ground.

"Did you find anything?" asked the elf after a moment.

"Just unicorn tracks."

"Are there any signs of a struggle?" suggested Mürgenstürm.

"You think maybe someone stopped to wrestle Larkspur two out of three falls before leading him away?" said Mallory irritably.

"I'm just trying to be helpful," apologized Mürgenstürm.

"You can start by shutting up," said Mallory. He straightened up, then began a systematic search of the yard.

"What are you looking for?" asked Mürgenstürm.

"I don't know," replied Mallory. "Footprints that don't belong to you or Larkspur, a scrap of clothing, anything that looks out of place." He walked through the knee-high weeds and grass for another minute, then shook his head, grimaced, and returned to the tree.

"No clues at all?" asked the elf.

"I have a horrible feeling that we're going to have to follow a trail of unicorn shit to solve this case," said Mallory. He walked carefully to the gate, followed by Mürgenstürm. "Think now!" he said. "Who else knew Larkspur was here?"

"No one."

"*Someone* had to know. Someone stole him. Who owns this place?"

"I have no idea. I suppose I could find out," said the elf. Suddenly his narrow shoulders slumped. "But not until the city offices open tomorrow morning, and then it'll be too late."

Mallory's eyes darted to the shadows, then focused again on Mürgenstürm. "Keep talking," he said in a low voice.

"About what?" asked the elf.

"Anything. It doesn't matter. We're being watched."

"You're sure?"

Mallory nodded.

"I wasn't aware of it. It must be your long experience as a detective."

"It's my long experience dodging bill collectors," replied Mallory. "Start talking about unicorns. Whoever it is, he's coming closer."

Mürgenstürm's face went blank. "I don't know what to say."

"Ten minutes ago I couldn't shut you up!" hissed Mallory. "Now talk!"

"I feel silly," said the elf.

"You're going to feel a lot worse than silly if you don't say something!"

"Give me a hint," said Mürgenstürm desperately.

Mallory cursed, and suddenly hurled himself into the darkness.

"Got you!" he cried triumphantly, and emerged a moment later with a scratching, spitting, clawing girl in his arms.

"Let me go!" she snarled.

Mallory felt her twisting free and released his grip. She hissed at him, then sprang lightly to the top of the fence and crouched there.

"Who are you?" demanded Mallory.

"I know her," said Mürgenstürm. "She's Felina."

"What are you doing here?" persisted Mallory.

"I have as much right to be here as you!" she replied hotly. "Maybe more!"

"She was probably just rummaging through the house, looking for garbage," said Mürgenstürm.

"Then why was she hiding?"

"I don't like people!"

As Mallory studied her more closely, he found to his surprise that she wasn't a girl after all—at least, not like any girl he had ever seen. She was young and slender, and her limbs were covered with a fine orange down faintly striped with black, while her face, neck, and chest were cream-colored. Her orange irises were those of a cat, her canines were quite pronounced, and she had whiskers— feline, not human—growing out of her upper lip. Her ears were a little too rounded, her face a touch too oval, her nails long and lethal-looking. She wore a single garment, a short tan dress that looked like it had been found on one of her garbage-hunting expeditions.

"What are you?" asked Mallory, genuinely curious.

"*Felinis majoris,*" she answered defiantly.

"She's one of the cat-people," explained Mürgenstürm. "There aren't very many of them left anymore."

"Why don't you like humans?" continued Mallory.

"They don't like anybody," said Mürgenstürm before
Felina could answer. "Dogs hunt them, humans shun
them, real cats ignore them."

"I can speak for myself," said Felina haughtily.

"Then start speaking," said Mallory. "What are you
doing here?"

"Looking for food."

"Do cat-people eat unicorns?"

"No." Suddenly her eyes widened and she smiled a
very feline smile. "It was *your* unicorn that was stolen!"

"His," said Mallory, jerking a thumb in the elf's direction. "I'm just helping him look for it."

She turned to Mürgenstürm. "They'll kill you at sunrise," she said, amused.

"Not if we find it first," said Mallory.

"You won't."

"How do you know?"

"Because I know who stole it," said the cat-girl.

"Who?"

She purred and licked a forearm. "I'm hungry."

"Tell me who stole it and I'll buy you any dinner you
want," said Mallory.

"I never *buy* dinners," she said, stretching languor-
ously. "It's so much more fun to hunt for them."

"Then name your price."

"My price?" she said, as if the notion of selling anything was totally new to her. Suddenly she smiled. "My
price is that I want to watch *his* face"—she pointed to
Mürgenstürm—"when I tell you."

"Fine," said Mallory. "Take a good look at him."

"Your unicorn, little elf," she said, watching Mürgenstürm as a cat watches a mouse, "was stolen by the
Grundy."

Mürgenstürm turned a pale green and reacted as if he'd
been hit with a sledgehammer.

"No!" he whispered, collapsing cross-legged with his back to the fence.

She grinned and nodded her head slowly.

"What's going on?" demanded Mallory. "Who is this Grundy?"

"He's the most powerful demon in New York!" moaned Mürgenstürm.

"Maybe on the whole East Coast," added Felina, delighted with the elf's reaction.

"He uses magic?" asked Mallory apprehensively.

"Magic doesn't work, John Justin," said Mürgenstürm in a dull voice. "You know that."

"Then what makes him a demon?"

"Nothing *makes* him a demon. It's what he *is*."

"All right," said Mallory. "What *is* a demon?"

"A malevolent entity of incomparable power."

"So is an IRS auditor," said Mallory irritably. "Be more specific. What does he look like? Has he got horns? A tail? Does he breathe smoke and belch fire?"

"All that and more," moaned Mürgenstürm.

"*Much* more," added Felina happily.

Mallory turned to Felina. "You're sure that it was this Grundy who stole the unicorn?" he asked. "You actually saw him do it?"

She nodded, grinning from ear to ear.

"Suppose you tell me exactly what happened."

"The Grundy and Flypaper Gillespie came up to the fence—"

"Just a minute," interrupted Mallory. "The Grundy and *who?*"

"Flypaper Gillespie," said Mürgenstürm. "He's a leprechaun who works for the Grundy. They call him that because things stick to him."

"What kinds of things?" asked Mallory.

"Wallets, jewelry, amulets—things like that," answered Felina.

"Go on."

"The Grundy opened the gate, pointed to the unicorn, and said, 'There he is. You know what to do.' And Flypaper Gillespie said that he sure did know what to do, and then the Grundy vanished, and Flypaper Gillespie untied the unicorn and led him away." Felina paused. "That's everything that happened."

"You're sure?" persisted Mallory.

"Yes."

"Where were you all this time?"

She pointed to a second-floor window.

"What were you doing there?"

"Hunting."

"Hunting what?"

"Something tasty," she replied.

"You say the Grundy vanished," noted Mallory. "Are you sure he didn't just walk away while you were watching the unicorn?"

"He vanished," Felina repeated firmly.

Mallory turned to Mürgenstürm. "Tell me more about this Grundy."

"What do you want to know?"

"Everything."

"Nobody knows that much about him," replied Mürgenstürm, "except that he's a malevolent entity who is the cause of most of the misery and despair in my Manhattan. He appears, and terrible things happen."

"What kinds of things?"

"*Terrible* things!" repeated Mürgenstürm with a shudder.

"Like what?"

"Don't ask!"

"It's my business to ask."

"He's responsible for everything bad that happens here.

If there's a natural disaster, he caused it; if there's an unsolved crime, he committed it; if there's an epidemic, he spread it.''

"Why?"

"He's a demon. It's his nature."

"How does he vanish into thin air?"

"He is a master of illusion and misdirection."

"But not of magic?"

"No. Although," added the elf, "he *is* capable of feats that, even to the experienced eye, are indistinguishable from magic."

"What are his weaknesses?" asked Mallory.

"I don't know if he has any."

"He must, or he'd own the whole city by now."

"I suppose so," said Mürgenstürm dubiously.

Mallory turned back to the cat-girl. "Think hard, Felina. Did the Grundy say anything else? Did he tell Flypaper Gillespie where to take the unicorn?"

Felina shook her head.

"Did he say how soon he'd be meeting him?"

"No."

"By the way, just for the record, what does a unicorn look like?"

"Just like a horse, only different," said Felina.

"Different *how?*" asked Mallory. "Just the horn?"

"Just the horn," she agreed. "And maybe the legs, and the face, and the flanks, and the tail."

"It looks like a horse except for the head, the body, and the horn?" suggested Mallory sardonically.

She smiled and nodded.

Mallory glared at her for a moment, then shrugged. "All right. Can either of you tell me anything about Flypaper Gillespie?"

"He's a leprechaun," said Mürgenstürm.

"I *know* he's a leprechaun!" snapped Mallory. "You told me that already!"

"That totally defines him," said Mürgenstürm. "What else did you want to know?"

"I almost hesitate to ask, but what does a leprechaun look like?"

"They're sort of . . . well, small . . . and they've got funny ears, though they're not really pointed . . . and, um . . ." began Mürgenstürm, struggling to come up with a description.

"They wear tweeds a lot," interjected Felina helpfully.

"Anyway, you'll know one when you see one," concluded Mürgenstürm confidently.

"How about behavior?" demanded Mallory, resisting the urge to snatch up the little elf and shake him. "What do leprechauns do?"

"They rob and steal and drink a lot," said Mürgenstürm. "Mostly Irish whiskey."

"And they lie," added Felina.

"Oh, yes," said Mürgenstürm. "They never tell the truth when they can tell a lie." He looked at Mallory. "You seem annoyed, John Justin."

"I can't imagine why," muttered Mallory. "I'll try once more. Where am I likely to find Flypaper Gillespie?"

"I don't know," said Mürgenstürm. "I apologize if my answers seem inadequate, but the truth of the matter is that nobody has ever tried to *find* the Grundy or Flypaper Gillespie before. Usually, people run in the opposite direction."

"So I gather," said Mallory. "In fact, I think it's contract renegotiation time. I've got a feeling that I'm being underpaid for this job."

"But you agreed to take the case!"

"The case didn't have a goddamned demon in it when I agreed!"

"All right," said the little elf with a sigh of resignation. "Twenty thousand."

"Twenty-five," said Mallory.

"Done."

Mallory stared at him. "Thirty-five."

"But you said twenty-five thousand and I agreed!" protested the elf.

"You agreed too damned fast," said Mallory.

"Well, I'm certainly not going to agree to thirty-five thousand dollars—fast, slow, or otherwise."

"That's your privilege," said Mallory. "Find Larkspur yourself."

"Twenty-eight and a half," said the elf quickly.

"Thirty-three."

"Thirty."

"Make it thirty-one and we're in business."

"You promise?" asked Mürgenstürm distrustfully.

"Word of honor."

The elf considered it for a minute, then nodded his assent.

"You're *really* going to try to find the unicorn?" asked Felina.

"That's right," said Mallory.

"Even knowing that the Grundy's behind it?"

"Even so."

"Why?"

"Because Mürgenstürm's paying me an awful lot of money," said Mallory. He paused. "Besides, I haven't been having much luck as a husband or a horseplayer or anything else lately. I think it's about time I got back to doing something I'm good at."

"I *like* you," said Felina, rubbing her hip against his and purring. "You're not like the others."

"Thank you," said Mallory. "I think."

"You're not like them at all," she repeated. "You're *crazy!* Imagine anyone *wanting* to fight the Grundy!"

"I didn't say I *wanted* to," replied Mallory. "I said that for the right price I was *willing* to."

She rubbed up against him again. "Can I come along?"

"I thought you were afraid of the Grundy."

"I am," she assured him. "I'll desert you in the end, but it'll be fun in the meantime."

Mallory stared at her for a moment.

"Can you follow a unicorn's scent?"

"I suppose so."

"Okay, you're hired. Now, let's get going. We're not going to find it by hanging around here talking."

She stared at the ground, nostrils twitching, then walked to the gate, opened it, and headed off down the twisting, deserted street.

"I'm sorry that events have taken this unexpected and distressing turn, John Justin," said Mürgenstürm as he and Mallory fell into step behind Felina.

"It could be worse. At least we know who we're looking for now—and we've still got most of the night ahead of us."

"True," said the elf. "But as you actively seek the Grundy, so he will actively defend himself." He paused. "Still, you're risking your life for me, and I'm grateful."

"You're overreacting," said Mallory. "The Grundy doesn't even know I'm here."

Suddenly there was a clap of thunder, and a flash of lightning momentarily illuminated the night sky.

"Don't bet on it, John Justin Mallory!" said a hollow voice from a nearby courtyard.

Mallory raced off in the direction of the voice, but found nothing except eerie shadows flickering on the stone gargoyles that stared down at him from a balcony overlooking the empty street.

Chapter
3 ────────────────────

They had proceeded for another block when Mallory noticed that his surroundings were getting brighter.

"I must have gotten turned around," he remarked to Mürgenstürm. "I could have sworn we were going back the way we had come."

"We are, John Justin," said the elf.

Mallory shook his head. "The street was dark before. Now look at it. The streetlamps are starting to glow, and a number of the apartments are lit up."

"They always were," Mürgenstürm assured him.

"Bullshit."

"They were," repeated the elf. "You simply couldn't see it before."

"Why not?"

Mürgenstürm scratched his head. "I suppose it's because you were an intruder who had wandered over from *your* Manhattan. Now, for better or worse, you're a participant."

"That makes a difference?"

"All the difference in the world."

47

"Why?"

"Excellent question."

"You don't know," said Mallory.

"I have never pretended to be anything other than what I am: a devilishly handsome elf of normal intelligence and sexual needs—"

"And severely diminished expectations of longevity," interjected Mallory.

"True," agreed Mürgenstürm unhappily. "At any rate, I have never claimed to be a scholar or a clairvoyant, and I find it thoroughly ungracious of you to constantly belittle me for these shortcomings."

Mallory was about to answer him, but at that moment they followed Felina around a corner and he realized that Mürgenstürm's Manhattan had come fully to life. It was still cold and raining, but the street was bustling with elves, gnomes, goblins, trolls, and even less human passersby, as well as an assortment of men and women. Sturdy multihued elephants and draft horses pulled an endless stream of carts and carriages, while odd little street vendors who were neither men nor elves were hawking everything from toys to mystical gemstones.

A large man with scaly skin and strange, staring eyes stood in front of a clothing store, slowly turning the crank on a music box with long, webbed fingers, while a little blond boy on a leash walked up to Mallory with a cup in his hand and a hopeful smile on his face. Mallory tossed him a coin, which he caught in the cup, and, after bowing deeply, he cartwheeled up to a passing woman and did a little jig until she, too, had made a contribution.

"I'm on retainer *plus* expenses, right?" said Mallory suddenly.

"That's right, John Justin," replied Mürgenstürm.

"I just wanted to make sure you remembered."

"Why?" asked the elf.

"Because I'm soaked to the skin and freezing my ass off," said Mallory, striding toward the front door of the clothing store. The organ grinder stepped out of his way, and Mallory noticed that he had a row of gills running up each side of his thick neck.

"Don't overdo it, John Justin," Mürgenstürm cautioned him. "My funds are quite limited."

"Then pull some more out of the air."

"That money's no good."

"*What?*" said Mallory ominously.

"Oh, it's perfectly good in *your* Manhattan," the elf assured him. "But where would we be if anyone in my world who needed money could simply produce it out of empty air?"

"Then give me some money that works *here*."

Mürgenstürm begrudgingly counted out $500 and gave it to him, along with a handful of change. Mallory inspected the money briefly, then placed it in his pocket and entered the store, which was surprisingly crowded given the time of night. The clientele wore everything from tuxedos to suits of armor, except for a portly, middle-aged man who wore nothing except a bowler hat and a gold-handled umbrella. Most of the mannequins displayed various satin and velvet robes and gowns, though a handful sported chain mail, and one was equipped with jodhpurs and a pith helmet. Two live models, one well over seven feet tall and the other shorter than Mürgenstürm, walked up and down the aisles showing off marked-down seersucker suits.

"Interesting," remarked Mallory.

"Pedestrian," replied Mürgenstürm, obviously unimpressed.

"May I help you?" asked a smartly dressed man, approaching them.

"Yes," replied Mallory. "I need an overcoat, preferably something with a fur collar."

"I'm afraid that's out of the question, sir," replied the man.

"How about a fleece-lined ski jacket?"

The man looked mildly distressed and shook his head. "I'm terribly sorry, sir, but we simply don't carry anything that exotic."

"You don't carry anything *exotic?*" repeated Mallory. "What the hell have you got on display?"

"You refer, doubtless, to our safari outfit," replied the man, gesturing toward the mannequin with the pith helmet. "I'm afraid that's our only truly *outré* outfit, sir."

"Look," said Mallory. "All I want is something that will keep me warm and reasonably dry."

"And it shouldn't be too expensive," added Mürgenstürm hastily.

"Well, let me take your measurements, and I'll see what we can do for you, sir," said the man, whipping out a pen and a note pad.

"Don't you need a tape measure?" asked Mallory.

The man looked amused. "Whatever for?"

"Damned if I know," admitted Mallory.

"Shall we begin, sir?"

"Go right ahead."

"Age?"

"Thirty-seven," said Mallory, puzzled.

"Legs?"

"Yes."

The man tried to hide his annoyance. "How many, sir?"

"Two," said Mallory.

"Eye color?"

"Brown."

"Any scars?"

"Any scars?" repeated Mallory, puzzled.

"Please, sir. Others are waiting."

Mallory shrugged. "One, from an appendectomy."

"Are you right-handed or left-handed?"

"Right."

The man looked up and smiled. "I believe that's everything. I'll be right back."

"Strange," muttered Mallory as he watched the man scurry across the store.

"Why should you say that, John Justin?"

"You didn't find that unusual?" asked Mallory.

"Not really. He should have asked about cavities and fillings, of course, but they're obviously understaffed."

Just then a woman screamed at the far end of the store, and a moment later Mallory saw Felina leap up onto a display counter, hissing furiously. She was wearing a hat that seemed to be composed entirely of bananas, grapes, and oranges, and it was apparent that she was prepared to fight to the death for it.

"If you won't pay for it, you *must* give it back!" said a saleswoman, approaching her.

Felina hissed again and leaped lightly to a chandelier.

"Cat-people really aren't at their best in places like this," said Mürgenstürm sadly. "They simply don't understand the capitalist ethic."

"Go buy the damned thing for her and get her out of here before she kills someone," said Mallory.

"*She's* not on an expense account," protested Mürgenstürm.

"Just do it," said Mallory. "You can take it out of my pay."

Satisfied, the little elf walked over to pay for the hat. A moment later Mallory's salesman returned, carrying a red satin robe with a coal black cape.

"How do you like it, sir?" he said, holding it up to the light.

"It's lovely," said Mallory. "But it's not what I asked for. I've got to wear it outside."

"Certainly," said the man. "That's why I chose red and black. They won't show the dirt as much as our more popular gold-and-white combination."

"I'm not so much concerned with the dirt as I am with the cold and the rain."

"Ah, you must be referring to the belt!" said the salesman. "Not to worry, sir. The new XB-223 belt has a much better control system." He held up the belt for Mallory's inspection.

"Mostly, I was referring to the fabric."

"Just try it on, sir," said the salesman, holding it out for him. Mallory decided that he would waste less time by humoring the man than by arguing with him, and allowed the salesman to help him into the robe. "Oh, it's *you*, sir, no doubt about it! Are you ready for our free field-testing?"

"Field-testing?"

"Certainly. We stand behind all our products. Come this way, sir."

He led Mallory to a small, transparent booth, and ushered him inside.

"Put the belt on the first notch," he instructed the detective.

Mallory did so, and a moment later he was bombarded by water from half a dozen hidden spray nozzles. The torrent continued for thirty seconds, then stopped abruptly.

"How do you feel, sir?" asked the salesman.

"Dry," said Mallory, surprised.

"Now, if you'll draw the belt into the second notch . . ."

Mallory did so, and the compartment quickly filled with snow. Then, a moment later, it vanished.

"Warm and cozy?" asked the salesman.

Mallory nodded.

"It's those XB-223 belts," said the salesman. "Absolutely fabulous!" He paused. "Would you care to field-test it for deserts, tropical rain forests, or mine shafts?"

"No," said Mallory, stepping out of the booth. "This will be fine."

"Shall I gift wrap it, sir?"

"No, I'll wear it. How much do I owe you?"

"Two hundred seventy-three rupees, sir."

"I beg your pardon?"

"Two hundred seventy-three rupees, with tax."

"How much is that in dollars?"

"It's an Indian product, sir. I'm afraid we can't accept American money for it."

"But I don't have any rupees."

"No problem, sir. Shall we bill it to your account?"

"Why not?" said Mallory with a shrug.

"I'll need your address," said the salesman.

Suddenly an idea struck Mallory. "Do the Grundy or Flypaper Gillespie have accounts here?"

The salesman turned pale. "The Grundy?" he whispered.

"Or Flypaper Gillespie."

"Why do you want to know?" stammered the man.

"They're old friends of mine, but I've misplaced their addresses."

"They're your *friends?*" repeated the salesman, horrified. "Take the robe! There's no charge!"

"How can I find them?"

"I don't know," whimpered the salesman, backing away from him. "But when you do, remember to tell them that I gave you the robe for free!"

He turned and rushed off into the crowd of shoppers. Mallory watched him for a moment, then walked out of the store, where he found Mürgenstürm and Felina waiting for him on the sidewalk. The cat-girl was smiling, showing off her hat to any and all passersby.

"You owe me one hundred fifty-six pesos," announced Mürgenstürm.

"We're even," said Mallory, setting the belt on the first notch and marveling at the way it instantly protected him from the rain. "I got the robe for free."

"How did you manage that?"

"I have friends in high places," said the detective dryly. "All right, Felina—can you pick up Larkspur's scent?"

The cat-girl walked up to Mallory, rubbed up against him, and purred.

"Don't do that," said the detective, looking around uncomfortably.

"Scratch my back," she said.

"Not in front of everyone."

She rubbed against him again. "Scratch my back or I'm leaving," she said insistently.

He grimaced and began rubbing her back. A blissful smile spread across her face, and she began writhing sinuously beneath his hand.

"Enough?" asked Mallory after a moment.

"For now," she replied smugly, starting off again with one hand securing her hat, and Mallory and Mürgenstürm fell into step behind her. She remained on the thoroughfare for two blocks, then turned onto a narrow street. She proceeded for a few yards, then paused, puzzled, looked around, walked over to a mailbox, jumped atop it, and began licking the outside of her left thigh.

"What's wrong?" asked Mallory.

She continued licking herself for another moment, then turned to him.

"I've lost the scent," she announced.

"But Larkspur definitely entered this street?"

She shrugged. "I think so."

"You *think* so?" he demanded, as she went back to licking her thigh.

"He came this far, but there have been too many people passing by. I don't know where he went next."

"Wonderful," muttered Mallory. He walked a few feet down the street. "How about here?"

She jumped off the mailbox, walked over to where Mallory was standing, sniffed the air, and shrugged again.

Mallory looked down the dimly lit street, which was practically devoid of pedestrians. A number of the buildings fronting it had been rehabilitated, and one of them boasted a brightly illuminated open-air restaurant. Due to the icy rain most of the tables were deserted, but one of them was occupied by two men. The man with his back to Mallory was wearing a trenchcoat and a felt hat, while the man seated opposite him, far smaller in size, wore a shopworn double-breasted suit and was continually wiping the rain from his face with a large silk handkerchief. As Mallory drew closer he saw that they were playing chess.

"Well, we've got to start somewhere," said Mallory, approaching the two chessplayers. He stood there for a moment while they continued staring intently at the board, then cleared his throat. "I beg your pardon."

"No offense taken," answered the man in the trenchcoat, without looking up from the chessboard. "Now, go away."

"I wonder if I might ask you a question," persisted Mallory.

"You might," said the man. "I probably wouldn't answer you, though."

"It'll only take a second."

The man looked up irritably. "It's already taken twenty seconds." He turned to his opponent. "This had better not be coming off my time."

"Of course it is," said the smaller man in a slightly

nasal accent that Mallory couldn't identify. "Remember V-J Day? I stood up and cheered, and you took a whole minute off my time."

"That was different," said the man in the trenchcoat. "Nobody said you had to get up."

"It was patriotic."

"It was *your* decision to be patriotic. I, on the other hand, was minding my own business when this inconsiderate dolt approached me."

"Thirty-nine days, eight hours, six minutes, sixteen seconds, and counting," said the smaller man firmly.

The man in the trenchcoat glared furiously at Mallory. "Now see what you've done!" he snapped.

"I heard you say something about V-J Day," said Mallory. "Have you guys really been playing since World War II?"

"Since February 4, 1937, to be precise," said the smaller man.

"Who's ahead?"

"I'm down one pawn," said the man in the trenchcoat.

"I mean, how many games have each of you won?"

"What a damnfool question! I hope you don't think I'd be sitting here in the rain on New Year's Eve if I'd already beaten him."

"You've never beaten him?" said Mallory. "Then why keep trying?"

"He's never beaten me either."

"You two must have set a record for consecutive draws," remarked Mallory.

"We've never played to a draw."

Mallory blinked the rain from his eyes. "Let me get this straight," he said at last. "You've been playing the same game of chess for half a century?"

"Give or take," acknowledged the man in the trenchcoat.

"Chess doesn't take that long," said Mallory.

"When *we* play it, it does," said the smaller man with a touch of pride.

"Right," agreed his opponent. "The game's the thing—at least the way me and the Weasel play it."

"The Weasel?" asked Mallory.

"That's me," said the smaller man with a self-effacing smile. "And he's Trenchcoat."

"Don't you have real names?"

"We know who we are," said Trenchcoat, lighting up a bent Camel cigarette.

"And you've been sitting right here for fifty years?"

"Not really," replied Trenchcoat. "We began in the back of a saloon down in the Village, but they lost their lease about thirty years ago."

"Thirty-two years, to be exact," corrected the Weasel.

"So we've actually only been here about a third of a century."

"Non-stop?" asked Mallory.

"Barring calls of nature," said the Weasel.

"We eat right at the table," added Trenchcoat. "It saves time."

"And of course I catch up on my sleep when it's his move," said the Weasel.

"Don't either of you ever wonder what's been going on in the world for the past half century?" asked Mallory.

"Every now and then," admitted the Weasel. "Are any wars still being fought?"

"Thirty or forty," replied Mallory.

"And is there crime in the streets?"

"Of course."

"What about the Yankees?" asked Trenchcoat. "Are they still winning pennants?"

"From time to time."

"Well, there you have it," said Trenchcoat with a shrug. "Nothing's changed."

"Think of all the money we've saved by not buying newspapers," added the Weasel.

"But you can't just drop out of the world and play chess for the rest of your lives," persisted Mallory.

"Of course we can," said Trenchcoat.

"At least until the game is over," said the Weasel.

"Will it ever be over?"

"Certainly," said the Weasel confidently. "I'll have him in another fifteen years or so."

"Dream on," said Trenchcoat contemptuously.

"It seems like such a waste," remarked Mallory. "You're just sitting here vegetating."

"*He's* vegetating," replied the Weasel. "*I'm* formulating a plan to break through his Indian defense."

Trenchcoat turned to stare at Mallory. "And what are *you* doing that's so important?"

"Hunting for a unicorn."

"Well, you won't find it in the city," said Trenchcoat. "Unicorns need water and green things. If I were you, I'd look in Africa or Australia or someplace like that."

"This one was stolen," explained Mallory.

"Is it yours?"

"No. I'm a detective."

"You know, it's funny that you should say that," said Trenchcoat.

"Oh? Why?"

"Because *I* used to be a detective."

"What about you?" Mallory asked the Weasel. "Were you a detective too?"

"*Au contraire*. I was a criminal."

"More to the point," added Trenchcoat, "he was *my* criminal."

"I don't think I understand you," said Mallory.

"It's really quite simple," said Trenchcoat. "What is

the one thing that detectives absolutely cannot do without? Criminals!''

''And I needed him just as badly,'' continued the Weasel. ''In fact, we defined each other. You can't have a criminal without laws, and you can't work at enforcing laws without criminals. You might say that we had a symbiotic relationship. I'd clock in every morning at eight o'clock and go out to rob, pillage, and loot . . .''

''And I'd clock in at nine—it seemed only fair to give him enough time to break some laws—and then I'd try to apprehend him.'' Trenchcoat paused, a pleasant smile of reminiscence on his face. ''We'd go at it hot and heavy all day long, him putting on disguises and ducking in and out of shadows, me gathering clues and trying to track him down . . .''

''Taking an hour off for lunch . . .'' interjected the Weasel.

''And then we'd clock out at five, get together for a drink, and prepare for the next day.''

''We even coordinated our sick time and vacations.''

''Right,'' said Trenchcoat. ''And then one day it dawned on us that the game was more important than the rewards.''

''I realized that matching wits with him was more gratifying to me than stealing things. After all, I had a warehouse full of toasters and I never ate at home.''

''And I didn't really care about catching murderers and bank robbers; most of them didn't present any kind of a challenge—and besides, the courts kept turning them loose anyway.''

''We also realized that we were both getting a little old to be chasing around the city and shooting at each other . . .'' said the Weasel.

''Not that we ever aimed to actually hit one another . . .''

''So, since it was the battle of wits that excited us, we

decided to rid ourselves of all the peripherals and get down
to the basic contest.''

"I found another job for my secretary, Velma," said
Trenchcoat as Mallory winced, "and then the Weasel
and I sat down and began discussing creative alter-
natives . . ."

"We gave serious consideration to cards—there's a poker
game over on the next block for the ownership of Lincoln,
Nebraska, that's been going on even longer than we have—
but we wanted something where chance didn't enter into
it . . ."

"So we hit upon chess," concluded Trenchcoat.

"And here we are. I strike in the dead of night and steal
his pawn . . ."

"And I trail him down dark twisting alleys between
bishops and rooks," concluded Trenchcoat with a contented sigh. "It's really much more satisfying than hunting
for murderers. Or unicorns, for that matter."

"Speaking of unicorns . . ." began Mallory.

"I thought we were speaking of chess," said Trenchcoat.

"Only some of us were," said Mallory. "Some of us
are looking for a stolen unicorn."

"I hardly see how we can help you."

"We tracked him to this street, and then we lost his
trail. Has he passed by in the last few hours? He would
have had a leprechaun with him."

"Who knows?" replied Trenchcoat with a shrug. "I've
been concentrating on my next move for two days now."

"How about you?" asked Mallory.

"I was watching *him* to make sure he didn't try to
cheat," answered the Weasel.

"At any rate, I wouldn't be in such a hurry to catch him
if I were you," remarked Trenchcoat.

"Why not?"

"Take it from a fellow detective: you're viewing this

from the wrong perspective. One unicorn, properly and thoroughly stolen, can provide a man with a lifetime's employment.''

"Thanks for your suggestion," said Mallory. "But the lifetime is *his*"—he jerked a thumb toward Mürgenstürm— "and it ends tomorrow morning if I don't find the unicorn."

"Who's going to kill him?" asked Trenchcoat.

"I have a feeling that it's going to be a race between his guild and the Grundy."

"The Grundy?" asked Trenchcoat, arching an eyebrow. "Is *he* involved in this?"

"Yes."

"Watch out for him," warned Trenchcoat. "He's a mean one."

"Can you tell me anything about him?" asked Mallory.

"I just did," said Trenchcoat.

"Do you know anything about a leprechaun named Flypaper Gillespie?"

"Just generically."

"Generically?" repeated Mallory.

"Leprechauns are a vicious and surly race."

"I don't suppose you'd care to join in the hunt?"

Trenchcoat surveyed the chessboard for a moment, then sighed and shook his head. "Not when I'm closing in for the kill."

"In that case, you could leave now," said the Weasel.

"You do seem to have him in a bit of trouble," agreed Mallory, taking a quick glance at the board.

"You think so?" said Trenchcoat triumphantly. "Then watch *this!*"

He reached forward, picked up his queen, and placed it on the next table, just behind a vase filled with artificial carnations.

"Mon Dieux!" muttered the Weasel, astonished. "The boldness, the effrontery, the sheer brilliance of it!"

He immediately fell silent as he began considering how best to protect his king's bishop from an attack launched from a neighboring table.

"There's no sense hanging around here any longer," said Mallory, shaking his head in disbelief. "Where the hell is our faithful tracker?"

Mürgenstürm pointed down the street to a mesh litter basket with a KEEP OUR CITY CLEAN sign affixed to it, where Felina, bareheaded, was rummaging for edible garbage.

"Call her over and let's get this show on the road," said Mallory. As Mürgenstürm went off to fetch her, the detective leaned over to the Weasel and whispered, "Saltshaker to queen's bishop five."

The Weasel's eyes widened. "You know," he said excitedly, "it's so crazy it just might work!" He went back to studying the board.

"What happened to your hat?" asked Mallory when Felina returned with Mürgenstürm.

"I got tired of it," she said with a shrug.

"What now, John Justin?" asked Mürgenstürm anxiously.

"We keep looking for Larkspur."

"But where? We've lost his trail."

"So much for shortcuts," said Mallory. "It looks like I'm going to have to do it the hard way."

"The hard way?"

Mallory nodded. "Before I go hunting for Larkspur, I've got to know exactly what I'm hunting for. What does a unicorn look like? What does it eat? Does it help to have a virgin handy? Where are they likely to hide it? What kind of trail does it leave besides unicorn shit? Is there a particular sound or scent it will respond to?"

"How should I know?" asked Mürgenstürm. "My job was just to guard the damned thing, not study it."

"Who *would* know?"

"I have no idea," replied the elf as they reached the corner of the main thoroughfare. While throngs of pedestrians passed by and scores of draft animals traversed the street, paying no attention to the traffic lights, Felina began climbing a lamppost in pursuit of a small bat that was fluttering around the light. "I mean, a person who could speak endlessly about the habits and habitats of unicorns is hardly my idea of good company."

"What about a zoologist?" suggested Mallory.

"Sounds good to me," replied Mürgenstürm. "Do you know any?" Mallory merely glared at him. Suddenly the elf snapped his fingers in triumph. "I've got it!"

"What?"

"The Museum of Natural History! They've got a stuffed unicorn on display there. They're bound to have all kinds of information about them."

"Will it be open?" asked Mallory dubiously.

"I know the night watchman. He'll let us in for a small financial consideration."

"How did a little green wimp like you ever come to spend any time in a museum?"

"There's a gallery there that's been closed for renovation, and the weather being what it is . . . ah . . . well, you know how these things are . . ."

"That's where you take your conquests?" asked Mallory incredulously.

"Sometimes," acknowledged the elf. "Just those who live in the vicinity. No more than three or four an evening." He drew himself up to his full, if minimal, height. "And they're not conquests," he added with dignity.

"They're not?"

"Well, not when I take them there," said Mürgenstürm. "Only when I leave."

Just then Felina dropped lightly to the ground beside

them and delicately wiped a piece of gray fur from her lips.

"I'm surrounded by appetites," commented Mallory disgustedly. He looked up the broad thoroughfare. "Well, let's be going."

Just then a newsboy, a huge stack of freshly printed papers folded under his arm, walked by.

"Grundy Issues Warning!" he cried, holding a paper above his head with his free hand. "Read all about it! Grundy Issues Warning!"

"See?" said Mallory confidently. "He's so busy with other things he probably hasn't even seen Larkspur since he stole him."

A second newsboy approached them from a different direction.

"Grundy Threatens Mallory!" he hollered. "Extra! Extra! Grundy Threatens Mallory! Props and Midgets Lose Again!"

Mallory walked over to the boy.

"Let me see one of those," he said, pulling some change out of a pocket.

The newsboy handed him a copy, and Mallory opened it up.

" 'Mallory, Go Home While You Still Can!' Warns Grundy," he read aloud.

"Does he mean you?" asked Felina.

"I suppose so."

She smiled and rubbed against him. "You're famous!"

Mallory stared at the paper again, then looked at Mürgenstürm. "How the hell did he get a photo of me?" he asked at last.

The little elf shrugged. "He's the Grundy."

Suddenly a small boy wearing an Eastern Union uniform raced up and handed an envelope to Mallory.

"What's this?" asked the detective.

"Telegram, sir."

"You're sure it's for me?"

"You're John Justin Mallory, aren't you?"

Mallory nodded. "How much do I owe you?"

"It's been prepaid."

Mallory flipped him a coin, which the boy caught on the run, then ripped open the envelope.

MALLORY, DO NOT, REPEAT, DO NOT GO TO THE MUSEUM OR MAKE ANY OTHER ATTEMPT TO FIND THE UNICORN OR FLYPAPER GILLESPIE STOP YOUR LIFE IS AT RISK STOP THIS IS YOUR ONLY WARNING STOP

Mallory handed the telegram to Mürgenstürm, who turned almost white as he read it. A few seconds later it dropped from his trembling fingers and fell to the wet sidewalk.

"We decided to go to the museum less than two minutes ago," said Mallory.

Mürgenstürm gulped. "I know."

"Even if we were wired for sound, it takes longer than that to write and deliver a telegram."

"Obviously not for the Grundy," said Mürgenstürm in a quavering voice.

"I thought you told me he didn't have any magical powers."

"That's absolutely right, John Justin. Magic doesn't work, and I've always held that it's ridiculous for anyone in this enlightened day and age to believe otherwise."

"That how do you explain the telegram?" demanded Mallory.

Mürgenstürm smiled a sickly smile. "Maybe I was wrong."

Chapter
4 ———————————————

Mallory looked around, studying the various stores.

"What are you looking for, John Justin?" asked Mürgenstürm. "I thought we were going to the museum."

"First things first," said Mallory. "Where can I find a gun shop?"

"There's one on the next block," said Mürgenstürm. "But I thought you never carried a weapon."

"I was never threatened by a demon before," said Mallory, heading off in the direction the elf had indicated. "Will it be open on New Year's Eve?"

"Why not?" responded Mürgenstürm. "More people are shot on New Year's Eve than any other night of the year."

They reached the store in another minute, and Mallory turned to the elf. "I think one shopping binge a night is enough for Felina. Why don't you stay out here and make sure that she doesn't wander off?"

"Why bother?" asked Mürgenstürm. "She's obviously no longer any use to us as a tracker."

"Because I have a feeling that we're going to need all the help we can get."

"Even incompetent help?"

"You can't always choose," replied Mallory. "Find me someone competent and we'll talk about leaving her behind."

"You're the boss," said Mürgenstürm with a shrug.

"We'll get along fine as long as we all remember that," said Mallory, and entered the store alone.

There were a number of customers inspecting the various weapons. A trio of uniformed military men seemed to be comparing notes on rapid-action repeating rifles; a huge, bearded warrior dressed in furs and a metal skullcap was hefting a number of battle-axes; a chalk-white woman with long black hair and high, arching eyebrows was holding an ornate dagger, striking assorted dramatic poses in front of a mirror; another woman, complaining about her husband in a loud voice, kept sending a clerk back for larger and larger handguns; a Gnome of the Subway, looking apprehensively at the doorway every few seconds, was examining various types of ammunition; and perhaps a dozen other customers of varying sizes and species were simply browsing aimlessly.

Mallory stopped at a display case of pistols, then wandered over to a wall that held a number of tribal spears in small metal clamps. He continued browsing, discovering a number of weapons that made absolutely no sense to him. Finally he walked up to the main counter.

"May I help you, sir?" asked a slight, balding man with a drooping moustache.

"I hope so," replied Mallory. "What kind of gun will stop a leprechaun?"

"Leprechauns?" said the man with a pleased smile. "Ah, there's nothing quite like hunting leprechauns in the rain! How many of the little beggars do you plan to blow away, sir?"

"Just one."

The man nodded sympathetically. "They're getting harder to find every year. Not like the good old days, eh?"

"I guess not."

"How much of a sporting chance do you want to give him?"

"None," said Mallory.

"Quite right, sir," said the salesman, trying unsuccessfully to hide his disapproval. "I assume your license is in order?"

"License?"

"For slaughtering leprechauns," explained the salesman patiently.

"I didn't know I needed one."

"I'll bet you left it at home, sir."

"I don't have one."

"Certainly you do, sir," said the salesman persuasively. "If you didn't have one, you couldn't buy a gun to kill the little bastard with, could you?"

"I left it at home," said Mallory.

"You look like an honest man," said the salesman. "I see no reason why I shouldn't take your word for it." He reached beneath the counter and withdrew a small pistol. "Here's just the ticket, sir. Ten shots, one in the chamber and nine in the stock, accurate up to two hundred feet." He laid the pistol down on the counter and placed a box of ammunition next to it. "Will there be anything else?"

"Yes," said Mallory. "How do you kill a demon?"

"It all depends. We have a complete line of talismans and amulets." The salesman reached into another cabinet and withdrew a long crystal wand. "Or you could use *this* little baby here! Sweetest little weapon you've ever seen. Guaranteed to demolish every demon below the level of the Fifth Circle."

"I don't feel comfortable with magic," said Mallory. "What kind of gun will do the trick?"

"None. And I'll thank you not to refer to this as a *magic* wand, sir," said the salesman haughtily. "This wand works by strict scientific principles, just the same as our amulets and talismans: it refracts light to create invisibility, it ionizes the air around your antagonist and thereby eliminates his oxygen supply, it seeds clouds to create thunder and lightning, it—"

"All right," said Mallory. "I'll take it." He picked up the wand and examined it. "How do you make it work?"

"The spells are included with the instructions."

"Spells?"

"There are certain key words that trigger various responses from the microchip in the handle," explained the salesman. "The rest of it is just for dramatic effect."

"And this will definitely work against any demon I run across?" asked Mallory.

The salesman shook his head. "Only those below the Fifth Circle. What type of demon do you expect to be confronting?"

"I don't know. But if it's any help, he's called the Grundy."

"You want to kill the *Grundy?*" gasped the salesman.

"Only if it's necessary."

"Your name wouldn't be Mallory, would it?"

"It would."

The salesman grabbed the wand back. "Go away!"

"You don't have anything that will help me?"

"You're in the wrong place!" whimpered the salesman, crouching down and hiding behind the counter. "The only thing you need is a Bible."

"The Grundy's affected by Bibles?"

"No, but you might want to learn a quick prayer or two before he finds you."

"What do I owe you for the gun?" asked Mallory.

"One hundred seventy-five dollars."

"All I have are hundreds," said Mallory. "You're going to have to get up and make change."

"Just put a hundred on the counter and leave!"

Mallory, aware that everyone in the store was staring at him with expressions varying from shock to pity, picked up the pistol and the box of ammunition, put them in his pocket, and walked back into the street, where he found Mürgenstürm and Felina waiting for him.

"What now, John Justin?"

"Now we go to the museum." Mallory paused. "I don't suppose they'll have a stuffed leprechaun?"

"Certainly not!" said Mürgenstürm, morally outraged. "You might as well ask if they have a mounted elf on display!"

It took them fifteen minutes, via elephant and subway, to reach the museum, a huge and ancient structure of stone and steps and spires.

"The perfect example of Gothic Baptist architecture," commented Mürgenstürm admiringly as they approached the main entrance.

"I didn't know there *were* any examples of Gothic Baptist architecture," replied Mallory.

"There are here," said Mürgenstürm, ascending the broad stairs. When he reached the top, he went to a small door about fifty feet to the right of the main entrance and knocked vigorously.

"Hold your horses!" said a voice. "I'm coming!"

A moment later the door opened and an elderly man, his white hair thinning and uncombed, stuck his head out. "Oh, it's you again," he said when his eyes fell on the little green elf. "You know, Mürgenstürm, you've really got to do something about that libido of yours."

"My feelings precisely," echoed Mallory.

The old man stared at him for a moment, then made a

face and turned back to Mürgenstürm. "Your tastes are getting more degenerate by the hour," he said.

"You misunderstand the situation," said Mürgenstürm.

"If I do, it's not without cause," said the old man.

"John Justin, I want you to meet my friend Jebediah," said the elf. "Jebediah, this is the world-famous detective, John Justin Mallory."

Jebediah squinted at Mallory and nodded. "World-famous, eh? Well, come on in—but leave the cat behind."

"You mean Felina?" asked Mürgenstürm.

"You see any other cats?" asked Jebediah.

"But she's not a cat. She's one of the cat-people."

"Same thing," said Jebediah with a shrug. "She'll upset the exhibits."

"I thought this was a museum," interjected Mallory.

"It is."

"Aren't the exhibits all dead?"

"Of course."

"Then how can she upset them?" persisted the detective.

"Look," said Jebediah. "It's cold and it's raining, and I've got no intention of standing here in the doorway answering stupid questions. If you want to come in, leave her outside."

Mallory turned to Felina. "Wait here," he instructed her. "We'll only be a few minutes."

She made no reply, but merely squatted down on her haunches, staring at some fixed point in space that only she could see. In the dim light it seemed to Mallory that her pupils had expanded to entirely cover her irises. He reached out to give her a reassuring pat on the shoulder, which she avoided without seeming to move, and finally he shrugged and followed Jebediah and Mürgenstürm into the interior of the museum.

"Impressive, isn't it?" asked the elf.

Mallory looked around the huge, marble-floored central

hall. The arched ceiling was a good forty feet high, and a pair of reconstructed pterodactyls seemed to be hovering over him, suspended by nearly invisible support wires. Dominating the hall was the skeleton of an enormous tyrannosaur, its jaws filled with row upon row of long, jagged teeth.

"Mean-looking son of a bitch," he commented.

"Didn't there used to be an elephant here?" asked Mürgenstürm, indicating the area where the dinosaur stood ready to pounce. "A big one, with huge tusks?"

Jebediah nodded. "We've still got him, but he's with the rest of the African animals now. The taxi drivers started objecting to him, so we brought old Rex up here from the basement." The old man paused to brush a piece of lint from his dark blue uniform. "Just as well. He was getting lonely down there; now at least he's got the birds to keep him company."

"Birds?" repeated Mallory.

"The pterodactyls," explained Jebediah. He turned to Mürgenstürm. "Well, if you're not here for an affair of the heart, just what is it that you want?"

"I need some information," said Mallory.

Jebediah sighed. "I didn't figure you were here just to keep a lonely old man company on New Year's Eve."

"Well, that, too," said Mürgenstürm quickly. "But mainly, we have to learn something about unicorns."

"So they stole the unicorn from you, did they?" asked Jebediah, amused. "I knew they would."

"That's none of your business!" snapped Mürgenstürm.

Jebediah turned to Mallory. "I keep on telling him. 'Mürgenstürm, you ugly little wart,' I say, 'you can't keep letting your gonads rule your mind. Mürgenstürm,' I say, 'this museum's filled with exhibits that became extinct because they never learned to control their baser passions. Mürgenstürm,' I say, 'I can understand an occasional roll in the hay, but you're the most compulsive little pipsqueak I've ever—' "

"That will be quite enough, thank you!" snapped the elf.

"He hired you to find it?" asked Jebediah, ignoring Mürgenstürm's furious gaze.

Mallory nodded.

"Well, Mr. Mallory, I can guarantee it's not here."

"I'm sure it isn't," said Mallory. "But I've never even seen a unicorn. Mürgenstürm tells me you've got one on display."

Jebediah checked his wristwatch. "Can you be through in fifteen minutes?" he asked.

"I don't see why not."

"You're sure?" insisted Jebediah.

"How the hell long can it take to look at a stuffed unicorn?"

"Okay," said Jebediah, heading off toward one of the dozen corridors that fed into the central hall. "Follow me."

Mallory and Mürgenstürm entered the corridor.

To the left was a diorama featuring a rhinoceros, three zebras, a pair of wildebeest, and a family of four giraffes at a savannah water hole. On the right was a leopard, poised to spring out of its tree onto an unsuspecting impala. The corridor continued for some forty yards and held at least a dozen more dioramas.

Mallory turned back and studied the leopard for a moment. He could see its muscles bunched as it prepared to jump, almost rippling under its dead skin. Its eyes seemed to glow with awareness, and he half-expected to see its tail twitch just before it launched its attack.

"We have to hurry, Mr. Mallory," said Jebediah, taking a few steps back in the detective's direction.

Mallory immediately began walking again. "They're

very lifelike," he said when he had caught up with the old man.

"That they are," agreed Jebediah as they passed a gorilla family and skirted around the bull elephant that had been moved from the central hall.

"How much farther?" asked Mürgenstürm, running on his short, stumpy legs to keep up with the two men.

"Just past the bongo and the okapi," replied Jebediah. "You look all worn out." He grinned. "They say sex does that to the wind."

"I haven't had any sex for hours," panted Mürgenstürm. "Obviously, it's a lack of sex that does it."

"Obviously," said Mallory caustically.

The corridor branched to the left, and a moment later, after passing some large antelope, they entered a small room that housed a trio of creatures in plain glass cases. To the right was a banshee, to the left a satyr complete with its musical pipe, and directly in front of them was a large white unicorn. Its prominent brown eyes looked straight ahead, the horn on its forehead reminded Mallory of a twisted candy stick, its body was sleeker than most herbivores, and its tail almost touched the ground. It wasn't exactly horselike—a zebra, or even the extinct quagga, resembled a horse far more—but he couldn't figure out what else to compare it with, for it resembled all other animals even less.

He walked around the case, wondering why he was bothering, since, having seen a unicorn, he knew he could never mistake it for anything else.

Finally he came to a placard that offered him some minimal information:

NORTH AMERICAN UNICORN

Unicorns occur on all continents and islands except Antarctica, though they are believed to be virtually extinct in Peru, Tibet, and the Italian Riviera.

Unicorns are usually herbivorous, although they have been known to eat everything from small rodents to parking meters. They are primarily nocturnal, and tend to congregate at right angles to where you are looking at the moment.

The North American Unicorn—*unicornis n. americanus*—differs from all other members of the unicorn family in that it lives in North America.

This specimen was shot by Col. W. Carruthers during a safari to the interior of Sioux City, Iowa.

"Seen enough?" asked Jebediah.

"In a minute," said Mallory, staring at the unicorn once again.

"Make it quick."

Mallory turned to Mürgenstürm. "Does Larkspur look like this?"

The elf nodded. "They could be twins."

"I need to know more about his habits," said Mallory. "The placard wasn't very helpful."

"Time's up," announced Jebediah. "Let's go."

"Gesundheit," said Mürgenstürm.

"I didn't sneeze," said the old man.

"Well, somebody did," replied the elf.

"Not me," said Mallory.

"I know what I heard," said Mürgenstürm stubbornly. "Somebody went—"

A guttural coughing sound came to their ears.

"Just like that," concluded the elf uneasily.

"Damn!" snapped Jebediah. "I *told* you to hurry!"

Suddenly Mallory could smell the acrid scent of animals.

"What the hell's going on?" he demanded.

"Shhhh!" whispered Jebediah, holding his finger to his lips.

He waited for a moment, then nodded his head and stepped into the corridor through which they had come.

"Quickly now!" whispered the old man.

Mallory and Mürgenstürm fell into step behind him and they proceeded down the corridor, past the okapi and bongo displays.

"Just a minute!" said Mallory, stopping short as they passed a diorama depicting two lions at a kill.

"What is it?" asked Mürgenstürm, bumping into him.

"I could swear one of those lions just looked up," said the detective. He stared at it again, then shrugged. "Overactive imagination," he announced at last.

"Hurry!" whispered Jebediah urgently.

Mallory began walking again, and soon came to the junction of corridors where the bull elephant stood. It was a huge animal, fully twelve feet at the shoulder, and its sudden appearance, with ears spread wide and trunk extended toward him, startled the detective for a moment. He quickly recovered his composure and walked around the elephant to where Jebediah was standing by the entrance to another corridor.

"Hold on," said Mallory after they had walked about twenty-five feet. "Where's Mürgenstürm?"

"I thought he was right behind you," said Jebediah.

Mallory walked back to the end of the corridor.

"Damn it, Mürgenstürm!" he said. "What the hell's keeping—" He choked off the last word of the sentence as he found himself staring into the bloodshot little eyes of the elephant, which stood facing him, ears spread, trunk extended.

"Right here," said Mürgenstürm, walking up to him. "I went into the wrong corridor." The elf looked up at Mallory. "What's the matter, John Justin? You look like you've just seen a ghost."

"He was facing the other direction not twenty seconds ago," said Mallory, still looking at the elephant.

"You must have gotten all turned around," said Mürgenstürm. "Stuffed animals don't move."

Suddenly they heard an ear-splitting roar that echoed through the empty, drafty corridors.

"Do they roar?" asked Mallory.

"Not to my knowledge," said the elf uneasily.

"Let's get the hell out of here," said Mallory urgently, walking briskly to the spot where he had left Jebediah. There was no trace of the old man.

"Maybe you're in the wrong corridor," suggested Mürgenstürm.

"This is where I left him," said Mallory firmly.

"Then maybe he moved."

"We'll see," said Mallory, retracing his steps.

When they came to the elephant they gave it a wide berth and entered a new corridor just as a bird screeched behind them. They walked about fifty feet into it, then stopped.

"He's not here," said Mallory.

"What do we do now?" asked Mürgenstürm nervously.

"We go back the way we came."

"I'm lost," admitted the elf.

"We'll go back to the elephant, and it'll be the second corridor on the left."

"Wait!" exclaimed Mürgenstürm suddenly.

"What is it?"

"I think I heard him."

"I didn't hear anything."

"This way," said the elf, continuing down the corridor. "Jebediah!" he yelled.

There was no response.

"You're wrong," said Mallory.

"Well, I heard *something*," said Mürgenstürm nervously.

"I didn't," repeated Mallory.

"It sounded like footsteps."

They had been walking as they talked, and now they found themselves just a few steps from a branch in the corridor.

"Which way did they seem to be coming from?" asked Mallory.

"From the right, I think," replied Mürgenstürm.

Mallory stepped into the junction of the corridors, turned to his right—

And found himself face to face with a growling, snarling bull gorilla.

"*Jesus!*" he muttered. Both man and gorilla remained motionless for an instant. Then Mallory turned on his heel and raced back down the corridor, practically flattening Mürgenstürm in the process. The gorilla screamed, pounded his chest with his hairy hands, and then began lumbering leisurely after them.

Mallory came to the elephant with Mürgenstürm just a step behind him and raced to his right. As he entered the nearest corridor, he heard shrill, angry trumpeting behind him. He ran halfway down the corridor, then chanced a quick look behind him.

"We're safe!" he panted to the elf. "He can't get through. The corridor's too narrow for him."

"Not for *him*, though," whimpered Mürgenstürm, pointing in the opposite direction, where a black-maned lion was slinking toward them, his belly skimming the marble floor.

Somewhere a public address system clicked on, and the static momentarily frightened the lion, which leaped into an adjoining corridor.

"Assuming that you're still alive, I suppose you'd like an explanation," said Jebediah's voice.

"It would be nice," muttered Mallory under his breath.

"I didn't mean to desert you, Mr. Mallory, but I simply couldn't wait any longer. You see, the animals in this museum were stuffed and mounted by Akim Ramblatt."

"Who the hell is Akim Ramblatt?" whispered Mürgenstürm.

"You're probably wondering who the hell Ramblatt was," said the old man's voice. "The answer to that is that he was the best taxidermist who ever practiced the art. By the time he went to work for us, he was already known as the Master Builder." There was a brief pause. "He makes his animals appear so lifelike that they simply don't know they're dead. They sit up there in their glass cases all day thinking about it, and along about eleven each night they can't see any reason why they shouldn't stretch their legs and walk around a bit."

The next line was drowned out by a scream from some unidentified beast.

"Anyway, they're usually only active for an hour or two before they remember that they're not really alive. Ramblatt may have been the Master Builder, but he was not, after all, God." Jebediah chuckled. "So, assuming that you can hear my voice, all you have to do is hide in a safe place for the next couple of hours and you'll be just fine. The one time I got caught out of the office, I dove into the water hole and breathed through a hollow tube— but of course, that was before Ramblatt added the rhino. Not that he's vicious—at least as rhinos go—but he does love his wallow, and it's a very small water hole." He sighed. "Oh, well, you'll figure something out. And now, if you'll excuse me, it's time for my nap. If you manage to live through this experience, stop by my office; I'll have some coffee on the stove." Another pause. "I really can't think of any other advice for you. Ten-four."

The public address system went dead.

"How long has it been since eleven o'clock?" asked Mürgenstürm weakly.

Mallory checked his watch. "Seven minutes."

"That's all?"

The detective nodded, as the sound of moving bodies came to their ears.

"We can't stay here," said Mallory. "We're right in the middle of the African exhibit."

The rustling sounds of movement became louder.

"What's on the second floor?" asked Mallory.

Mürgenstürm shrugged. "Just bones and fossils, I think."

"It can't be any more dangerous than here," concluded the detective. "Let's find a staircase."

He headed off to his left, then froze as the gorilla lumbered into sight.

"The other way! Quick!"

They returned to the junction where the elephant had been mounted. At the moment it was inspecting the entrance to one of the other corridors, and Mallory and Mürgenstürm, backs to the wall, began edging gingerly around the area, looking for a sign that might point either to a staircase or an exit.

Suddenly the elephant wheeled around, flattened its ears, and charged toward them without a sound. Mürgenstürm backed into a corridor while Mallory looked desperately for an escape route. At the last instant he dove to the floor, slid beneath the startled pachyderm's outstretched trunk, regained his feet, and hurled himself into a new corridor. The elephant followed him instantly, and with a sinking feeling in the pit of his stomach, Mallory realized that he had chosen the one corridor through which it could move with ease.

He took a hard right at the next juncture, barely avoiding the elephant's trunk, and skidded to a halt as he found himself no more than twenty feet away from a rhinoceros that was grunting and pawing at the marble tiles with a forefoot.

He heard the elephant scream once, and then the building seemed to shake as it bore down upon him with thunderous, bone-crunching steps. He took a quick look back, found his entire field of vision filled by elephant, and dove into the diorama from which the rhinoceros had emerged.

He expected to be lifted high above the floor, wrapped in the elephant's trunk, and hurled against a wall, or perhaps impaled on its long miscolored tusks—but although the hideous sounds of thudding bodies came to his ears, he was still alive and intact half a minute later, when he finally forced himself to open a terrified eye.

The rhino, a gaping wound on its left shoulder, was racing down the corridor, pursued by the enraged elephant.

Mallory considered remaining where he was, hidden by weeds and grasses, then remembered that sooner or later the rhino would return to its diorama, probably little the worse—but considerably the more enraged—for wear.

Cautiously the detective got to his feet, crawled to the edge of the diorama, and stuck his head out into the corridor. It was empty, and he immediately began walking rapidly in the opposite direction from the one the elephant and the rhino had taken. He took two more turns, heard the chattering of monkeys, decided that their shrieks would warn him of any approaching predators, and entered their corridor. Their screaming and chattering increased, and a number of them threw fruits and nuts at him, but none left their dioramas, and finally he saw a small stairway at the end of the corridor. He broke into a trot, and had almost reached it when he found the bull gorilla blocking his way.

Mallory suddenly remembered the pistol he had purchased. He reached into his robe, pulled it out, and pumped four quick shots into the gorilla's chest.

"You can't kill something that's already dead," mumbled the gorilla in harsh, guttural tones.

Mallory blinked rapidly.

"I warned you not to come to the museum," continued the gorilla, glaring balefully at the detective.

"Are you the Grundy?" asked Mallory.

"For the moment," growled the gorilla, approaching him slowly. "And a moment is all you have remaining, John Justin Mallory!"

Mallory looked around desperately as he backed away. Finally his gaze fell on some dry weeds in one of the dioramas. He grabbed them, set fire to them with his pocket lighter, and thrust them at the gorilla's harsh, dry hair.

The gorilla instantly burst into flame. The cold light of the Grundy's intelligence left its eyes and, screaming, it raced away down the corridor. Mallory watched it for a moment, then quickly walked the rest of the way to the staircase and began climbing up to the second floor—and collided with Mürgenstürm, who was racing down the stairs.

"Where the hell were you?" demanded the little elf, his face flushed from exertion.

"Downstairs," said Mallory. "Where the hell do you think I was?"

"How do I know? One minute you were there and the next minute I was all alone!" Mürgenstürm tried unsuccessfully to push him aside. "Let me by!"

"You're going the wrong way."

"You go your way and I'll go mine!" said the elf desperately.

"But there's nothing upstairs!" protested Mallory. "All the stuffed animals are on the first floor!"

"You may know it, and I may know it, but try telling him!"

"Try telling who?" demanded Mallory.

"*Him!*" whimpered Mürgenstürm, pointing a trembling finger toward the top of the stairs.

"Wait here," said Mallory, cautiously climbing the remainder of the stairs.

When he reached the doorway to the second floor he was confronted by a huge green panel that completely blocked his way. As he tried to figure out what it was, he became uncomfortably aware of the fact that it was *moving*, and a moment later he realized that it was the tail of a brontosaur.

"How can that be, John Justin?" whispered Mürgenstürm, who had followed him up. "Nobody's ever stuffed and mounted a dinosaur. They're just skeletons!"

"It's the Grundy's work," said Mallory grimly.

"The Grundy stuffs dinosaurs?" asked Mürgenstürm, bewildered.

Mallory nodded. "He also makes mistakes."

"He hasn't made any that I'm aware of," said Mürgenstürm devoutly.

"He made one a couple of minutes ago," said the detective. "And now he's made another one. This damned thing is a vegetarian; it won't bother us."

"Elephants are vegetarians too," Mürgenstürm reminded him.

"You've got a point," admitted Mallory, his sense of triumph evaporating. "Well, we sure as hell can't stay here."

"Why not?" asked the elf.

"Take a look," said Mallory, pointing to the foot of the stairs, where a leopard was slowly climbing up toward them. When it saw that its prey was aware of its presence it looked full into the detective's eyes and snarled.

"Shoot him!" cried the elf, suddenly noticing the pistol in Mallory's hand.

"It wouldn't do any good. He's already dead."

Mürgenstürm raced ahead of the detective and bolted into the enormous hall. Mallory followed him, securing the door behind them.

The brontosaur was at the far end of the hall, some 200 feet away from them, casually inspecting its surroundings and looking for food.

"There aren't any other doors," said Mürgenstürm, "just this one and the main stairway—and what do you want to bet that Rex and his flying friends are waiting there for us?"

"How about elevators?"

"I can't see any."

"Wonderful," muttered Mallory. Suddenly he turned to the little elf. "Can you stop time for them the way you did for the two hoods in my office?"

"That's the best idea you've had all night, John Justin!" replied Mürgenstürm. "A truly phenomenal notion. I *knew* I picked a good man!"

"Why not?" asked Mallory wearily.

"It only works with creatures who are *aware* of time to begin with," explained Mürgenstürm. "And obviously a dinosaur who is walking around in the twentieth century has only the haziest conception of the passage of time."

"I don't suppose you'd care to try it anyway?"

"I already did."

"Have you got any other parlor tricks you can do?"

"Like what?"

"I don't know—levitation, teleportation, anything like that."

Mürgenstürm shook his head unhappily. "Stopping time is my *pièce de résistance*." He paused. "And it only works for about five minutes anyway,'' he added apologetically.

Mallory made no reply, but stared intently at the brontosaur, which stood between them and the main staircase.

Mürgenstürm grabbed the detective's sleeve, shaking it. "Are you all right, John Justin?"

"Shut up!" snapped Mallory. "I'm thinking."

"About what?"

Mallory was silent for another moment. Then he looked down at the elf.

"Do you have to be in the same room with whomever you stop time for?"

"It helps."

"But it's not absolutely necessary?"

Suddenly Mürgenstürm turned a pale green. "Oh, no!" he said. "You can't be serious, John Justin!"

"Why not?"

"He'll kill me!"

"In case it's escaped your attention, he's trying to kill you already."

"But he's the Grundy!"

"He's the guy who's animating these animals. If you stop time for him, maybe *they'll* go back to sleep when *he* does."

"But he's got powers!"

"Do you want to find that damned unicorn before tomorrow morning or don't you?" demanded Mallory.

"He's too far away!"

"Try!"

"And he's stronger than I am."

"We don't need *five* minutes," said Mallory. "Sixty seconds will do. We'll run right down the main stairway and out the front door."

"But—"

The brontosaur suddenly noticed them and began approaching.

"All right!" whimpered the elf.

"Well?" asked Mallory as the brontosaur drew nearer.

"I did it."

"It isn't working."

"I told you it wouldn't!" said Mürgenstürm, darting back into the stairwell.

And then, between one step and the next, the dinosaur froze.

"Mürgenstürm!" yelled Mallory.

"Don't hit me!" whined the elf. "It's not my fault!"

"It worked!" shouted Mallory. "Let's get the hell out of here!"

He raced across the hall to the head of the main staircase, slid down the long, curving banister, and ran to the front door.

"What's the matter?" asked Mürgenstürm, joining him a few seconds later.

"It's locked!"

"Of course it's locked."

"I thought it would be one of those doors that you could open from the inside!" Mallory looked around desperately. "Where's the door we came in through?"

"This way!" said Mürgenstürm, heading off at a run.

Mallory fell into step behind him, and suddenly heard a loud hissing noise.

"Faster!" he yelled. "Rex is waking up!"

The elf reached the door ten steps ahead of Mallory and hurled himself through it. Mallory dove after him, just as the talons of Rex's tiny forelegs ripped his pants from the knee to the ankle, and then the door slammed shut behind him.

"Made it!" wheezed Mürgenstürm, lying on his back and panting, completely oblivious to the freezing rain.

Mallory, bent over, hands on knees, was too busy catching his breath to answer immediately. Finally he rasped out, "That was too damned close!"

"We were lucky, John Justin," said the elf. "But it won't work again. He'll be ready for it the next time."

"He's some guy, this Grundy," said Mallory. "I keep expecting to look up and see some witch on a broomstick skywriting SURRENDER, DOROTHY!"

"Who's Dorothy?" asked Mürgenstürm.

"Never mind." He looked around. "By the way, where's Felina?"

"Right here," said a voice from above him.

Mallory looked up and saw the cat-girl perched on a ledge, right next to a window.

"What are you doing up there?"

"I was watching you with the dinosaur," she said. "You're not very fast."

"I hope you enjoyed yourself," said Mallory dryly.

She smiled and nodded.

"I suppose it never occurred to you to help us."

She continued smiling and shook her head slowly.

"I take it that your sympathies lie with the predator rather than the prey."

Her smile widened.

"What next, John Justin?" asked the elf. "We can't go back into the museum, and Larkspur's trail is cold."

"Next we find a phone book."

"And look under *U?*" suggested Mürgenstürm sarcastically.

Mallory shook his head. "Under *C.*"

"*C?*" repeated the elf. "Who's that?"

"Colonel W. Carruthers."

"I never heard of him."

"He's the guy who killed the unicorn in the museum."

"So you still insist on educating yourself about unicorns?'' complained Mürgenstürm. He pointed to Mallory's wristwatch. ''It's eleven-eighteen and we're no closer than when we started. By the time you learn anything useful about unicorns, it will be sunrise!''

''The alternative is learning about the Grundy,'' replied Mallory, ''and I already know more about him than I want to. Besides, maybe we can hire this Carruthers to help us.'' He looked up at Felina. ''Are you coming along or not?''

In response, she stood up and prepared to jump off the window ledge.

''Don't!'' shouted Mallory. ''It's a twenty-foot drop!''

She laughed and flung herself out into space. Mallory closed his eyes and turned his head away, waiting for the sound of a *splat!* as her body crashed onto the pavement.

Instead, he soon became aware of a soft purring, and an instant later Felina was rubbing her back up and down against his hip.

''I'm hungry,'' she said.

''Don't you ever think of anything except your stomach?'' asked Mallory.

''Eating makes more sense than chasing a unicorn through the rain on New Year's Eve,'' she replied.

The detective stared at her. ''It was starting to seem pretty logical until you put it that way.'' He shook his head. ''You know, every time I think I'm starting to understand this city, something like *this* happens.''

''Something like what?'' asked the elf.

''Like the animals coming to life in the museum.'' He uttered a curse. ''Damn, but I thought I had him there for a minute!''

''Him?''

''The Grundy. He was speaking to me through a gorilla, and I set him on fire. I should have known it wouldn't be that easy.''

"You actually set the Grundy on fire?" repeated Mürgenstürm, wide-eyed.

Mallory shook his head. "I set the gorilla on fire." He paused. "I'll get him the next time."

"You don't know what you're saying, John Justin!" said the elf fearfully.

"He had hundreds of animals and dinosaurs at his disposal, and we got out in one piece. He stole a unicorn, but he left a witness behind. He tried to kill me, but he let me get close enough to set him on fire." Mallory paused thoughtfully. "He may be powerful, but he's not perfect."

Suddenly Felina hissed and dove into the grass. She stood up a moment later, covered with mud, proudly holding a small rodent in one hand.

"You're not going to eat it like that, are you?" asked Mallory.

"Of course not."

"Good," replied Mallory, relaxing.

"I'm going to play with it first," she said with a predatory grin.

"Not in front of *me*, you're not!" snapped Mallory.

"You mustn't judge her too harshly, John Justin," said the elf. "It's her nature, just as yours is solving mysteries."

"By the same token, it's the Grundy's nature to steal unicorns and kill oversexed elves. Why hold it against him?"

"Let's not carry this line of reasoning to ridiculous extremes," said Mürgenstürm haughtily.

Felina, who had been looking off into the distance, turned to Mallory.

"If you don't stop saying bad things about me, I won't tell you what I see."

Mallory peered into the darkness.

"I don't see anything."

"Of course not. You're only a Man."

"All right," said Mallory. "What do you see?"

"Are you sorry that you criticized me?" she replied with a cunning smile.

He stared at her for a moment. "All right—I'm sorry."

"And you'll never, ever do it again, no matter what?"

"I said I'm sorry. That's enough."

"But did you *mean* it?" she purred.

"I meant it!" yelled Mallory. "Now, what the hell do you see?"

"A unicorn."

Chapter

5 ———————————————————

11:20 PM–Midnight

"Where is it?" demanded Mallory.

"Over there, on the bridle path. Can you see it now?"

Mallory wiped the rain from his eyes and squinted. "I can't even see the bridle path. Is someone with it, or is it running loose?"

"I can't tell," said Felina.

"Can you tell if it's Larkspur?" asked Mallory.

Felina shrugged. "All unicorns look alike." She paused thoughtfully. "All men look alike, too."

"How far away is it?" persisted the detective, still trying unsuccessfully to discern its shape.

"Not very," said Felina, turning her attention back to the rodent in her hand. "Hello, little appetizer," she purred.

"Let's go!" said Mallory.

Felina sat down cross-legged on the grass. "Cute little cold cut," she said. "I think I'll put you on a cracker."

"Felina, get up!" demanded Mallory.

"I'm busy," said the cat-girl, releasing the rodent, then grabbing it just before it could race beyond her reach.

"Damn it! We need your help!"

"Just follow the bridle path and you'll catch up with it sooner or later."

"Where *is* the bridle path?"

"That way," she said, holding up the rodent and pointing it to the east.

Mallory turned to Mürgenstürm. "Let's go."

"We might need her," protested the elf.

"If we stick around long enough to watch her torture her dinner, we may never catch up with the damned unicorn," said Mallory, setting off across the soggy grass in the direction Felina had indicated. Mürgenstürm opened his mouth to say something, thought better of it, and fell into step behind him.

They walked for almost 300 yards, and finally came to the cinder bridle path.

"Which way now, I wonder?" mused Mallory, looking up and down the path.

Mürgenstürm shrugged. "Shall I go back and ask?"

Mallory shook his head. "It'll take too long." He looked both ways again, then set off to the north.

"What made you decide on this direction, John Justin?" asked the elf after they had walked in silence for a couple of minutes.

"It's less crowded," answered Mallory. "If someone has got a unicorn that doesn't belong to him, it stands to reason that he won't want to take it where everyone can see him. Now, in *my* Manhattan you've got the Plaza and the Park Lane and all those stores at the south end of the park."

"It's the same in this Manhattan," said Mürgenstürm. He paused. "So you're saying that if it turned south, it probably wasn't Larkspur?"

"Right," said Mallory. "I hope."

A cold wind whipped across the park, and suddenly the

rain changed to light snow. Within five minutes it was snowing heavily, and Mallory came to a stop.

"I have a feeling we're going the wrong way," he announced.

"Oh? Why?"

"Because the Grundy hasn't tried to warn me off yet."

"Maybe he knows you're expecting him to do so, in which case the proper strategy from his point of view is to do nothing." Mürgenstürm's brow furrowed in thought. "Unless, of course, he anticipates that you might be expecting just such a tactic, in which case—"

"Enough," interrupted Mallory.

"I was just trying to be helpful," said Mürgenstürm petulantly.

"Why don't you try being quiet instead?" suggested Mallory.

A harpy that had been perched in a nearby tree suddenly took wing and circled over them.

"Go back, John Justin Mallory!"

Mallory turned to Mürgenstürm. "Thanks a lot, you little green bastard!"

"What did *I* do?"

"Two minutes ago I would have known what the hell that meant!"

"Don't listen to her!" cried a large owl that sat shivering on a barren, leafless tree. *"Press on, Mallory! Press on!"*

"Wonderful," muttered Mallory.

"What are you going to do, John Justin?" asked Mürgenstürm.

"Keep walking."

"What factor led to this decision?" queried the elf.

"It's too damned cold to stand here wondering what to do next," replied Mallory, finally remembering to tighten his belt to the second notch and feeling somewhat more comfortable as his robe began generating heat.

They walked another fifty yards, and then the little elf tugged at Mallory's sleeve.

"What now?" asked the detective.

"Do you think you could manage to do without me for, oh, about fifteen minutes?" asked Mürgenstürm.

"Why?"

"Do you see that apartment building opposite us?" said the elf, pointing to a decaying structure with spires and a turret that Mallory was sure couldn't co-exist in *his* Manhattan.

"It looks like mad scientists build monsters in the basement," remarked the detective.

"I don't know what goes on in the basement, though I suppose anything's possible," answered Mürgenstürm.

"Get to the point."

"I have an ongoing . . . ah . . . *friendship* with the housekeeper, if you know what I mean."

"You're facing death in seven hours if you don't find the unicorn, and you want to take time off from the chase to get laid?" demanded Mallory unbelievingly.

Mürgenstürm sighed. "I see your point, John Justin," he said. "It was thoughtless and selfish of me to suggest deserting you." Suddenly his homely little face brightened. "I could see if she's got a friend."

"Forget it."

"You're absolutely right, John Justin," agreed Mürgenstürm contritely. "I have to learn to control my passions. Taking fifteen minutes out of our limited remaining time was insensitive and wrongheaded." He looked at Mallory out of the corner of his eye. "How about ten minutes?" he suggested very softly.

Mallory turned to him. "How about a kick in the groin to get your mind back on business?"

"Ohhh!" moaned Mürgenstürm as if in pain, pressing his knees together and clasping his hands over the area in question. "Don't even suggest it! What kind of monster are you?"

"A very cold one," replied Mallory, wishing his robe had been equipped with a hood. "Now, do you think we can get this show back on the road?"

"All right," said the elf, his expression still pained. "But no kicking."

"No deserting," responded the detective.

"It wasn't desertion," protested Mürgenstürm. "It was more in the nature of physical and psychic renewal." He paused. "Are you absolutely positively sure we can't spare even five minutes?"

Mallory grabbed the elf by his scrawny neck. "Now, you listen to me—" he began fiercely.

"Out of the way!" yelled a voice. "Clear the path!"

Mallory released his grip and jumped aside just in time to see a slender man, clad only in track shoes, shorts, and a T-shirt with the number 897 emblazoned on its chest, collide with Mürgenstürm. The little elf went flying into the snow that was accumulating beside the bridle path, but the man managed to maintain his balance and began running in place.

"Terribly sorry," said the man as Mürgenstürm slowly picked himself up. "But I *did* have right-of-way."

"I didn't know there *were* right-of-way rules on a bridle path," remarked Mallory.

"Bridle path?" repeated the man, confused. "You mean this isn't Highway A-98?"

Mallory shook his head.

"Then I suppose those aren't the lights of the Via Veneto glimmering in the distance?" said the man unhappily, pointing to Fifth Avenue without losing a step.

"They're the lights of Manhattan," answered Mallory.

"Manhattan?" repeated the man, surprised. "Are you quite sure?"

"Not as sure as I was yesterday," replied Mallory. "But pretty sure."

"Hmm," said the man thoughtfully. "I seem to be farther off course than I thought."

"Where are you heading?" asked Mallory.

"Rome, of course."

"Of course," repeated Mallory dryly.

"But where are my manners?" said the man. He extended his hand without losing a step. "My name is Ian Wilton-Smythe."

"British?" asked Mallory, shaking his hand.

Wilton-Smythe nodded. "To the core. Kill the Irish! Plunder the colonies! God save the Queen!" He paused. "It *is* still the Queen, isn't it? Or have we a King now?"

"It's still the Queen," said Mallory. "I take it you haven't been home in some time?"

"Not since the spring of 1960," acknowledged Wilton-Smythe. "Went over to Rome for the Olympics that summer."

"As a spectator?"

"As a marathon runner. In fact, I'm still running it. I seem to have taken a wrong turn somewhere along the course."

"I don't know how to lay this on you," said Mallory, "but we've had quite a few Olympics since then. The race is over."

"Not until I cross the finish line, it isn't," said Wilton-Smythe adamantly.

"Why not just stop?"

"Not cricket," replied Wilton-Smythe. "Rules of the game, you know."

"There's nothing in the rules that says you have to keep

running for decades after everyone else has finished," said Mallory.

"Slow and steady wins the race," quoted Wilton-Smythe.

"Not *this* race," replied Mallory. "It's already been won."

"That's hardly my fault, is it?" shot back Wilton-Smythe. "My job is to plug away and do the best I can." He paused. "You don't see any photographers around here, do you?"

"No."

"Pity."

"Why?" asked Mallory. "Were you expecting some?"

"Well, I *am* the sporting world's greatest news story," said Wilton-Smythe. "With every step I take, I extend my record."

"What record? You lost."

"The record for the longest time required to complete an Olympic marathon, of course," said Wilton-Smythe. He looked puzzled. "I keep expecting the Guinness people to interview me or measure my stride or something for their record book, but so far they haven't shown up. I wonder why?"

"Maybe they don't know you're still running," suggested Mallory.

"Impossible!" scoffed Wilton-Smythe. "Probably they're waiting for me five or ten miles farther up the road."

"Perhaps," said Mallory without much conviction.

Wilton-Smythe yawned. "I'm getting sleepy. I think I'd better take a little nap before I reach them. I wouldn't want to look other than my best for the interviews and picture-taking."

"I don't think you're going to have much luck finding a room," said Mallory. "It's New Year's Eve."

"Why would I want a room?"

"I thought you said you were sleepy."

"I sleep on straightaways and wake up for the turns," explained Wilton-Smythe. "I wouldn't ever want it said that I cheated."

"Do you eat on the run, too?"

"Of course."

"Forgive my asking," said Mallory, "but how the hell did you ever wind up on a bridle path in Central Park?"

"I wish I knew," admitted Wilton-Smythe. "I think I probably should have turned left at Melbourne."

"Melbourne, *Australia?*"

The runner nodded. "Puzzling, isn't it?"

"To say the least," agreed Mallory.

"Well," said Wilton-Smythe, "I've enjoyed our little chat, but I really must be toddling along."

"If I were you, I'd pick up a road map," Mallory shouted after him.

"What for?" he yelled back. "All roads lead to Rome."

Then they were out of earshot, and Mallory turned to Mürgenstürm.

"What did you make of that?" he asked.

"He's a fool," answered the elf promptly. He frowned and scratched his head. "On the other hand, he's been working steadily for more than a quarter of a century, whereas most of the truly intelligent people I know can't seem to hold a job. I find it intensely puzzling."

"Not really," said Mallory. "It's pretty much the same in *my* Manhattan."

"It is?"

Mallory nodded. "The bright ones can solve most of the problems of the world—but putting on matching socks or learning how to change a tire seems a little beyond them."

"How comforting," said Mürgenstürm. "I was afraid it was an isolated phenomenon."

"No such luck," said Mallory. He began walking to the

north again. "Let's keep moving. Robe or no robe, it's goddamned cold out."

"Maybe the snow will prove to be an advantage," said Mürgenstürm hopefully. "We should be able to pick up the unicorn's tracks."

"If our marathon runner doesn't obliterate them," said Mallory.

They walked, shoulders hunched and heads lowered against the driving wind, for another half mile. Then Mürgenstürm suddenly sat down heavily on the ground.

"I can't go any farther," he said. "I'm cold and I'm wet and I'm exhausted."

"And you think you're going to get warm and dry and energetic by sitting on the ground in the middle of a snowstorm?" asked Mallory sardonically.

"I don't care anymore," moaned Mürgenstürm. "Let them come looking for me tomorrow at sunrise. All they'll find are the frozen remains of a noble little elf who never meant any harm to anyone."

"Can you think of anything that would make you feel better?"

"Absolutely nothing," said Mürgenstürm emphatically.

"Not even a ladyfriend?"

"Well . . . maybe."

"Look," said Mallory. "If I let you go off and get laid, do you think you can keep your mind on business when you get back?"

"Oh, absolutely, John Justin!" cried the elf enthusiastically. "I see it all now! It's not the weather. It's just my metabolism."

"Stop drooling or you'll freeze your chin off," said Mallory disgustedly.

"I'll be back in ten minutes," said Mürgenstürm, leaping to his feet. "Fifteen at the most." He paused. "Maybe twenty."

"Take thirty, and see if you can find out anything about Flypaper Gillespie."

"Right," said Mürgenstürm. "I'll meet you here in half an hour."

"I hope you don't think I'm going to stand here in the snow waiting for you to get your rocks off," said Mallory.

"What *are* you going to do?"

"I'm a detective," replied Mallory. "I'm going to try to find that damned unicorn."

"You were never this single-minded in your own Manhattan," noted Mürgenstürm.

"Things were never this black-and-white in my own Manhattan," said Mallory. "There were always legal ramifications and extenuating circumstances and moral ambiguities. This is a lot simpler: something was stolen by a villain and I'm being paid to get it back."

"I thought you said you preferred *your* Manhattan," said the elf.

"I said I *understood* my Manhattan," replied Mallory. "That's not the same thing."

"How can you prefer something you don't understand?"

"I don't understand the form. The substance makes a lot of sense."

"I don't know what you're talking about," said Mürgenstürm.

"Then you'll have something to think about while you're hunting up one of your many true loves."

"How will I find you when I'm done?"

"The same way I'm trying to find Larkspur. Follow my tracks."

"What if the snow melts, or you go indoors?" persisted Mürgenstürm.

"Hire a detective," said Mallory, heading off along the bridle path.

"That's not very funny, John Justin."

"If you're worried about it, you can put your romance on hold and come along with me."

"I'll follow your tracks," said Mürgenstürm hastily. He began trotting across the park toward the bright lights of Fifth Avenue.

Mallory watched the little elf for a moment, then turned back to the bridle path and continued walking.

He had gone no more than fifty yards when he came to a small wooden lean-to, occupied by a pudgy man in a bright gold-and-green-checkered sports jacket.

"Evening, neighbor," said the man with a friendly smile.

"Hello," said Mallory.

"Terrible night, isn't it?"

Mallory nodded.

"Can I interest you in a little suntan lotion, friend?" asked the man.

"You're kidding, right?" said Mallory.

"Friend, if there's three things I never kid about, it's religion, blondes named Suzette, and business. This is business. I can sell you a case at fifty percent off the retail price."

"What the hell would I do with suntan lotion?"

"Go to Jamaica. Take a safari to Africa. Keep it in your garage until summer. Mix it with vodka and tonic. Scrub your floors with it. Friend, there's no end of things you can do with a case of cut-rate suntan lotion."

"Forget it," said Mallory, starting to walk again.

"For you, sixty percent off," persisted the man, leaving the lean-to and running after him.

"It's New Year's Eve!"

"Happy New Year!" cried the man, pulling a kazoo out of his pocket and blowing a few notes on it. "Sixty-five percent off, and that's my last offer."

"I hope you don't seriously expect to sell suntan lotion in the middle of a snowstorm," said Mallory.

"It's the very best time to sell it," replied the man, struggling to keep pace with the detective.

"How do you figure that?"

"How many stores are open right now? Maybe five hundred," he answered himself. "And how many of them are selling suntan lotion? None! If you want suntan lotion, you've got to come to me."

"But I don't want suntan lotion," said Mallory irritably.

"Friend, you drive a hard bargain. Seventy percent off, but only if you promise never to tell my accountant."

"Not a chance."

"All right!" snarled the man. "Seventy-five percent, and I'll hate myself in the morning."

"Keep nagging me and you'll have a lot of company."

"I'll throw in a beach ball."

"Just what I need on New Year's Eve in Central Park," said Mallory.

"Good!" cried the man. "Have we got a deal?"

"No."

"What kind of person are you?" screamed the vendor. "I've got a wife and two kids and a mortgage. I just bought a new television set, I'm late on my car payment, and my daughter needs braces. Where's your compassion?"

"I must have left it in my other suit," said Mallory. He stopped and turned to the man. "You wouldn't happen to have any gloves or earmuffs for sale, would you?"

"Unloaded 'em all last July," said the man. "Ninety percent, and I'll pay the sales tax."

Mallory shook his head and began walking again. "Not interested."

"What does interest have to do with it?" demanded the man. "I'm a merchant, you're a consumer. Doesn't that mean something to you? Don't you feel your moral responsibility to me?''

"Do *you* feel any moral responsibility to *me?*'' asked Mallory.

"Certainly.''

"Good. I'm a detective who's looking for a unicorn. Did one pass by here recently?''

"Yes,'' said the man.

"When?''

"Maybe five minutes ago.''

"Was there a leprechaun with it?''

"I really didn't pay that much attention,'' said the man. "Now, let me total up what you owe me for the suntan lotion.''

"I'm not buying any suntan lotion.''

"But I told you about the unicorn!''

"For which I thank you.''

"Then do your duty and buy my suntan lotion.''

"No.''

"Ninety-five percent off list.''

Mallory shook his head.

"All right,'' said the man with a sigh of defeat. "How much do you want?''

"For what?'' asked Mallory, puzzled.

"To take the damned stuff off my hands.''

"I keep telling you—I don't want it.''

"You can't do this to me! It's New Year's Eve! I have a right to be home in the bosom of my family! I'll pay you twenty percent of its list price to haul it away.''

"It's been nice talking to you,'' said Mallory, increasing his speed.

"Thirty percent,'' said the man, finally coming to a stop. "And that's my final offer.''

Mallory continued walking.

"Fifty, and that's my absolute final penultimate offer!''

The man was up to double the list price before Mallory walked out of earshot.

He had proceeded another 100 yards when he was joined by a tall, unkempt man in a raincoat, carrying a cardboard box in one hand.

"Good evening to you, sir," said the man, falling into step beside him.

Mallory merely nodded and kept walking.

"I'm pleased to see that you managed to get away without buying any suntan oil." He chuckled. "Imagine anyone being stupid enough to try to sell that stuff in a blizzard!"

"What are *you* selling?" asked Mallory.

"Selling? My dear sir, you cut me to the quick! Do I look like a salesman?"

"Don't ask."

"As a matter of fact, I'm giving something away."

"I'm in a hurry."

The man increased his pace. "Take a look inside, sir," he said, thrusting the cardboard box into Mallory's hands.

Mallory took the box and opened it without slowing his pace, then made a face. "It looks like a bunch of worms."

"Not merely worms, sir," said the man with a show of outraged dignity. "Nightcrawlers!"

"What's the difference?"

"What's the difference between a skateboard and a Rolls-Royce?" replied the man. "These are purebred nightcrawlers, sir, each with a five-generation pedigree, each registered with the A.E.S."

"The A.E.S.?" repeated Mallory, handing the box back to him.

"The American Earthworm Society," explained the man. "It's been our governing body since 1893."

"What the hell do I want with nightcrawlers?"

"They're for fishing."

"It's snowing out, in case you hadn't noticed."

"It won't bother their furry little bodies in the least."

"They look more slimy than furry."

"Right you are, sir," agreed the man, looking into the box. "It won't bother their slimy little bodies in the least."

"What I meant was, who's crazy enough to go fishing in a blizzard?"

"Almost no one, sir. Think of it: you'll have the field to yourself!"

"I'm on a bridle path in Central Park. There aren't any fish around here."

"Ah, but if you *do* find one, think of how hungry he'll be!"

"Go trade them for the suntan lotion," said Mallory.

"I'm also having a sale on tombstones," said the man persuasively.

"A sale on tombstones?" repeated Mallory.

"If your name happens to be Jessica Ann Milford and you died of drowning in August of 1974," qualified the man.

"It's not, and I didn't."

"It's really quite a bargain," continued the man eagerly. "Marble, with beer cans rampant on a field of hypodermic needles. Very tasteful."

"I'll think about it," said Mallory, starting to walk again.

"I'll be right here, waiting for your decision," said the man.

Mallory shook his head and increased his pace. The snow continued to fall, and the wind began whipping across the park so fiercely that visibility became almost nil. A few minutes later he was sure he had wandered off the bridle path, but when he turned around to retrace his steps he found that the snow had totally obliterated his footprints. He looked around for the lights of Fifth Ave-

nue, but the snow completely obscured them, and he
realized with a sinking sensation in his stomach that he
was lost.

He cursed Mürgenstürm under his breath, then began
searching for some form of shelter. The blanket of snow
stretched endlessly before him, but he thought he could
discern a structure off to his left and, lowering his head
against the wind, he slowly made his way toward it.

Just when he was sure that he had been mistaken, the
wind died down and he found himself only a few steps
away from a large stone building. It was dark, but its two
chimneys were belching smoke into the frigid night air. He
covered the remaining distance at a run and pounded on
the door. When there was no response he pushed it open
and stepped inside, panting heavily.

He brushed the snow off his cloak, felt around for a
light switch, couldn't find one, and pulled out his cigarette
lighter. It didn't provide much illumination, but it was
enough for him to realize that he was inside a barn with
two rows of box stalls. The place smelled strongly of
horses, and he could hear the occasional thumping of
hooves on straw.

Finally he found a bare light bulb descending from the
rafters. He walked over and pulled on the frayed string that
hung down from it, and suddenly he stood in a pool of
harsh white light, surrounded by flickering shadows as the
bulb swung to and fro.

"Is anyone here?" he asked, then jumped in surprise
when he received an answer.

"Yes."

"Where are you?" he said, looking around apprehensively.

"Right here."

"Where is *here*?"

"Look down."

Mallory looked down and found a miniature horse, no more than nine inches at the shoulder, standing right next to him.

"Was that *you* talking?" he asked, squatting down to inspect the elegant little animal.

"Yes," said the horse. "There's a small towel hanging up there," it added, nodding its head at the edge of a nearby stall. "I wonder if you would be so kind as to retrieve it and place it over my back?"

Mallory walked over, picked up the towel, and laid it gently across the little horse's back and withers.

"Thank you," said the horse, not quite able to repress a body-wrenching shiver. "It was getting quite cold in here."

Mallory stared at the tiny animal. "I didn't know horses could talk," he said at last.

"Of course they can."

"I've never heard them."

"Perhaps they had nothing to say to you."

"Perhaps," agreed Mallory. "By the way, you *are* a horse, aren't you?"

"Certainly."

"And this is a stable?"

"That's right."

"You wouldn't happen to have any unicorns stabled here, would you?" asked Mallory.

"I'm afraid not. Why?"

"I've been following one up the bridle path. I thought it might have stopped here to get out of the weather."

"I wish I could help you," said the horse, "but we haven't boarded any unicorns here in more than a month." The little animal paused. "They're quite rare, you know. I don't imagine there can be more than two dozen of them in all of Manhattan. In what direction was this unicorn heading?"

"North, I think. I never got close enough to it to be sure."

Mallory opened the door, stuck his head out, determined that visibility was still about nil, and decided to wait a couple of minutes before braving the snow again.

"I've never seen a horse as small as you before."

"I wasn't always this small," answered the horse.

"You weren't?"

The horse shook its head ruefully.

"What happened?" asked Mallory.

"You can't tell it to look at me, but I used to be a racehorse."

"Maybe I saw you run," said Mallory. "I get out to Belmont and Aqueduct three or four times a week."

"I wasn't good enough. They had high hopes for me when I was born, but I spent most of my career running at places like Thistledown and Latonia and Finger Lakes."

"What's your name?" asked Mallory.

"The name my owner gave me, or my real name?"

"Your real one, I guess."

"Eohippus."

"Never heard of you."

"That's not the name I ran under," replied Eohippus. "It's the one I chose for myself once I understood my destiny." The little horse snorted, then continued. "As I said, I wasn't a very good racehorse."

"You're just the kind I always seem to bet on," remarked Mallory dryly.

"My owner and trainer did everything they could to make me better," said Eohippus.

"Like what?"

"The first thing they did was geld me."

"That makes you faster?" asked Mallory dubiously.

"It makes me faster whenever I see a veterinarian approaching, I can tell you that," said Eohippus bitterly. He whinnied; it sounded like a sigh in the cavernous interior of the barn. "As soon as I recovered I was back on the track."

"Maybe they should have tried blinkers," suggested Mallory.

"They did."

"Did it help?"

"Blinkers are for horses who look around, who don't pay attention to business. That wasn't me. I tried my very best with every stride I ever took. All the blinkers did was close off two-thirds of the world to me." He paused. "Then there were the drugs."

"Illegal ones?"

Eohippus shook his head. "They were perfectly legal. My trainer thought that I might have sore muscles, and the drugs were designed to mask the pain." He whinnied again. "They crippled my sister, who didn't know her ankle was sore until it shattered, but I was perfectly healthy."

"Just slow," said Mallory.

The little horse nodded his head sadly. "Just slow," he agreed unhappily.

"Well, not everyone can be Seattle Slew."

"He was my uncle," noted Eohippus.

"Really?" said Mallory. "I almost went broke trying to find horses to beat him."

"He'd run down the backstretch and the trees would sway," recalled Eohippus in awestruck tones. "And I wanted so badly to be like him! It's what I was born to do—to run so fast that my feet barely touched the ground, to pierce a hole in the wind. And, oh, how I tried! I ran my heart out"—he paused tragically—"but I just didn't have the ability."

"So what happened?"

"One day I was running at a bush-league track in New

Mexico, and I was losing touch with the leader, like I always did after half a mile or so, and my jockey began whipping me—and suddenly my saddle slipped and he fell off.''

"Your trainer didn't tighten the girth properly."

"That's what *I* thought," said Eohippus. "But that night I noticed that I had to reach a little higher than usual to eat my oats. And when my exercise girl kicked me during a workout the next day, my saddle slipped again. That's when I realized I was shrinking. Every time I was hit, I got a little bit smaller." He paused. "Finally I got too small to run, and they retired me—but I kept right on shrinking. Then the entire truth finally dawned on me— that anytime *any* horse was whipped or abused in a losing cause, I got smaller. That was when I changed my name to Eohippus—the first horse. There's something of me in all racehorses, and something of them in me."

"How long has it been going on?" asked Mallory.

"For about ten years now," said Eohippus.

"You don't seem to have shrunk since we started talking," said Mallory, "yet they must be running races and whipping racehorses *somewhere* in the world right at this moment."

"They are," answered Eohippus. "But now that I'm so small, the change in me is proportionately small, so that you can hardly notice it from one week to the next."

"How did you wind up here in Central Park?"

"This is a stable for used-up old racehorses who escaped the glue factory," explained Eohippus. "Most of them pull wagons; a few carry fat little children around the bridle paths."

"Don't tell me you pull wagons," said Mallory.

"No," said Eohippus. "But I feel comfortable here."

Mallory heard a very distinct horse-laugh directly behind him. He turned, and saw a dark equine face looking at him.

"There's nothing comfortable about it," said the dark-faced horse. "We're a bunch of broken-down wrecks, just marking time on the way to the grave or the dog-food factory."

"You sound bitter," said Mallory.

"Why shouldn't I?" replied the horse. "We're not all like Eohippus here, any more than we're like Man o' War or Secretariat."

"Very few horses are like Man o' War or Secretariat," remarked the detective.

"That's because very few are as healthy!" snapped the horse. "I was a racehorse for six years, and I never took a sound step, never spent a day without pain. I used to feel my jockey's whip dig into me while I was running on swollen legs and inflamed ankles, and I'd wonder what I had done to make God hate me so."

"I'm sorry to hear it," said Mallory.

"You weren't so sorry the day you threw your tickets in my face and told my trainer to chop me up for fishbait."

"*I* did that?" asked Mallory, surprised.

"I never forget a face."

"Then I apologize."

"That gives me a lot of comfort," said the horse bitterly.

"I get emotional at the track," said Mallory uncomfortably.

"*People* get emotional at the track. Horses never do."

"That's not entirely true," said Eohippus gently. "There are exceptions."

"Name one," challenged the horse.

"I remember Ruffian," said Eohippus, his tiny face lighting up at the recollection. "She *loved* the racetrack." He turned to Mallory. "Did you ever see her?"

"No, but I've heard she was really something."

"The best filly that ever lived, bar none," said Eohippus decisively. "She was in front from her first stride to her last."

"And she was dead six hours later," said the dark-faced horse. "Her last stride shattered her leg."

"True," said Eohippus sadly. "I lost a whole inch that night." He shook his head. "You'd almost think the Grundy had bet against her."

"The Grundy?" said Mallory eagerly. "What do you know about him?"

"He's the most powerful demon in New York," replied Eohippus.

"Why would he want to steal a unicorn?" continued Mallory.

"Other than the usual reasons?"

"I don't know. What are the usual reasons?"

"Ransom, for one."

Mallory shook his head. "No. He hasn't made any demands."

"Well, there's always the horn. It's worth a fortune on the black market."

"Does he *need* a fortune?"

"No."

"What else is a unicorn good for?"

"Not much," said the dark-faced horse contemptuously.

"Under what circumstances was it stolen?" asked Eohippus.

"It was in the care of an elf named Mürgenstürm, and it was stolen about ten hours ago by the Grundy and a leprechaun called Flypaper Gillespie."

"I've heard of him," said Eohippus thoughtfully. "He's a formidable character in his own right."

"Do you have any idea where I can find him?" asked Mallory.

"No. But I don't like the thought of *any* animal being

abused. If you'll wait until the snow lets up tomorrow morning, I'd like to join you."

"I can't wait," said Mallory. "In fact, I've already stayed here longer than I should. There's a deadline."

"What kind of deadline?" asked Eohippus curiously.

"Mürgenstürm's guild is going to kill him if I don't find Larkspur by sunrise."

"Larkspur?" whinnied Eohippus, startled, and all up and down the row of stalls the name was repeated in awed tones.

"Is he something special?" asked Mallory.

"He is if the Grundy's got him!" said Eohippus.

"I don't think I understand."

"Once every millennium a unicorn is born that possesses a nearly perfect ruby embedded in its forehead, just below the horn," said Eohippus. "It's rather like a birthmark."

"I take it Larkspur has one."

"He does," said the tiny horse.

"And that makes him worth enough money to interest even the Grundy?"

"Money has nothing to do with it," said Eohippus. "The ruby provides a doorway between worlds—and it is a source of enormous power in itself. The Grundy has two such stones already, which is why he is the Grundy. Who knows what he'll become once he adds a third one?"

"Everyone keeps telling me that magic doesn't work here," complained Mallory, "and yet it seems to be the single governing force of this place."

"The stones aren't magical," said Eohippus. "They have certain properties, totally consistent with the laws that govern the physical universe, that create a permeable membrane between universes and allow their possessor to channel his electromagnetic brain waves more efficiently than anyone else."

"What would they do if they were magical stones?" asked Mallory, confused.

"The same thing," said Eohippus.

"Then the difference is semantic."

"The difference is scientific," the little horse corrected him.

"But the result is the same."

"In essence."

"What do you suppose the Grundy plans to do with this power?"

"He's already got everything he wants from *this* world," said Eohippus. "I would imagine he'll want to expand into your world next. Forgive me for jumping to conclusions, but you *are* from that other Manhattan, aren't you?"

"Yes."

"I *thought* you didn't go there just to bet on horses."

"Why?" asked Mallory.

"All this harping about magic, as if the means were more important than the result. All that really matters is *what* the Grundy will do with Larkspur's stone, rather than *how* he will do it."

"I'll go along with that," agreed Mallory, walking to the door. "I'd better be on my way."

"Where will you go?" asked Eohippus. "Whether the unicorn you were following was Larkspur or not, you'll never be able to pick up his trail in this blizzard."

"I know. I think the only option left to me is to find a phone book."

"Why?"

"I need to hunt up a Colonel Carruthers, if he lives in Manhattan."

"What does Carruthers have to do with Larkspur?" asked Eohippus.

"Nothing. But he seems to be the only unicorn expert around; at any rate, he's the only one I know about." He paused. "If Mürgenstürm shows up, tell him to check out Carruthers' address and catch up with me there."

"I'm coming with you," said Eohippus decisively. "You're a stranger here; you could waste hours just trying to find a phone book, let alone hunt down this Colonel Carruthers."

"I'll have to carry you," said Mallory, bending down to lift the tiny animal into his arms. "The snow is over your head."

"It's not over *my* head!" said a huge chestnut horse at the far end of the barn. "I can carry you both."

"No," said a roan gelding, "I'll carry them."

"Silence!" thundered the dark-faced horse, reaching down and opening the latch to his stall door with his teeth. *"I'll* carry them."

"I thought you hated me," said Mallory as the horse approached him.

"I do," replied the horse coldly.

"Then why—?"

"To reinforce my hatred. Rage is all I have left—and rage, like love, takes constant nurturing."

"Yeah. Well, when you start slipping and sliding, just keep telling yourself that you hate the Grundy more."

Mallory opened the door, carried Eohippus to a mounting block, and gingerly mounted the dark-faced horse.

"Well, for better or worse, here we go," said Mallory as they went out into the blinding snow.

"Hold onto my mane," said the horse as he walked out into the blinding snow.

"You're not thinking of *running* through this stuff, are you?" asked Mallory apprehensively.

"Time is of the essence, is it not?"

"Getting there in one piece is at least as essential, and I've never ridden bareback before."

"Then you'll have to learn, won't you?" said the horse with a note of satisfaction.

"The ground is covered with ice. You'll hurt your legs again."

"I will cherish my pain. It will remind me of you."

"Your name doesn't happen to be Flyaway, does it?" asked Mallory sardonically.

"My name," answered the horse, "is legion."

The horse broke into a run, while Mallory, with Eohippus tucked under his arm, clutched at its snow-covered mane with desperate fingers, his black cloak flapping in the wind like some giant winged creature of the night.

Chapter
6 ——————————————————————

Eohippus stood shivering in the snow as Mallory leaned against the side of the booth, thumbing through the pages of the phone book.

"Is Carruthers listed?" asked the little horse.

"Colonel W. Carruthers," read Mallory. "I don't suppose there can be two of them."

He pulled a coin out of his pocket, inserted it in the phone, and dialed the number.

"No answer," he announced a few moments later.

"He's probably ushering in the New Year," suggested Eohippus. "What about his address?"

Mallory checked the book again. "124 Bleak Street," he said, frowning. "I've never heard of it."

"It's between Sloth and Despair," said the dark horse.

"Those are streets?" asked Mallory.

"They are in *this* Manhattan."

"And you've been to Bleak Street?"

The dark horse nodded. "I pulled a death cart after one of the Grundy's plagues."

"A death cart?"

"The Grundy plays for keeps," said Eohippus grimly.

"I guess he does," acknowledged Mallory. He laid Eohippus across the dark horse's withers and clambered awkwardly onto the horse's back. Then he clutched Eohippus to his chest and wrapped the dark horse's mane around the fingers of his right hand. "All right," he announced. "Let's go."

The dark horse started trotting across the stark white landscape of Central Park, which seemed to shimmer and glow in the ghostly light. After they had proceeded for a quarter of a mile, Mallory noticed that the flat landscape had become punctuated with eerie shapes.

"What the hell is *that?*" he asked, pointing toward the largest of them.

"A snowman," replied Eohippus.

"It's not like any snowman *I* ever saw," said Mallory.

"Well, actually, it's a snow gorgon."

"Some kid's got a hell of an imagination," said the detective.

"Yes," agreed the tiny animal. "The feet should be much larger."

"You mean something like that actually exists in this world?" demanded Mallory.

"Of course," replied Eohippus.

The snow structures became increasingly complex, culminating in a castle that could have housed a small battalion.

"Beautiful work," commented Eohippus. "Notice how all the bricks are made of ice—and I'll bet the drawbridge actually works."

"Who could have built it?" asked Mallory, looking around for some sign of life. "It's only been snowing for twenty or thirty minutes."

"Who knows?" replied the tiny horse. "Why not just appreciate it before it melts?"

"Not knowing things bothers me," said Mallory. "I suppose that's why I became a detective."

"It's just as beautiful whether you know who created it or not," said Eohippus.

"Not to me, it isn't," replied Mallory doggedly.

"Philistine!" muttered the dark horse.

Mallory decided not to press the issue and turned his attention back to the snow sculptures, some delicate and crystalline, others straight out of his worst nightmares. Here and there some enterprising ad men had rushed out into the snow and indulged their creative instincts: exquisitely detailed snowmen and women displayed carefully textured smoking jackets, robes, bras, and shoes, each with pricetags and store locations prominently displayed, and an antiquarian car dealer had even sculpted a Duesenberg and a Tucker, complete with drivers in the proper period attire.

"Well, what do you think?" asked Eohippus after they had passed yet another castle.

"I haven't made up my mind," replied Mallory. "Part of me thinks it's fascinating." He paused. "And the part that's a detective thinks these things provide muggers with an awful lot of places to hide."

"We don't have any muggers in Central Park," said Eohippus.

"Don't count on it," said Mallory. "I just saw some movement behind that snow sphinx."

Eohippus looked in the direction he indicated.

"It's just a puppet show," he announced after a moment.

"Outside, at midnight, in a blizzard?" demanded Mallory in disbelief.

"What better time or place?" replied Eohippus. "Lots of children are permitted to stay up late to usher in the New Year. This keeps them from becoming nuisances at their parents' parties."

As they drew nearer, Mallory could see a number of small children, all wearing robes similar to his own, sitting cross-legged on the ground, laughing happily as a man and a woman, totally covered with snow, went through an elaborate Punch-and-Judy routine. As Mallory studied the children more closely, he could see furry and scaled tails poking out from under almost half the robes. A pair of teenaged girls, one quite human, the other sporting a huge pair of leathery wings, both of them obviously assigned to watch the children, stood at either side of the group, looking incredibly bored.

"Don't they get cold?" asked Mallory.

"They're wearing protective robes and cloaks," answered Eohippus.

"I meant the actors."

"I can't imagine why," said Eohippus.

"They're covered with snow," Mallory pointed out.

"Of course they are. They're snow inside and out."

"Are you trying to tell me that there aren't any people under all that snow?" demanded Mallory.

"That's right," replied Eohippus.

"I don't believe it!"

"It's the truth," said the tiny horse. "Every time we get a measurable snowfall, the kids run out to this spot for a Punch-and-Judy show. I don't know how, but the snowmen remember the scripts from one winter to the next."

Just then Judy hit Punch on the head with a rolling pin made of snow, and Punch, weeping and wailing, collapsed to the ground while the children laughed and cheered.

"You see?" said Eohippus. "That blow would have killed a *real* person."

"I agree," said Mallory. He paused. "I guess I'm just used to *my* Central Park."

"This isn't to imply that this Manhattan is without its

dangers," continued the tiny horse. "But they come from different sources."

"Such as the Grundy?"

Eohippus nodded.

Then the children were behind them, and they came to a bleak, barren area that was punctuated only by an occasional snow sculpture. Finally the dark horse reached the end of the park and turned onto a narrow, freshly plowed street.

"Where are we now?" asked Mallory.

"On Sorrow Street," said Eohippus.

"Never heard of it," said Mallory.

"It's only a block long," replied the little horse. "It runs from Gluttony to Lust."

"They don't exist in my Manhattan."

"Of course they do," said Eohippus. "They just have other names."

They came to an intersection, and the dark horse stopped for a red light. Mallory took the opportunity to look down the cross street.

Every building had a doorman, each dressed more exotically than the last. The interiors seemed to be plush and dimly lit, and high-pitched laughter pierced the cold night air. The doorman of the building nearest the corner, a tall bronzed man dressed in a turban, a metallic gold vest, velvet pantaloons, and shoes with toes that curled upward, was persuasively describing the delights of his establishment to a well-dressed gentleman who seemed normal in every respect except for a huge pair of white wings that stuck out through the back of his overcoat; finally he nodded, passed some money to the doorman, and entered the building, where a pneumatic and suggestively clad young woman immediately took him by the arm and led him out of sight.

"Lust Street?" asked Mallory.

Eohippus nodded.

"Why is it adjacent to Sorrow Street?" asked the detective. "Are they all rip-off joints?"

"No," replied the tiny horse. "They give the customer exactly what they promise: unbridled carnality, with absolutely no uncomfortable emotional involvements."

"Sounds like everyone's getting their money's worth," commented Mallory.

"True," agreed Eohippus. "Yet almost all of them wind up on Sorrow Street sooner or later."

"I assume that Gluttony Street is composed of restaurants?" continued Mallory.

"Each and every one a four-star establishment."

"They also give the customer what he wants?"

"More," said Eohippus grimly.

The light turned green, and they proceeded for a short block, turned left, went another block, and took a right. Once again the ambience of the neighborhood changed: the brownstone apartment buildings managed to look dusty even while covered with snow, rusted Nashes and Studebakers and Packards that hadn't run for years lined the street, beneath every streetlight huddled an undernourished beggar, and most of the stores had OUT OF BUSINESS signs posted on their doors.

"Bleak Street?" guessed Mallory.

Eohippus nodded, as the dark horse came to a stop.

Mallory looked at the black-draped windows confronting him. "There must be some mistake," he said.

"This is 124 Bleak Street," replied the horse.

"But it's a funeral home!"

"That is hardly *my* fault."

Mallory dismounted and placed Eohippus on the sidewalk, then turned to the dark horse.

"Stick around," he said. "I've got a feeling the phone book was wrong."

"You needed transportation to Bleak Street. I provided it. My obligation to you is ended."

The horse turned and trotted away down the street.

"A nice loyal friend you've got yourself," remarked Mallory caustically.

"He's in terrible pain," answered Eohippus. "His legs are unsound, and between our weight and the snow . . ."

"I know," said Mallory. "I just get the feeling that he blames me personally for all his misfortunes."

"He blames all men," said Eohippus.

"Well, I think a little silent suffering would do wonders for his personality," said Mallory, turning his attention back to the building. He stared at it for a moment, then approached the front door and tried the handle.

"That's curious," he muttered.

"What is?" asked Eohippus.

"It's open."

He entered, followed by the little horse, and found himself in a candlelit circular foyer. Along the back wall were three doors, each decorated with a funeral wreath. To the left were four gilt chairs facing an elegant mahogany desk.

An elderly man wearing a dark, double-breasted pinstriped suit a somber tie sat at the desk, writing in a black, leather-bound ledger with a quill pen. He was incredibly gaunt, with deep, hollow cheeks and sunken eyes. His hair, which was steel gray, formed a prominent widow's peak just above his thin eyebrows.

"Are you here to claim a body?" he asked in a deep, cadaverous voice.

"No," said Mallory. "I'm looking for a Colonel Carruthers."

He smiled, displaying a row of crooked yellow teeth. "Ah! Then you want the Morbidium."

"I do?"

"Yes," said the man. He squinted down at Eohippus. "I'm afraid we don't allow dogs."

"He's a horse," said Mallory.

The man stood up and took a step toward them, then bent over and stared at Eohippus. "So he is," he said at last. He straightened up. "We don't have any rules barring horses, but it's highly irregular." He looked at the little horse again, then shrugged his narrow shoulders. "I don't suppose one more irregularity will make any difference. Please follow me, sir."

He went through the nearest doorway, and Mallory and Eohippus fell into step behind him. They walked through a narrow corridor that was illuminated by evenly spaced candles in pewter holders affixed to the walls, then came to a spiral staircase and began climbing down.

"Exactly what is this Morbidium?" asked Mallory, lifting up Eohippus and carrying him.

"It's the storeroom for the mortuary upstairs," answered the old man.

"They store bodies down here?"

"Coffins."

"And that's where Carruthers lives?" persisted Mallory suspiciously.

"That's right."

"This may be a silly question," continued Mallory, "but is the Colonel alive?"

"Certainly."

"And you and the Colonel work in this Morbidium?"

The old man laughed. "We *live* here."

"In a mortuary?" asked Mallory unbelievingly.

"Not everyone is fortunate enough to set aside sufficient funds for his retirement, sir," replied the old man as he reached the bottom of the staircase. "The mortuary supplies us with a warm, dry room in which to visit and a fine supply of truly luxurious caskets in which to sleep—and in exchange we do such maintenance work as may be required."

"And they leave the caskets down here for you permanently?"

"Goodness, no!" answered the old man. "They're a business. Every casket is for sale. But as each is sold, they must restock; it would be quite embarrassing for them to find themselves with more corpses than coffins." He paused. "Actually, it's like changing beds every couple of days; it helps break up the monotony."

"It sounds uncomfortable," remarked Mallory.

"Oh, no, sir," said the old man. "Modern caskets are quite spacious and luxurious. In fact, I can honestly say that I never owned a bed half so comfortable."

The old man led them along a corridor.

"Here we are, sir," he said. "I'll point the Colonel out to you."

He opened a door, and Mallory and Eohippus followed him through into a large room.

There were upwards of forty coffins at the far end of the chamber, many of them quite elegant but a few rather mundane and nondescript, each positioned upon its own table. All but a handful of them were supplied with blankets and pillows, and as Mallory looked at them more closely, he noticed that half a dozen elderly men and women lay sleeping in them. One old man had on a set of Walkman earphones, and was tapping his fingers against the side of the coffin in time to the music.

The remainder of the room resembled the lobby of an aging hotel that, while in good repair, was badly in need of redecorating. The chairs and couches, though deep and comfortable, were sadly out of date, the pattern of the carpet had been discarded as old-fashioned sometime before World War II, the ashtrays were more elegant than functional, and the gilt-framed prints on the walls were by painters who were long dead and even longer-forgotten. A phonograph that displayed a representation of a dog listening to his master's voice was playing a 78 RPM recording of one of Rudy Vallee's less memorable love songs.

A number of men and women, most of them quite elderly, were seated on the furniture. A couple of the men were dressed informally in white tennis togs and another wore a sports shirt, a sleeveless sweater, a leather golf cap, knickers, and spiked shoes, but the remainder were clad in dark suits, high-collared white shirts, and somber ties. All of the women wore either print dresses or business suits and most wore hats with veils; some of them wore kidskin gloves, and one, an ancient white-headed woman with regal bearing, was enveloped in a fur wrap that seemed to be composed almost entirely of foxes' heads, tails, and feet, with each head chewing vigorously on the tail ahead of it. Almost all the men and women held dainty little demitasses filled with coffee, and most of them were also munching on cookies or pastries.

A burly woman, vibrant with life, sat at the end of the room nearest to the caskets. Her auburn hair, coiled tightly in a bun, was unmarked by gray, though Mallory estimated her age at between sixty and sixty-five. She wore a brown tweed jacket, a wool skirt, a very businesslike tan blouse, and a silk tie.

"That's her," said the old man.

"That's who?" asked Mallory.

"The Colonel."

"You mean the Colonel is a woman?"

"Have you got something against women?" asked the old man.

"Not at all," said Mallory hastily. "I was just surprised."

The old man caught her attention, and the Colonel got to her feet and walked briskly across the room.

"I have someone who's here to see you, Colonel," he said.

She stared at Mallory. "Do I know you?"

"Not yet," said Mallory, extending his hand. "My name is John Justin Mallory."

She took his hand and shook it vigorously. "I'm pleased to meet you, Mallory. You may call me Winnifred." She looked at Eohippus, who was still tucked under Mallory's arm. "What have we here?"

"A horse," said Mallory.

"Quite a small one," she said, unsurprised. "Has he got a name?"

"Eohippus," said the tiny horse.

"Well, I'm pleased to meet you, Eohippus," she said, reaching out a hand and gently tousling his forelock and mane as he wriggled with pleasure. "You've got a manly little voice."

"Thank you," said Eohippus.

She turned back to Mallory. "Can I offer you some tea, or perhaps a scone with some clotted cream?" She paused. "To be perfectly truthful, they're not all that good, but one does what one can."

"No, thank you," said Mallory. "What I'd really like is some information, and perhaps even some help."

She chuckled. "I'm having enough trouble just helping myself these days. It comes from spending all my time studying the beasts of the jungle instead of the beasts of Wall Street." She shrugged. "But that's neither here nor there. What kind of information do you need?"

"I understand that you know something about unicorns," began Mallory.

"Wrong! I know *everything* about unicorns. I've been studying them for close to forty years." She looked at him sharply. "What's *your* interest in them?"

"I'm hunting for one."

"Excellent!" she said happily. "I'm always glad to talk to a fellow sportsman, Mallory. There's nothing quite so invigorating as staring into the bloodshot little eyes of a bull unicorn as he prepares to charge!"

"I believe that this particular unicorn has been domesticated," replied Mallory.

"What a shame!" said Winnifred. "They're such noble sport in the wild! Ah, that's the life, Mallory—the sun overhead, the wind in your face, surrounded by your loyal trolls, hot on the trail of a unicorn with a record horn! And, oh, the smell of unicorn steak cooking over an open fire! It makes my heart beat faster just to think of it! *That's* where you should be, Mallory—out in the wilderness, not hunting some poor brute who has probably been reduced to wearing a bridle and saddle." She paused. "You know, if this were even ten years ago and I still had my trusty .550 Nitro Express, I'd volunteer to take you along on a *real* unicorn hunt."

"I'd be honored to have you with me on this one," said Mallory.

She smiled wistfully, then sighed deeply. "I'd just be in the way, a fat old woman who's short of breath and spends most of her time living in the past. You don't need me, Mallory."

"You're exactly what I *do* need," said Mallory. "I'm not a hunter; I'm a detective."

"A detective?"

He nodded. "The unicorn I'm after was stolen this afternoon. I've got until daybreak to find it."

"You mean it's right here on the streets of Manhattan?"

"Well, I doubt that he's still on the street," replied Mallory. "But he's somewhere in the city. And," he added, "I don't begin to know how to go about finding him."

"It's quite a challenge," she mused, trying unsuccessfully to hide her interest. "Your employer wants it by dawn, you say?"

"That was the stipulation."

"Hmmm. That doesn't give us—excuse me: *you*—much time." She turned to him. "Who do you think stole it?"

"I *know* who stole him: the Grundy, and a leprechaun named Flypaper Gillespie."

Winnifred frowned. "Why would the Grundy want to steal a unicorn?"

"It was Larkspur," said Eohippus.

"*Larkspur?*" she exclaimed. "That puts an entirely different light on it! Of course I'll help you, Mallory." She frowned. "The problem is that you're going to need more help than I can give you."

"I thought you knew everything about unicorns," said Mallory.

"About their habits, and how to track them down, yes," explained Winnifred. "But I don't know very much about that ruby in his head, or what the Grundy can do with it. We're going to have to enlist the aid of an expert."

"On unicorns?" asked Mallory, confused.

"On magic."

"Then the ruby *does* have magical powers?"

"If its powers aren't magical, they're so close to magic that it makes no difference."

"Shouldn't we make some attempt to find out if it's magical?" asked Mallory. "There may be certain precautions we have to take."

"That's why we're going to pay a call on the Great Mephisto," she said firmly. "He'll know—and if the stone *is* magical, he'll be able to tell us what to do."

"He's a magician?"

"The best."

"Where can we find him?" asked Mallory.

"He's very fond of a little bar on the next block," replied Winnifred.

"Would he go there on New Year's Eve?" asked Mallory.

"Why not?" replied Winnifred. "He has nowhere else to go." She checked her wristwatch. "There's every likelihood that he'll be there in the next twenty or thirty minutes."

"He'd better be," said Mallory. "I've still got a deadline. My client will be put to death at sunrise if I haven't got Larkspur back by then."

"Oh? Who are you working for, Mallory?"

"An elf named Mürgenstürm. Ever hear of him?"

She shook her head. "The name is unfamiliar to me. What's his connection to Larkspur?"

"He was supposed to be guarding him when the Grundy stole him."

"That's very curious," said Winnifred.

"What is?"

"Placing such a valuable animal in the care of a single elf. He must be quite formidable, this Mürgenstürm."

Mallory smiled wryly. "As a matter of fact, he's the most scatterbrained, oversexed, cowardly little bastard I've ever met."

"That doesn't fit," Winnifred announced firmly. "Something's very wrong here, Mallory."

"Oh?"

She nodded. "Why would the elves' guild entrust Larkspur to someone like that? They've got a reputation for being the finest security force around. Why should they take the most valuable thing they've ever had to protect and place it in the charge of an elf such as you've described?"

Mallory frowned. "It doesn't make much sense, does it?"

"It certainly doesn't," agreed Winnifred. "Could he

have lied to you, Mallory? Could it be an inside job from start to finish?"

"I doubt it."

"Why?"

"Three reasons," answered Mallory. "First, he hired me to clear him with his guild. Second, he was genuinely terrified when he found out that Larkspur was in the Grundy's possession. And third, the Grundy keeps trying to scare me off and has already tried to kill me." He shook his head. "No, the Grundy stole the unicorn; I'm sure of it. But suddenly I've got a batch of questions about that little green wart."

"You mean Mürgenstürm?" asked Eohippus.

Mallory nodded.

"For example?" said Winnifred.

"I know you have detectives in your Manhattan. Why did he come to *my* Manhattan for one?"

"That's easy enough to answer," said Winnifred. "Any detective from *this* Manhattan would have spotted the flaws in his story. This addle-pated, incompetent act you describe wouldn't have fooled anyone who knew Larkspur's value." She frowned. "But as for why he wanted a detective in the first place, or why he's putting on this act . . ." Winnifred shrugged. "I have no idea."

"You and me both," muttered Mallory. "And then there's Felina."

"Felina?"

"A cat-girl. She's been tagging along with us since half an hour after I arrived. I wonder if *she's* in on whatever's going on?"

"I wouldn't worry too much about a cat-person," said Winnifred. "If they have any loyalty at all, it isn't for sale, and I certainly wouldn't trust one to keep a secret." She paused and looked at him sharply. "Perhaps you'd better return home, Mallory. Since Mürgenstürm obviously lied to you, you're under no obligation to remain here.''

"Most of my clients lie to me the first time around," replied Mallory. "It's an occupational hazard. And this one is paying me enough for me to officially believe him until dawn." Suddenly he got to his feet. "Get your coat. We can't stay here."

"But Mephisto almost never shows up before one o'clock," protested Winnifred.

"Then we'll wait for him."

"What's the matter, Mallory?"

"I left a message for Mürgenstürm to meet me here. And while I may officially believe him, I don't think I trust him."

Winnifred walked immediately to a closet, pulled out a white, ankle-length fur coat and a pair of boots lined with the same fur, and led the detective and Eohippus out of the room and up the long flight of stairs.

The snow had stopped when they reached the street, and Winnifred started off to her right.

"Hi, John Justin Mallory," purred a familiar voice. "That's a tasty-looking little animal you have with you."

Mallory looked up and saw Felina perched atop a streetlamp.

"What are you doing up there?" he asked.

"Sitting," she said, her eyes never leaving Eohippus, whom Mallory had set down on the ground.

"How long have you been here?"

"I don't know."

"How did you find me?" demanded Mallory.

She smiled and jumped lightly to the ground. "You're much easier to follow than a unicorn," she said, squatting down next to Eohippus. "Cute little, sweet little, fat little, chewy little tidbit," she crooned in a singsong voice.

"Uh . . . Mallory?" said Eohippus nervously.

"This is Felina?" asked Winnifred.

Mallory nodded. "She was helping me track down a unicorn in the park when dietary considerations intervened."

Felina reached out her hand to touch Eohippus, and Winnifred slapped it. The cat-girl jumped back quickly, spitting and hissing.

"You are to leave him alone," said Winnifred firmly. "Do you understand?"

Felina snarled at her.

"Do that again, young lady, and I'll put a leash on you," said Winnifred.

Felina's demeanor abruptly changed from aggressive to subservient.

"A high-spirited species," Winnifred explained to Mallory. "You have to lay out the ground rules and let them know who's in charge right at the start, or you're just asking for trouble." She looked at Felina. "Now, we're not going to have any more problems about touching the little horse, are we?"

Felina smiled and shook her head. Mallory decided that it was a little too toothy a smile, and decided to pick Eohippus up and tuck him under his arm.

"The bar is just on the next block," said Winnifred. "Actually, it's a very pleasant place. Large drinks, small prices."

"Then let's go," said the detective.

"Right," she agreed, striding off vigorously. "Suddenly I feel alive again. I'm out of that musty mortuary, and the game's afoot!" She took a deep breath. "Ah, smell that invigorating air, Mallory! It reminds me of the time I hunted the yeti in the Himalayas."

"I didn't know yetis really existed," remarked the detective.

Winnifred laughed and turned around to better display her white fur coat. "What do you think I'm wearing?"

"I'm glad you're on *our* side," said Mallory.

"And I'm glad you rescued me from another New Year's Eve surrounded by a batch of people who are just sitting around waiting to die," she replied earnestly.

"What the hell is a vibrant person like you doing with them anyway?" asked Mallory.

"I really don't know," she replied honestly. "I just drifted into staying there, and they made it so comfortable that before long it became too much of an effort to leave."

"That's why I stay in Manhattan," agreed Mallory. "It may not be much, the air may stink and the streets may be unsafe, but somehow getting through the day has always seemed like less work than moving."

Suddenly she stopped and lifted her gaze to the cloud-covered heavens.

"Be on your guard, Grundy!" she shouted. "We may not look like much, we may lack your dark powers, we may not have your evil allies—but we're going to give you a run for your money, I promise you that!"

Chapter
7 ——————————————————————

12:27 AM–12:45 AM

"Do you like ragtime?" asked Winnifred as they approached the tavern.

"It beats the hell out of the stuff that passes for music these days," replied Mallory. "As far as I'm concerned, it's been going straight downhill ever since the Andrews Sisters stopped recording."

"Good," said Winnifred. "I think you'll like this place."

Mallory stopped in front of the building. "Are you sure you've got the right spot?" he asked her. "This joint's a Chinese laundry."

Winnifred chuckled heartily and opened the door, and a blast of frenzied ragtime music emanated from the dimly lit interior.

"Follow me," she said.

Mallory, carrying Eohippus and followed by Felina, fell into step behind her as she briskly made her way to an empty table at the far end of the crowded room. Couples, foursomes, and even larger groups clustered around the tables and at the long mahogany bar, obviously enjoying themselves, while a number of white-jacketed waiters carried drinks on silver trays.

Most of the men were dressed in old-fashioned tuxedos, and Mallory noticed that a number of them wore spats. The women, all with short hairstyles and shorter dresses, seemed to be engaged in a contest to see which of them could look the most like Clara Bow.

"Mephisto's not here yet," announced Winnifred after scanning the low-ceilinged, smoke-filled room. When they finally reached their table and seated themselves, she turned to Mallory. "Isn't this a charming little bistro?"

"The place is filled with gents and flappers," he replied wryly, as the piano player ripped into a new tune and half a dozen patrons began dancing the Charleston. "Are they the cast of some Broadway show?"

"No, they're customers just like you and me."

"They may be customers," responded Mallory, "but they're sure as hell not like you and me. What is this place, anyway?"

"The Forgotten Speakeasy," answered Winnifred.

"Speakeasy?" he repeated.

She nodded, amused by his reaction. "It's been in continuous operation since 1925." She lowered her voice confidentially. "In fact, they still make their own gin in one of the upstairs bathtubs. It's quite good, actually."

"Don't the customers know that Prohibition is over?" asked Mallory as he observed the clientele at play. "Or isn't it?"

"Oh, it's over," she assured him. "And to be perfectly truthful, some of them probably don't know. This place is so popular that a number of them have never gone home. They talk about Lucky Lindy and Big Al, they wonder if talking pictures are just a passing fad, they think the market will never crash." She pointed surreptitiously to a tall man who stood in a corner, his back to the wall, a toothpick in his mouth, flipping a silver dollar in his right hand. "See him?"

Mallory nodded.

"He was hired to assassinate a famous bootlegger," she whispered. "Nobody's had the heart to tell him that the bootlegger died more than forty years ago."

A waiter approached them, and Mallory noticed that his hair, like that of all the other men, had been slicked down with grease.

"May I take your orders?"

"I'll have a hot toddy," said Winnifred. She turned to Mallory. "You really should try one. They're quite invigorating."

"I'll try anything that won't make me go blind," said the detective.

"Make that two hot toddies," Winnifred instructed the waiter. "And when Mephisto comes in, tell him that I want to see him."

"Will the . . . ah . . . young lady have anything?" asked the waiter, indicating Felina.

"Milk," said the cat-girl.

The waiter made a face. "We don't have any."

"Can you make a Brandy Alexander?" asked Mallory.

The waiter nodded.

"Good. She wants one—and hold everything except the cream."

The waiter looked at Mallory as if he were crazy, but finally shrugged, nodded again, and departed toward the bar.

"Oh, dear!" said Winnifred suddenly. "We forgot about Eohippus!"

"It's all right," said Eohippus, who was sprawled across Mallory's lap. "I don't drink."

"You must be uncomfortable like that," said Winnifred. "Let me put you on the table."

She lifted Eohippus up and placed him next to a bowl of peanuts. Felina stared at the tiny animal and leaned forward slightly.

"If you do, I'll thrash you to within an inch of your life," said Winnifred earnestly.

Felina, all innocence, leaned farther forward and straightened the tablecloth, then tilted her chair back on two legs and pouted.

Suddenly a tall man with very thick horn-rimmed glasses entered the tavern, walked up to the bar, exchanged greetings with the bartender, and began wending his way toward their table. He wore a modern tuxedo, a red and black satin cape that would have been right at home in a Dracula movie, and a pointed hat that had all the signs of the Zodiac embroidered on it.

"Hi, Winnie," he said, pulling up an empty chair and sitting down. "You wanted to talk to me?"

"Yes," said Winnifred. "Mephisto, this is John Justin Mallory. And these," she added, gesturing in turn to his companions, "are Eohippus and Felina."

"The Great Mephisto, at your service," said the magician, extending his hand to the detective.

"Pleased to meet you," said Mallory. He reached forward, only to discover that a small rabbit had suddenly appeared in the palm of the magician's hand. Mephisto placed it in a pocket just before Felina could pounce on it.

"Colonel Carruthers tells me you're the best magician in New York," continued the detective.

"In the world," Mephisto corrected him. "You want proof?" he added, producing a deck of cards out of empty air and fanning them out. "Pick a card. Any card."

"I'm not interested in card tricks," said Mallory.

"You should be," said Mephisto. "They're all the rage at parties these days." He flicked his hand and the cards vanished.

"Do you just do tricks, or are you really a magician?" asked Mallory.

"What's the difference?" asked Mephisto.

"Life and death, in this case," said Mallory.

"Oh?" said Mephisto, suddenly interested. "Then I'm a magician, adept at creation, prognostication, and spells. What can I do for you, my friend?"

"Tell me about the ruby embedded in Larkspur's head."

Mephisto turned to Winnifred. "Larkspur?" he repeated petulantly. "I thought you were offering me a job!"

"No whining!" she snapped. "Now, behave yourself and answer his questions."

"A magician could starve to death in a place like this," he muttered. "The way everyone wants free advice, you'd think I was a doctor!"

"The question, Mephisto," urged Winnifred. "Or are you simply a sleight-of-hand artist after all?"

"O ye of little faith," he said with a sigh, and turned to Mallory. "What do you want to know about Larkspur's precious gem?"

"Everything," said the detective.

Mephisto stared at him for a moment, and then suddenly snapped his fingers triumphantly. "Now I've got it! You're the guy that the Grundy is after!"

Mallory nodded.

"Hah!" grinned Mephisto. "Then he's trying to steal the stone!"

"He's already stolen it," said Eohippus.

"If he's stolen anything, it's the unicorn, not the ruby," said Mephisto.

"There's a difference?" asked Mallory.

The magician nodded. "A friend of mine just ushered in the New Year at what we used to call 'a house of ill repute.' Since his wife is aware of his favorite haunts in this Manhattan, he chose to do his carousing in *your* Manhattan.'' He paused. ''He couldn't have done that if the Grundy possessed the ruby.''

''Why not?''

''Because, among its other properties, the ruby permits transit between your world and mine.''

''I find that hard to believe,'' said Mallory. ''There are an awful lot of people here from my Manhattan, and none of us used a ruby to get here. Hell, I came in an elevator.''

''Nevertheless, the ruby made it possible.''

''How?''

''It's difficult to explain,'' said Mephisto. ''You see, there's a membrane between the two worlds.''

''You mean like a skin?'' interrupted Mallory.

The magician chuckled. ''Nothing so tangible; it's more like a very special zone that connects your world with mine. At any rate, as long as Larkspur lives, the membrane is permeable and passage between the worlds is possible. When he was born, it became possible to pass from one world to the other. When he dies—and the only thing other than old age that can kill him is the removal of the ruby—the membrane will harden within a matter of a few hours, and our worlds will be closed off from each other.''

''Until the next ruby-bearing unicorn is born in 1,000 years,'' suggested Mallory.

''Forever,'' replied Mephisto.

''But I thought that a unicorn was born with a ruby every millennium or so,'' said Mallory.

''That's true,'' acknowledged Mephisto. ''But each ruby gives us access to a different world. Once Larkspur dies—from whatever cause—your world is inaccessible to us for all eternity. The next ruby will open up some other world, just as the last two did.''

''How long should Larkspur live?'' asked Mallory.

''Let's see,'' said Mephisto, rubbing his bony chin. ''He

must be about sixty now." He turned to Winnifred. "What *is* a unicorn's life expectancy?"

"Between one hundred and one hundred and twenty years," she replied. "But that's for a normal unicorn. With one like Larkspur, who can say?"

"But he's not likely to die of natural causes in the next few years?" persisted Mallory.

"No."

Mallory frowned. "Then I can't understand why the Grundy wants the ruby. The second he removes it, Larkspur will die, and the second Larkspur dies this world is sealed off for another thousand years. That just doesn't make sense, given a demon who can reasonably be expected to want plunder from both worlds."

Mephisto smiled and leaned across the table, squinting at Mallory through his thick lenses. "Nothing is ever quite as simple as it seems," he said, producing a lit cigarette out of the air and taking a puff of it as Felina, startled, hissed and crouched atop her chair. "Especially in the world of master magi such as myself and the Grundy. For one thing, the possessor of the stone always has free passage between the worlds. For another, allowing transit through the membrane is only one of the ruby's properties."

"What are the others?" asked Mallory, raising his voice in order to be heard over the patrons, who were now singing "Lili Marlene" to the accompaniment of the pianist.

"The Grundy has certain talents," said Mephisto uncomfortably. "Insignificant and amateurish compared to those of a magician like myself, you understand"—he paused, frowning—"but they do seem to make him rich and powerful, while mine are only appreciated at parties and produce barely enough income to keep my rabbits fed." He sighed. "At any rate, the ruby tends to amplify its possessor's abilities—and of course the Grundy does have two other rubies already."

"What will this one enable him to do that the others didn't?" asked Mallory.

"You don't understand," explained Mephisto patiently. "This particular ruby has no properties the others don't also possess. But adding its potency to that of the others will give the Grundy even greater power than he already possesses. It's like running on three cylinders instead of two—which is all the more impressive when you consider that nobody else has any cylinders at all. He will be virtually invulnerable to attack; he'll be able to dominate not only people but events by sheer force of will; he may even be able to hasten the birth of the next ruby-bearing unicorn."

"Back up a sentence or two," said Mallory. "You said that Larkspur's ruby, added to the other two, will make the Grundy invulnerable to attack."

"Virtually," repeated the magician.

"Then he's not invulnerable now," said Mallory. "How do I get at him? What weapon do I use?"

"Well, you certainly can't use physical force," said Mephisto. "He's quite capable of destroying a gorgon with his bare hands. And weapons are out of the question, too—the two rubies he's got are more than sufficient to protect him." He paused. "I suppose magic is the only way to get to him."

"All right. How do I go about it?"

"You don't," said Mephisto. "You're not a magician."

"Can you teach me?"

"In one night?" laughed Mephisto. "Do you know how long it took me just to master that card trick I was trying to show you?"

"Then will you help us?" asked Winnifred.

Mephisto frowned and straightened up in his chair. "I don't know," he said. "I'd like to, I really would—but he's the *Grundy!*"

"I thought you were the greatest magician in the world," said Felina with a feline purr.

"I am," said Mephisto. He paused. "But for reasons that somehow elude me, he seems to be the most successful one."

"He'll be even more successful if he gets his hands on that third ruby," Eohippus pointed out.

"I'll have to think about it," said Mephisto. He turned to Mallory. "I need more details."

"Ask away," replied the detective.

"Why are you here in the first place? You're not even from this Manhattan."

Mallory paused for a moment as the waiter approached, then answered when it became obvious that the drinks were for another table. "I was hired by an elf named Mürgenstürm."

"What's he got to do with this?"

"I'm not sure yet," admitted Mallory. "He was ostensibly in charge of the unicorn when it was stolen by a leprechaun named Flypaper Gillespie, who works for the Grundy."

"Then the Grundy may not have it in his possession yet?" asked Mephisto.

"It's a possibility."

Mephisto got to his feet.

"Well?" said Winnifred.

"You can't rush a decision like this," he replied. "I'm going over to the bar to meditate."

He snaked his way between a number of couples who, having tired of the Charleston, were lining up for the Bunny Hop.

"He'll join us," predicted Winnifred confidently.

"I hope you're right," said Eohippus.

"I know I am. It's a matter of pride."

"He thinks he can beat the Grundy?" asked Mallory.

She chuckled. "Not really. But he'd die of shame if we won without his help."

"And," added Eohippus seriously, "he'd probably like to own a ruby or two himself."

"Let's worry about one problem at a time," said Mallory.

"I agree," said Winnifred. "We have more serious things to consider."

"Such as my cream," pouted Felina.

"I'm sure it will be here very soon," replied Winnifred soothingly. "Tonight is the busiest night of the year for them."

Felina sniffed and turned away.

"You were about to mention some serious considerations?" asked Mallory.

Winnifred nodded. "We have to decide how best to utilize our forces."

"I'm open to suggestions," replied the detective.

"I think you should return to the Morbidium."

"Why?"

"Because if Mürgenstürm shows up, we need someone there who recognizes him."

He shook his head. "It's not necessary."

"Oh? Why not?"

"Because if he's a party to the theft, he won't show up. And if he does show up, he'll identify himself. I think it would be better simply to phone the Morbidium in an hour or so to see if he's arrived yet."

"That makes sense, Mallory," agreed Winnifred. "All right; this frees you to help us search for Flypaper Gillespie."

"And the Grundy," he added.

"We don't want to confront the Grundy unless it's absolutely necessary," she said adamantly. "We'll let Mephisto find out whether he's got Larkspur or not. He has more circumspect means than you or I do."

"I didn't notice much about him that was subtle," commented Mallory.

"He may not be socially adept," said Winnifred, "but he's a fine magician. You'll have to take my word for it."

"Then you think that we should go hunting for Gillespie?" asked Mallory.

"He was the last one to have Larkspur, and he's much less formidable than the Grundy." She paused thoughtfully. "If we split up, we can cover twice as much territory."

"I haven't got the foggiest notion where to begin looking."

"He's a criminal," said Winnifred. "Scour the underworld. That's what *I* plan to do."

"I don't even know where to *find* the underworld," replied Mallory wryly.

"Hunt up some shady characters. Spread some money around. Ask a policeman." Winnifred stared severely at him. "You're a detective, Mallory. You'll find a way."

"We'll need a meeting place," said Mallory.

"Let me see," she mused. "The Morbidium is too far out of the way, Times Square is too crowded on New Year's Eve. So are the hotels and the theater district." Suddenly she smiled. "I have it! We'll meet at the New York Stock Exchange!"

"Where is it located?" asked Mallory.

"On Wall Street."

"Just making sure it's at the same address as the one in my world," he explained. He paused. "Just out of curiosity, what's so great about the Stock Exchange?"

"It's centrally located, and it will be completely deserted. They don't do any business on New Year's Day."

He shrugged. "Okay. What time do you want to meet?"

Winnifred checked her wristwatch. "It's nearly twelve-forty-five now. How would two-fifteen be?"

"That's only an hour and a half," he pointed out.

"I'm an optimist," she replied. "And it's harder than you might think to hide a unicorn in Manhattan. Besides," she added, "we'll want to exchange information by then."

She looked up as the waiter finally arrived with their drinks.

"Thanks," said Mallory. "What do I owe you?"

"Sixty cents," said the waiter.

Mallory handed him three quarters, and he departed.

"This is some place, this tavern," he said. "I guess no one ever told them about inflation, either."

"I believe this is yours," said Winnifred, placing the cream in front of Felina. The cat-girl glared sullenly at her, then reached out for the glass, downed its contents in a single swallow, and turned to face the wall.

"Not bad," said Mallory, taking a sip of his hot toddy. "By the way, I've been wondering: how did you ever become a big-game hunter?"

"My Manhattan may seem new and interesting to you," replied Winnifred, "but I grew up here. I always wanted to see what lay beyond the next hill, to visit the wild places before they had all been tamed, to see clear to the horizon with no buildings blocking the view."

"So you took up hunting?"

She nodded. "I went out to pit myself against animals no one had ever seen before, to climb mountains that had never been scaled and cross rivers that had never been crossed, to explore lands that no civilized man had ever seen." She paused. "I did it, too. I spent twenty-seven years in the bush, and the zoos and museums are filled with my trophies."

"Is that when you joined the army?"

"I never joined the army," she replied. "I don't think I'd have liked the regimentation."

"But you're a colonel," noted Mallory.

"Oh, *that*," she said with a shrug. "They made me a colonel when I helped put down an uprising among some trolls out in the bush."

Mallory finished his hot toddy. "You must have had some fascinating experiences," he said idly. "Which was your favorite?"

"My favorite experience?" she repeated, closing her eyes and allowing a nostalgic expression to cross her face. "I remember the silver moonlight over a tropical lagoon, the feel of a strong hand on mine, and the whisper of words over the rippling of water. Mostly, I remember the jasmine, sweet and fragrant on the cool night breeze."

"It sounds very romantic," said Eohippus.

"It does, doesn't it?" agreed Winnifred. She smiled a bittersweet smile. "The funny thing is that it never once happened, not to me."

"I beg your pardon?" said Eohippus, confused.

Winnifred sighed. "I went into the bush a fat, awkward young girl, and I came out a fat, wrinkled old lady." She paused. "Still, I remember it as if it were yesterday. They say that the heart plays tricks on you, but don't you believe it: it's the mind. That memory is more real to me than any of the things that really happened. I can still smell the overpowering fragrance of the jasmine. The faces are hazy—mine looks prettier than it was, and I can't quite recall my lover's—but the scent and the feelings are real, as real as if it had actually happened." She paused. "Isn't it funny that that should be my strongest memory of a life in the wilderness?"

"I don't think it's funny at all," said Mallory sincerely.

"You don't?"

He shook his head.

"Well," said Winnifred, suddenly uncomfortable, "so much for nostalgic nonsense." She straightened up in her chair. "We've still got a job to do. Is everyone ready to proceed?"

"I suppose so," said Mallory. "How do you want to divide up the troops?"

"I'm going with Mallory," put in Felina suddenly, grabbing his hand and rubbing her cheek against it.

"Then I think I'll take Eohippus," said Winnifred.

"I'm happy to accompany such a famous hunter," said the little horse. "But I should warn you that I don't know anything about leprechauns."

"That's not why I'm taking you," said Winnifred.

"Oh?" said the little horse.

"Do you really want to be alone in Felina's company while Mallory is busy making his underworld contacts?"

Eohippus trotted across the table to Winnifred. "I see your point," he said earnestly.

"Then let's go," said Winnifred, picking him up and walking vigorously toward the door.

Mallory got to his feet and turned to Felina, who remained seated.

"Are you coming?"

"I don't like her," hissed the cat-girl.

"She probably doesn't like you either," said the detective dryly.

"I like *you*, though," she replied with a feline smile.

"Then let's go."

She considered it for a moment, then leaped to her feet so quickly that a passing waiter jumped and spilled a tray filled with drinks.

"I'll protect you, John Justin Mallory," purred Felina.

"That's very comforting," replied Mallory.

"If she touches you . . ."

"Colonel Carruthers isn't the enemy," said Mallory wearily.

"You choose your enemies and I'll choose mine," said Felina.

When they joined Winnifred at the door, she turned to the bar.

"Well, Mephisto?" she said in a loud voice.

The lean, angular magician got grudgingly to his feet.

"All right," he said unhappily. "But I'm going to hate myself in the morning, assuming I live that long."

He joined them as they walked out into the frigid night.

"I've been assigned to the Grundy, I suppose," he said.

Winnifred nodded. "Don't try to fight him. Just find out if he's got Larkspur with him." She paused. "We rendezvous at the New York Stock Exchange at two-fifteen."

"I keep wondering if ninety minutes is enough time to gather any useful information," said Mallory.

"It will have to be," said Winnifred. "You may be on an even tighter schedule than Mürgenstürm."

"What do you mean?" he asked apprehensively.

"It occurs to me that if you're here when the Grundy gets his hands on the stone, you could be stuck in this Manhattan forever."

Chapter
8 ———————————————

The rain had started again as Mallory reached Times Square. It looked remarkably like the Times Square of his own world, right down to the cut-rate theater-ticket booth, the steam rising from the subway through the grates in the street, the street vendors, the souvenir shops, the pimps and pushers and prostitutes of both sexes. A huge Camel billboard out of his Manhattan's recent past featured a contented face blowing great gobs of smoke into the air.

Mallory stood under the bright lights of Broadway and peered down the length of 42nd Street. Most of the celebrants had already gone off to parties, and what remained were the regular denizens of the area. He spent a few moments scrutinizing the pedestrians who scurried past the novelty shops and massage parlors, observing the humans and nonhumans who struck beckoning postures in front of the run-down movie theaters, and watching the drunks and the addicts weave their ways down the filthy sidewalk.

"Christ!" he muttered. "They *all* look like criminals."

He sighed, then turned to Felina, who was hungrily eyeing a trash container.

"Come on," he said.

She took one last loving look at the trashcan, then fell into step beside him as he turned onto 42nd Street.

"Howdy, neighbor," said a sibilant voice as he passed a darkened building.

Mallory stopped and turned, and found himself facing a large man with green skin and cold, lifeless eyes.

"Looking for sssomething unusual?" hissed the man, and Mallory noticed that his tongue was quite long, and forked at the end.

"As a matter of fact, I am," he replied. "Where can I find a leprechaun?"

The man wrinkled his face in distaste. "You don't want a leprechaun, pal; they're nothing but trouble." He grinned. "But I can fix you up with a nice ssscaly lady. You've never made it until you've made it with a lizard!"

"No, thanks," said Mallory.

"We can take care of your ladyfriend, too," said the man persuasively. "Cat-girlsss go crazy over lizardsss."

Mallory shook his head. "I'm after leprechauns"—he flashed the wad of bills Mürgenstürm had given him—"and I'm especially after one named Flypaper Gillespie."

"If your ladyfriend isss into leashesss and collarsss, my brother Izzy can show her a real good time," continued the man, ignoring Mallory's query.

"If you can't tell me where to find Gillespie, who can?" persisted Mallory.

"You're *sssick!*" hissed the man. "I'm offering you an unforgettable night of ssslime and sssin, and all you want are leprechaunsss!"

He disappeared into the shadows, and Mallory, after waiting a moment to see if he would return, shrugged and resumed walking. He passed a number of sex stores which displayed an endless variety of odd-looking devices, most of which couldn't possibly have been worn or used by human men and women.

"Goblin girls!" whispered another voice. "Pretty young goblin girls!"

Mallory didn't even turn to see who was speaking to him, but grabbed Felina by the hand and increased his pace. He crossed Eighth Avenue, walked past another row of sleazy theaters and pornography shops—including one that promised a full refund if any customer could suggest anything that made one of their college-educated masseuses blush—and turned north when they got to Ninth Avenue.

The flashing neon lights vanished and the street, though darker, felt safer and less sleazy. They passed, in quick succession, a Greek restaurant that featured human and inhuman belly dancers, an English tea shop populated by gray-haired military types who all carried riding crops under their arms, a tavern that seemed to be a hangout for elves, and a cafeteria that claimed to have the rawest meat in the city and was filled to overflowing with goblins and trolls who made hideous growling and ripping sounds as they ate. Finally they came to the Emerald Isle Pub, and Mallory stopped abruptly.

Felina peered in the window. "There aren't any leprechauns in there," she announced.

"But there *are* Irishmen," replied Mallory. "And if they can't tell me where to find leprechauns, nobody can." He looked at her sternly. "Are you going to behave yourself, or am I going to have to leave you out here in the rain?"

"One or the other," answered Felina with an inscrutable smile.

"Outside it is, then," he said firmly.

"Wait!" she said as he approached the door.

"You'll sit still and keep quiet?"

"Probably."

"All right," he assented. "But the minute you start making a pest of yourself, out you go."

In answer, she rubbed up against him and purred, just as he opened the door.

"Not in front of everyone!" he whispered, embarrassed.

She grinned and stepped back as he ran a hand through his rain-soaked hair and surveyed the interior of the pub.

It was a small room, containing a bar and half a dozen tables, but it felt warm and cozy rather than hot and cramped. The tables were circular and well worn, the chairs were sturdy and functional, the floor was bare and unvarnished, and the walls contained a number of framed prints of the Irish countryside, plus a few autographed photos of Irish actors, athletes, and authors. The bar's stock was prominently displayed, and Mallory noticed that while there were literally hundreds of bottles of whiskey, there was no wine, nor were there any clear drinks such as gin or vodka. It was as if the management knew its clientele's tastes and saw no reason to display anything that wasn't in demand.

A huge, redheaded, freckle-faced bartender was staring curiously at him, as were a trio of old men who were sitting at a small table in one corner. Two more men, dressed in tweeds and turtlenecks, stood in the middle of the room, throwing darts into pictures of Queens Elizabeth I and II. A dozen others were scattered in twos and threes about the room; most of them wore tam-o'-shanters and about half of them had long scarves wrapped with careful nonchalance about their necks. A jukebox played an unending series of bouncy Irish melodies, most of them about girls named Kathleen or Molly.

"Good evening to you," said the bartender in a very thick brogue as the dart players tallied up their scores and sat down to do some serious drinking. "Can I be offering you a glass of good Irish whiskey?"

"Why not?" assented Mallory, approaching the bar while Felina leaped atop a stool and stared, unblinking, at the dart throwers.

"I've not seen you here before," said the bartender.

"That's not surprising," replied Mallory. "I haven't been here before."

"Would you be an Irishman?" asked the bartender, studying him carefully.

"John J. O'Mallory," replied Mallory.

"Then the first drink is on the house," said the bartender with the delighted smile of a man who has found a new source of income.

"That's very generous of you."

"And what will your friend be drinking?"

"Nothing," said Mallory as the bartender poured him a shot of whiskey. "You don't seem to mind her presence."

"Why should I? Cats originated in Ireland, you know."

"No, I didn't."

The bartender nodded. "Cats, whiskey, fine·linen, and revolution—our four gifts to the world."

"How about leprechauns?" asked Mallory.

"The Little People?" said the bartender contemptuously. "They may be Irish, but they're hardly a matter of pride. A vicious, untrustworthy race, if you ask my opinion."

"Do they ever come here?"

"I wouldn't have one in the place!" bellowed the bartender.

"Are you talking about the English?" asked one of the old men who were sitting in the corner. "Shooting's too good for them!"

"No," said the bartender. "We're discussing the Little People."

"Oh—*them*," said the old man. "Shooting's plenty good enough for them." He looked at Mallory. "What do *you* think of the English?"

"I've told the Sons of Erin not to goad my customers," said the bartender ominously.

"Just starting a pleasant little conversation," said the old man. "And you watch your tongue. The Sons of Erin remember who their friends are."

"Better by far than they remember who their creditors are," retorted the bartender caustically. "Or would you like to bring your bill up to date?"

"Maybe you'd better go back to the old country," shot back the old man. "America's turning you into a capitalist bloodsucker."

"There's nothing *in* the old country except a lot of rocks, and a batch of old men sitting around in pubs plotting revolution," said a ruddy-faced middle-aged man at another table.

"I heard that, Fitzpatrick," said the first old man, "and all I can say is that if the Knights of the Shamrock would do a little less talking and a little more fighting, we might all be able to go back to the old country."

"Hah!" shot back Fitzpatrick. "When did the Sons of Erin ever kill anything except a bottle of whiskey?"

"Fighting words!" cried the old man, scrambling to his feet.

"If they are, maybe I'd better tell the English to use them on you!" snapped Fitzpatrick, also rising.

"Would you care to step outside and repeat that?" said the old man.

"Indeed I would," said Fitzpatrick, taking his coat off, rolling up his sleeves, and spitting on his hands. He walked to the door. "Marquis of Queensberry rules?"

"Absolutely," agreed the old man, picking up a shillelagh and following him out onto the sidewalk.

Three or four customers followed them out, but the rest paid no attention to them—except for Felina, who walked to the window and pressed her face up against it curiously.

"Does this happen very often?" asked Mallory, turning to the bartender.

"No more than three or four times a night," replied the bartender, obviously unconcerned.

"Maybe we'd better break it up," suggested the detective.

"There's no hurry."

"Shillelagh or no shillelagh, the old man hasn't got much of a chance."

The bartender smiled. "They're just going to trade insults to get their blood properly boiling—and before that happens, they'll get so cold that they'll come back inside."

"You mean they're just going to *talk?*" demanded Mallory.

"There's a big difference between talking revolution and fighting one. If they liked to fight, they'd be in Belfast, setting off bombs."

"And this happens every night?"

The bartender nodded. "Except on Sundays."

"Why not Sundays?" asked Mallory, curious.

"We're closed on Sundays."

Felina returned to the bar and perched on the stool next to Mallory.

"I thought you were going to watch the fight," said the detective.

"All they're doing is yelling at each other," she replied with a shrug. Suddenly a bowl of peanuts captured her attention, and she began playing with them, arranging them in simplistic patterns on the surface of the bar.

The bartender noticed Mallory's empty glass. "Can I be giving you a refill, O'Mallory?"

"Why not?" said Mallory, shoving his glass toward the

bottle. He looked at the bartender. "I'd also like a little information."

"If it's within my power to give, it's yours."

"Thanks. I'd like to know where to find a leprechaun named Flypaper Gillespie."

"No, you wouldn't," said the bartender. "He's a mean one, Gillespie is."

"I know he is," said Mallory, pulling out his wallet and flashing his detective's license. "He took something that doesn't belong to him. I've been hired to get it back."

"Well, I'll be!" cried the bartender with delight. "A genuine shamus, right here in my pub!"

"Can you help me?"

"*I* can't, but maybe I can introduce you to someone who can. Finnegan!" he bellowed.

A slender, bearded, auburn-haired man in a wrinkled corduroy suit got up and walked over to the bar, carrying a small notebook in his hand.

"O'Mallory," said the bartender, "this is Finnegan, our resident poet. Finnegan, say hello to Detective John J. O'Mallory."

"Pleased to meet you," said Finnegan.

"Likewise," said Mallory. "I don't think I've ever met a poet before. Do you have any books out?"

"I'm our resident *unpublished* poet," said Finnegan dourly. "The list of markets I haven't yet cracked is truly phenomenal. I've been turned down by everyone from *Playboy* and *Atlantic Monthly* to college publications that pay with free copies instead of money." Finnegan paused and shook his head. "Sometimes I marvel at my consistency."

"What do you write about?" asked Mallory.

"What does *any* Irish poet write about?" replied Finnegan wryly. "I attribute my failure entirely to a secret consortium of highly placed and influential British editors."

"He's written a lot of poems about the Little People," added the bartender. He turned to Finnegan. "O'Mallory is looking for Flypaper Gillespie, and I figured an expert on the Little People might know where the slippery little bastard is."

"What's he done this time?" asked Finnegan, lighting up a foul-smelling pipe.

"Robbery."

"Was it bigger than a breadbox?" asked Finnegan.

"I beg your pardon?"

"That wasn't a facetious question, O'Mallory," said the Irishman. "Please answer it."

"A lot bigger," said Mallory. "Why?"

"Leprechauns keep pots of gold," replied Finnegan. "I thought everyone knew that. Oh, they're not at the end of the rainbow—in fact, most of them are buried in Central or Grammercy Parks—but as long as what he stole won't fit in the pot, at least you don't have to go out looking for it with a shovel."

At that moment Fitzpatrick and the old man and their partisans reentered the pub, their arms around each other's shoulders in good fellowship.

"A round for the house," said Fitzpatrick.

"Right," said the old man. "And in honor of the new bond we've just forged between the Sons of Erin and the Knights of the Shamrock, I'm paying."

"The hell you are," said Fitzpatrick. "*I* was at fault. *I'm* paying."

He slapped some money on the bar, and the old man brushed it onto the floor. "The Sons of Erin are paying, and that's final."

"If you were half the man you think you are, you'd let a real Irishman pay and keep your mouth shut!" bellowed Fitzpatrick, throwing the old man's money back at him and placing another bill on the bar.

The old man spat on the bill, turned on his heel, and walked back out the door. Fitzpatrick, growling threats and curses, followed him. Felina glanced at them, but remained where she was.

"I guess they're going to have to have another fight to see who won the last one," said the bartender. He turned to Mallory. "Can I fill you up again?"

Mallory shook his head. "No, I've got to keep my wits about me. In fact, I think I'd like to slosh a little cold water on my face and freshen up."

The bartender pointed to a door at the back of the room, and Mallory, after making sure that Felina was still engrossed with her peanuts, went through it. He found himself in a tiny vestibule, confronted by three more doors: one for men, one for women, and one for staff. He chose the first and entered the room.

There were three urinals, one no more than a foot above the ground, one of normal size, and one that stood well above his eye level. Mallory stood before the middle one and tried not to think about what kind of being would use the one on his right. Then he walked over to a trio of sinks that were built in the same proportions, turned on the cold water in the middle sink, and splashed a few handfuls on his face. He groped blindly for a paper towel, found it, and wiped off his face.

Then, refreshed, he returned to the bar, where Felina was still arranging the peanuts in geometric patterns.

"Ah, O'Mallory!" said Finnegan, looking up from his notepad. "I wrote a couplet while you were gone. Would you care to hear it?"

Mallory shrugged. "Why not?"

The poet cleared his throat, looked down at his notepad, and read in a deep voice: "*Revolution, devolution, achievable, believable, cleavable; Eire, fire, pyre, shire, per-*

ceivable, grievable, relievable.'' He looked at Mallory. ''What do you think?''

''What does it mean?'' asked Mallory.

''Mean?'' repeated Finnegan. ''My dear O'Mallory, a poem doesn't *mean;* it simply *is!''*

''I don't know,'' said Mallory, deciding that Felina's peanut designs made more sense than Finnegan's poem. ''It seems to me that if you're exhorting your audience to expel the British, you really ought to let them know.''

''Spoken like a true detective,'' said Finnegan in exasperation. ''Just the facts, ma'am. What happened on Friday night at eight-thirteen?'' He downed his drink, then looked over at Mallory. ''This couplet is a clarion call to arms, a promise of the Good Life, a rejection of all things British, an appeal to reject Protestant values, and a cunningly concealed erotic double entendre, all brilliantly reduced to the most subtle symbolism.''

''It sounds like a bunch of words strung together without any verbs,'' said Mallory.

''Must everything sound like 'Roses Are Red' to you, O'Mallory?'' demanded Finnegan. ''Where is your Irish soul? *Perceivable, grievable, relievable,''* he intoned again. ''My God, it's brilliant!''

''Well, it rhymes, anyway,'' said Mallory.

''It does, doesn't it?'' said Finnegan, frowning. ''I'll have to do something about that.'' He began scribbling furiously.

''Just a minute,'' said Mallory. ''Before you get too engrossed in that, I've got a few more questions.''

''What were we talking about?'' asked Finnegan.

''Flypaper Gillespie.''

''Ah, yes. Detestable little nuisance. Totally immoral, like all leprechauns, but he's got a certain animal cunning that most of them lack.'' He paused, then nodded his head. "Yes, there's no question about it—Gillespie is the nastiest of them all."

"Tell him about the poem," suggested the bartender.

Suddenly Finnegan's eyes blazed with hatred. "Do you know what that dirty little bastard did last month?"

"He wrote a poem?" guessed Mallory.

"He not only wrote it!" raged Finnegan, as Felina jumped away from the bar at the sound of his voice. "He actually *sold* it, just to humiliate me! Not only that, but the meter was off, the imagery was totally mundane, and he didn't even mention Ireland!"

"Have you got any idea where I can find him?" asked Mallory.

"He's probably on some college campus, giving dramatic readings and signing copies of his damned poem!" said Finnegan bitterly.

"At one in the morning?" asked Mallory dubiously.

"No," admitted the poet. "He's probably at home, counting all his ill-gotten loot and framing the reviews of his poem." He slammed a fist down on the bar. "He must have slipped somebody at the *Times* some money. No critic with any taste at all could actually *like* that poem!"

"Maybe the reviewer was a leprechaun," said the bartender soothingly.

"That's got to be it!" exclaimed Finnegan. "I should have known!" He turned to a new page in his notebook and began writing a letter of protest to the *Times*.

"Excuse me," said Mallory. "But if you can just tell me where he lives, I'll be on my way."

"Nobody knows," replied Finnegan. "At least, nobody who isn't a Little Person. The best thing to do is catch one of them and beat it out of him."

"Where can I find one?"

"Well, that's a bit of a problem," admitted Finnegan. "They're very good at hiding; when one of them turns sideways to you, he vanishes—even at high noon on an empty street.'' Finnegan paused. ''I suppose the best thing to do would be to visit one of their regular hangouts and stick around until you can grab one—and once you've got your hands on him, don't let him go until you've found Gillespie. They're a totally treacherous, deceitful race who cheat and lie for the sheer joy of cheating and lying.''

''Then why ask them anything?''

''Because they're the only ones who know where to find Gillespie—and you do have one thing in your favor: every last one of them is a coward.''

''So if I threaten to kill one I may get the truth?'' said Mallory.

''Possibly.''

''And since I won't know whether he's told the truth until I actually arrive at Gillespie's place, I should keep my informant around, just to be on the safe side?''

''Precisely,'' said Finnegan emphatically.

Fitzpatrick and his antagonist entered the pub once again, walked directly to their respective tables without a word, and sat down, glaring at each other. Felina walked over curiously to inspect each of them for non-existent bruises.

''One last question,'' said Mallory, as the two dart players stood up and recommenced their game. ''Where do the leprechauns hang out?''

''I guess the nearest place is the Rialto Burlesque,'' replied Finnegan. ''They sit in the balconies and scream and cheer and catcall and make general nuisances of themselves—especially if the stripper happens to be a redhead, or an emerald green lizard.''

''How far away is it?''

''Go up Ninth Avenue to 48th Street and take a left,'' said Finnegan. ''You can't miss it.''

''Thanks,'' said Mallory.

''How about one for the road?'' suggested the bartender.

"I'd better not," said Mallory, placing some money on the bar. "This should cover my—"

Suddenly there was a commotion behind him, and Mallory turned to see what had happened.

"Damn it!" yelled one of the dart players, glaring at Mallory. "If you can't control her, you shouldn't bring her in here!"

"What happened?" asked Mallory, looking around for Felina.

She was crouched atop a table near the pictures of the Elizabeths, a feathered dart in her mouth.

"Felina, what the hell did you do?" he demanded.

"It looked like a bird," she said, shrugging and spitting the dart onto the floor.

"Out," he said firmly.

She licked her forearm and paid no attention to him.

"You heard me!" snapped Mallory.

She continued licking.

He took a step toward her. "If I have to pick you up and throw you out, I will."

She jumped lightly to the floor, stuck her nose in the air, and exited with all the dignity she could muster.

"I'm sorry," said Mallory to the dart player.

"Well, you'd damned well better be!" shot back the enraged man. "It's getting to where a man can't take the Queen's eye out in peace!"

Mallory returned to the bar, pulled a dollar bill out of his pocket, and handed it to the bartender. "Buy him a drink on me," he said.

"That I will," replied the huge redhead. He reached beneath the bar and pulled out a shamrock, attaching it to Mallory's robe with a pin. "For luck," he said when he had finished adjusting it.

"Thanks," said Mallory. "I've got a feeling I may need it."

"O'Mallory!" said Finnegan suddenly, as Mallory reached the door.

"Yes?"

"If you do find Gillespie, get the name of the editor who bought his poem."

Chapter
9

Mallory walked out the door and found Felina sitting with her back against the side of the building, just out of reach of the rain.

"Come on," he said. "We've got work to do."

She stared off into space and made no response.

"Don't blame *me*," he said irritably. *"You're* the one who misbehaved."

She shrugged. "I got bored."

"That's no excuse. We're on an important job."

Felina got to her feet. "Maybe I'll forgive you," she said.

"You'll forgive *me?"* repeated Mallory.

Suddenly she caught sight of the shamrock and, before he could stop her, she grabbed it and stuffed it in her mouth.

"It's terrible!" she said after chewing for a moment, spitting out the remains.

"Nobody told you to eat it," said Mallory. "That's the kind of behavior I'm talking about."

She stared at him, her pupils like two black slits, then very slowly turned her back to him.

165

"Well, if that's your attitude," said Mallory, "I'll send you off with Colonel Carruthers when we meet in an hour."

He started walking away, and suddenly she flung herself onto his back, wrapping her legs about his waist and clutching his neck with her arms.

"I'll stay with you," she purred, her whole body vibrating. "You're forgiven."

"How comforting," said Mallory, wincing as her claws dug into his neck. "Now, get off."

She leapt directly from his back to a lamppost, spun once around it, hurled herself into the air, and, to Mallory's amazement, landed lightly on her feet.

They walked past a number of cheap nightclubs, many of which were populated entirely by elves and goblins, and then came to a row of dilapidated hotels, two of which had signs posted to the effect that they were for humans only, while another catered exclusively to females of any species. After that came an entire block full of taverns, most with live bands; one, which seemed to fascinate Felina, had a jazz trio composed of three shaggy, apelike creatures wearing top hats and playing primal rhythms on a huge drum made from the skin of some incredibly large animal.

When they reached 48th Street they turned left, and were soon standing in front of the Rialto Burlesque Theater, an ancient building that had once presented Shakespeare and Shaw, but was now reduced to an endless string of stripteasers.

Photographs of the headliners were displayed in glass cases that had once held pictures of the Barrymores and the Lunts, and Mallory, who hadn't seen a strip show in years, was surprised at the plethora of gimmicks that had evolved since the days of his youth. There were wild untamed jungle strippers and high-class society strippers. There were strippers who claimed to be Nazis and strippers who swore they had teleported here from Andromeda. There were strippers who boasted about their multitude of college degrees and came out dressed in caps and gowns, strippers who spoke only in monosyllabic squeals and whines and came out swathed in diapers and baby bunting, baton-twirling strippers, contortionist strippers, and tap-dancing strippers. There was even a vampire stripper who finished her act in a coffin.

"Doesn't anyone just take their clothes off anymore?" muttered Mallory as he stared at the photographs.

He was about to approach the box office when the theater doors swung open and he was almost trampled by a mad rush of sailors, followed by three fat, bald men in raincoats.

"Is the show over?" Mallory asked one of the bald men.

"Call that a show?" said the man bitterly. "When I yell, 'Take it all off!' I don't mean her goddamned *skin!*" He shuddered involuntarily at the memory.

"But it's over?" persisted Mallory.

The bald man grunted affirmatively and raced across the street, where the Follies was featuring Tassel-Twirling Tessie Twinkle, who purportedly had curves in places where most girls didn't even have places.

Mallory walked up to the box office.

A bored-looking woman sat in the dirty glass-enclosed booth, chewing a mouthful of gum and reading a well-worn copy of a gossip magazine.

"Yeah?" she said when she became aware of Mallory's presence.

"When's your next show?"

"Three AM."

Mallory thanked her and returned to the photo display, which Felina was studying with rapt attention. He knew that he couldn't wait for the next show and still make his

scheduled rendezvous with Winnifred Carruthers and the
Great Mephisto, and was considering returning to the Emerald Isle Pub to ask Finnegan for another location where
he might find some leprechauns, when he noticed a well-
dressed, distinguished-looking man walk up to the box
office, purchase a ticket, and enter the theater. A moment
later two middle-aged women, heavily laden with furs and
jewelry, did the same.

He walked back to the ticket booth.

"Back again?" said the woman in the same bored voice.

"I thought you said your next show was at three."

"That's right."

"Then why did those three people buy tickets and enter
the theater?" he asked. "It's not even one-twenty."

"Beats me," she replied. "I just sell tickets. It's you
perverts who watch the shows."

Mallory looked at the door to the theater, puzzled.

"You're taking up space," said the woman. "Do you
want tickets or don't you?"

He reached into his pocket. "Two, please," he said,
shoving a bill through the small hole in the glass.

She shoved two tickets and some change out to him,
then went back to reading her magazine.

"Come on," he said to Felina. "We're going inside."

"I want one of those," she said.

"One of what?"

She led him to a photo of a stripper. "One of *those*,"
she said, pointing to a silver-sequined G-string.

"Don't be silly," he said, taking her arm and starting to
lead her to the door.

"It's pretty!" she protested, twisting free of his grip and
running back to stare at the G-string.

"I'll make you a deal," said Mallory. "If you help me
find Flypaper Gillespie, I'll buy you one."

She nodded enthusiastically, and joined him as he walked to the entrance.

They entered the large lobby, which in the halcyon days of its youth had been lush and immaculate. Now it was old and seedy, with empty beer cans and candy wrappers carelessly strewn over its once-elegant carpet.

An ancient, formally tailored usher came up to greet them.

"Your tickets, sir?"

Mallory handed the tickets to the usher, who examined them, tore them in half, and returned the stubs to the detective.

"If you'll just follow me, sir," said the usher, leading them into the darkened theater and down the center aisle. When they reached the fifth row he stopped.

"Third and fourth seats, sir," he whispered.

"Thank you," said Mallory.

He and Felina sat down, and as his eyes became accustomed to the darkness he saw the three other patrons sitting in the row ahead of him. Off to his left, the usher was leading four couples down to the third row.

The well-dressed man checked his wristwatch and shook his head. "They're late," he muttered to himself.

"Excuse me," said Mallory, leaning forward.

"Yes?"

"I thought the show didn't start until three."

"That's ridiculous!" said the man. "It would run into the burlesque show if it did. No, the curtain was due to go up five minutes ago."

"What are we watching?" asked Mallory.

"You're new to the Rialto, aren't you?" asked the man, turning to him and casting a disapproving look at Felina.

Mallory nodded. "It's our first time."

"We never know what play they're going to perform

until the curtain goes up, though of course it's certain to have ghosts in it."

"It is?"

The man nodded emphatically. "Last week it was *Macbeth*, the week before it was *Outward Bound*, and so on."

"I like ghosts!" exclaimed Felina.

The two women turned to her and held their fingers to their lips. She hissed at them and turned her attention back to the stage.

"Why ghosts?" asked Mallory, curious.

"The Rialto is almost two centuries old," said the man, "and every night, right after the midnight striptease show, the ghosts of old actors return to perform in forgotten plays. Why shouldn't they pick plays with ghosts in them?"

"There's nothing forgotten about *Macbeth*," noted Mallory.

"You're doubtless referring to the Shakespeare version," said the man with just a touch of condescension. "What we saw was the Roger Bacon original."

"Who performs here?" asked Mallory. "Sarah Bernhardt and Edmund Kean?"

"I wish they did," said the man sincerely. "But of course, they've so many other theaters fighting for them that they rarely make an appearance at the Rialto. No, most of the actors are as thoroughly forgotten as the plays."

"Are there ever any leprechauns in the plays?"

"Never!" said the man firmly. "They would disrupt the entire presentation!"

"How about in the audience?" persisted Mallory.

"Don't be ridiculous!" snapped the man, turning his attention back to the stage as the curtain went up and a quartet of shadowy, translucent shapes, clad in classic Greek dress, began emoting in hollow, tremulous voices.

"There are the ghosts!" said Felina, standing atop her seat and pointing.

"If you can't keep her quiet, I'm going to complain to the management!" hissed one of the ladies.

Mallory tugged on Felina's hand until he got her attention.

"Sit down," he whispered. "We're not looking for ghosts. We want leprechauns."

"They're here."

"They are?"

She nodded.

Mallory stood up and looked around the theater. "Where?"

"In the balcony."

"I don't see anything up there except empty seats."

"That's because you're a man," she said smugly. "Cats see things that men can never see."

"How many of them are there?" asked Mallory.

She counted on her fingers. "Seven," she announced in a loud voice.

"Sir, you and your companion are creating a disturbance!" said the well-dressed man irritably.

"Sorry," said Mallory. He motioned to Felina. "Let's go," he said, heading up the aisle just as a Greek chorus of ethereal shapes began chanting in unison.

"Damned tourist!" muttered the well-dressed man.

When they reached the lobby Mallory walked over to the broad, winding staircase that led to the balcony.

"We'd better grab one quick, before they leave," he told Felina.

She grinned. "One just walked past you."

"Grab him!" snapped Mallory.

She pounced toward the doorway, and an instant later he could see her lifting a writhing, wriggling, cursing little leprechaun into the air. He was approximately two feet tall, wiry and redheaded, human in appearance except for his pointed ears and sharp, ski-slope nose, and dressed in the grubbiest clothes Mallory had ever seen.

"Put me down!" demanded the leprechaun.

"In a minute," said Mallory, approaching him. He grabbed the leprechaun's arm. "You can let go now," he told Felina. "I've got him." She released her grip and he pulled the leprechaun around to face him. "What's your name?"

"None of your business!" snarled the leprechaun.

Mallory twisted his arm. "Let's try again," he said. "What's your name?"

"Filthy McNasty!" squealed the leprechaun. "You're breaking my arm!"

"Kill him!" shouted a number of gleeful voices, and Mallory looked up to see three more leprechauns standing on the stairs.

"Blood!" cried another. "We want blood!"

Mallory turned to them without releasing McNasty.

"Where can I find Flypaper Gillespie?"

"You're holding him," giggled a leprechaun.

Mallory looked questioningly at Felina, who shook her head. He twisted McNasty's arm again. "Where's Gillespie?"

"I'm Gillespie!" cried one of the leprechauns.

"No, I am!" said another.

Felina shook her head again, and Mallory increased his pressure on McNasty's arm.

"I never heard of him!" screamed the leprechaun, aiming a kick at the detective's shins which Mallory narrowly dodged.

"You're lying," said Mallory. "I'm not even from this world, and *I've* heard of him."

McNasty shook his head. "Never, ever," he said sincerely. "Never never ever."

"Twist his arm off!" yelled a leprechaun. "He's lying!"

"He's cute," said Felina, a predatory smile on her lips. She flexed her fingers in front of McNasty's face, and the nails seemed to grow. "Can I play with him?"

"If he doesn't answer me, I don't see why not," said Mallory. He turned to Filthy McNasty. "I'm going to ask you one last time: where can I find a leprechaun named Flypaper Gillespie?"

"Oh, you mean the *leprechaun* Gillespie!" said Filthy McNasty, shrinking back from Felina in terror. "That's a whole different matter. Of course I know him! One of my closest, oldest friends, old Flypaper." He looked at Mallory out of the corner of his eye and lowered his voice. "Who did he kill?"

"Where is he?" repeated Mallory.

"Top floor of the Empire State Building," said McNasty quickly. "I'm meeting him there in half an hour."

"No, he's not!" smirked yet another leprechaun.

"All right," said Mallory, carrying McNasty to the door and slapping him when the little leprechaun tried to bite his hand. "Let's go."

"I'm not going anywhere!" protested McNasty.

"You're coming with us."

"But I'll miss Bubbles Malone and Her Educated Snake!" he wailed.

"We all have to live with disappointments," said Mallory dryly.

"Have some compassion!" begged McNasty. "It would break her insecure little heart if I wasn't up there in the balcony, leading the cheers and screaming, 'Down in front!' "

"She'll adjust."

"It's okay, Filthy," said a leprechaun. "I'll keep her company, and except for the improvement she'll never notice the difference." He picked up an empty beer can and hurled it at McNasty's head, giggling hysterically.

"But I already told you where to find Flypaper Gillespie!" screamed McNasty in desperation. "He'll be at the top of the World Trade Center in half an hour."

"You said the Empire State Building before."

"Did I? It must have been a slip of the tongue. No, I'm meeting him on the roof of the World Trade Center. You can never tell when an oversized monkey might come climbing up the side of the Empire State Building."

"Good," said Mallory. "Let's go."

"But you already know where to find him!"

"Right," said Mallory. "But if by any chance he's not there, I'm going to throw you over the side."

"Just a minute!" said McNasty. "Just a minute," he repeated. "Now that I dome to think about it, I was meeting him there *tomorrow* night."

"Oh, good show!" giggled a leprechaun.

Mallory twisted McNasty's arm again. "I'm not a patient man," he said. "I'm only going to ask you once more: where can I find him?"

"You're killing me!" screamed Filthy McNasty.

"No," said Mallory. "That comes next."

"All right!" shrieked the leprechaun.

"Where is he?" demanded the detective, easing up on the pressure.

"What's in it for me?" asked McNasty with a sly smile.

"You may live long enough to see Bubbles Malone," replied Mallory. "I should think that would be a pretty good deal from your point of view."

"And twenty bucks," said McNasty.

"Not a cent."

"I say twenty and you say zero," said McNasty reasonably. "Let's split the difference: fifteen bucks."

"*I'll* tell you for ten," offered a leprechaun.

"Five!" yelled another.

Mallory turned to the cat-girl. "Felina, he's all yours."

"Kill him! Kill him!" chanted two of the leprechauns.

"No!" screamed McNasty, grabbing Mallory and trying to use him as a shield. "You can't do this to me! I'm just an innocent bystander! *Help!*"

"We'll save you, Filthy!" cried one of the leprechauns, and suddenly the lobby was filled with half a dozen of the Little People, all racing about madly with no seeming purpose. One of them brushed by Mallory and stuck a hat pin into his calf. As the detective bellowed a curse and tried to kick his attacker, two others grabbed Filthy McNasty by his free arm and began pulling, while a third, standing back, hurled an ashtray at Mallory's head, missing him by less than an inch. Then, as quickly as they had begun, they stopped and returned to the stairway.

"Well, we tried our best, Filthy," panted one of them.

"Even friendship has its limitations," agreed another. He turned to Mallory. "Okay, you can kill him now. The slower the better."

Felina had been edging over toward the stairway, and suddenly she pounced on one of the leprechauns.

"What the hell are you doing?" demanded Mallory, as she turned the cursing, snarling leprechaun upside down and shook him. An instant later Mallory's wallet fell onto the floor. She casually tossed the leprechaun halfway up the stairs, retrieved the wallet, and returned it to the detective.

"Thanks," he said. "Now, shag all these others out of here."

She grinned, crouched down, and began slinking toward them, and suddenly they all broke for the door and raced out into the street.

"Three dollars and I'll tell all!" said McNasty, still struggling to free himself from Mallory's grasp. "That's my final offer. You'll never get information this cheap again!"

"We're all through dealing," said Mallory. "Felina?"

"Two-fifty!" said McNasty desperately.

The cat-girl approached the leprechaun with a hungry leer on her face.

"I give up!" wailed Filthy McNasty. "I'll tell you everything I know, but call her off!"

"Felina—stop," commanded Mallory.

She hissed at him, but held still, staring intently at the little leprechaun.

"All right," said Mallory. "Start talking."

"Flypaper Gillespie stole Larkspur, and nobody's seen him since," said McNasty.

"Where's the unicorn?"

"Nobody knows."

"Where does Gillespie live?"

"I can give you the address."

"You can do better than that," said Mallory, removing the leprechaun's belt and starting to bind his hands behind him. "You can take us there."

"But I don't want to see Gillespie! I don't even like him!"

Mallory removed his own belt from his pants and tightened it around Filthy McNasty's legs.

"Felina, pick him up."

Felina leaped forward, swooped the leprechaun off his feet, and slung him over her shoulder.

"Okay," said Mallory, walking to the door. "I think we're ready."

"*You* carry me!" pleaded McNasty. "I don't trust her!"

"I don't doubt it," said Mallory.

"All the blood is rushing to my head! I'm seeing religious images!"

"Obviously you're undergoing a spiritual experience," said Mallory sardonically. He held the door open while Felina passed through with her cargo.

Suddenly she shrieked and clapped a hand to her left buttock, and a moment later the leprechaun howled in anguish as she raked her claws down his leg.

"That's what you get for biting her," said Mallory.

"But it was a *friendly* bite!"

"Well, she probably gave you a friendly scratch."

"I'll remember this!" promised the leprechaun. "When I'm plucking out your eyeballs and cutting off your nose and you're begging for mercy, I'll remember this!"

"Just make sure you remember where Flypaper Gillespie lives," replied Mallory. "Because if you give us the wrong address, I'm going to let her keep you."

"I'd like that," purred Felina, as they walked through the windswept, rain-slick streets of Manhattan.

Chapter
10 —————————————————

It began raining harder.

They walked for more than a mile, with Filthy McNasty directing them down side streets and alleyways that Mallory was sure didn't exist in his own Manhattan. At one point he was certain that the little leprechaun was making them walk in a circle. They took four left turns in a row—but when they reached the point where Mallory thought they had started, none of the buildings looked familiar and he was standing on a street he had never heard of before.

The area began changing almost imperceptibly, and finally Mallory found himself in a seedy neighborhood filled with brownstones and hotels that had all seen better days. At last they came to a halt before a tall, narrow, brick building. The exterior was in need of a thorough sandblasting, and that portion of the interior that Mallory could see through a pair of dirty windows didn't look much better. The stone steps leading up to the front door were cracked, and three of the neon letters in the VACANCY sign were dark.

"This is it," said McNasty. "Let me go now."

"When I *know* this is where Gillespie lives," said Mallory, climbing the stairs. He turned to Felina. "You wait out here with him."

"Hey!" complained the leprechaun. "A deal is a deal!"

"Right," agreed Mallory. "And you'd sure as hell better have kept your end of it."

"I hope he didn't," purred Felina hungrily.

Mallory entered the building and found himself in a small, musty foyer. The furniture—two chairs and a sofa, all with cushions that were worn at the edges—had been purchased very inexpensively and was long past retirement age. The walls, which displayed a series of waist-high scuff marks from the chairs, were gray, the exact shade varying with the amount of grime on any given area. The rug was threadbare, and almost showed the pattern it had come with some generations earlier. A plastic Christmas tree, its branches discolored with age, many of its light bulbs missing, stood sedately in a corner, topped by a tarnished silver star that had once possessed five points but now had only two.

A balding, middle-aged man sat behind a battered reception desk, marking a copy of the *Racing Form* with a felt-tipped pen. He, like the foyer, had seen better days. His jacket was worn at the elbows, his shirt was missing a button, and his bow tie was slightly askew. He had a dapper little moustache, and a toothpick peeked out from the corner of his mouth. When he finally became aware of Mallory's presence he sighed, put the *Form* aside, and got wearily to his feet.

"Ho ho ho," he said in a bored tone of voice.

Mallory looked around. "Are you talking to me?" he asked at last.

"You got it, Mac," said the desk clerk. "Ho ho ho, and welcome to the Kringleman Arms, New York's finest boardinghouse. Is it still raining out?"

Mallory nodded.

"Shit!" He picked up his *Form* and drew a long line through a horse's name. "That takes care of the third race, ho ho ho."

"What's all this ho ho ho crap?" asked Mallory.

"It goes with the job," said the man. "If I don't say it, I get fired."

"Why?"

"Beats the hell out of me," admitted the man. "I suppose being the Kringleman Arms has something to do with it."

"I never heard of the Kringleman Arms before."

"That's not surprising. We're the most specialized boardinghouse you'll ever find." He pointed to a white-bearded old man who emerged from an ancient elevator and walked out into the night. "See that old geezer there?"

Mallory nodded.

"Well, we've got two hundred sixty-four of them."

"You're a retirement home?"

The man chuckled humorlessly. "We're a home for unemployed Santa Clauses. We fill up right after Christmas, and don't start emptying out until November." He grimaced. "The thing that sticks in my craw is that most of these old farts don't even pay rent."

"How do you stay in business?"

"We're owned by some old duffer who lives up north of here. He runs it like a charity." He shrugged. "I guess he feels sorry for all these old Santas. Still, he must be a real high roller to be able to afford to give all these rooms away."

"What's his name?"

"Nick."

"Not Nick the Greek?" said Mallory.

The man shook his head. "Nick the Saint. Ever hear of him?"

"I'm not sure," replied Mallory noncommittally.

"Well, he's the guy who made the rule about laughing." He snorted contemptuously. "Just wait until the Kristem starts paying off. I'll give him laughing, all right—I'll laugh my head off when I tell him I'm quitting this lousy job."

"What's the Kristem?"

The man smiled. "I invented it myself," he said confidentially. "It's a totally new, revolutionary way to analyze a race. None of that old crap that just concentrates on front-runners or breeding or post position, no sir. This takes *everything* into account: the position of Mars and Venus, the Gross National Product, the annual precipitation in Butte, Montana, the fiscal expenditure situation in Zambia—everything!"

"Why do you call it the Kristem?" asked Mallory curiously.

"Because my name's Kris and I invented it." He winked at the detective. "It's a little play on words. Classy, huh?"

Mallory shrugged. "I suppose so."

"And the best part of it is that it absolutely guarantees a six hundred percent daily return if you just follow the formula."

"I hate to ask the obvious question," said Mallory, "but why are you still working here?"

"There are still a few bugs in the system," admitted Kris reluctantly. "Oh, it works perfect on paper. I can sit here with the *Form* and give you seven winners out of nine races on tomorrow's card."

"You can?" asked Mallory, interested.

"Like clockwork," Kris assured him. "It works every single time." A puzzled frown crossed his face. "Until I bet on them, that is. I don't know why, but the second I put my money down, the whole thing goes to hell in a handbasket. Curious, isn't it?''

"How long have you been working at getting the bugs out?''

"Oh, fifteen or twenty years,'' said Kris. "But once they're out, I'm going to clean up. I may even market it myself.'' He looked sharply at Mallory. "You're not from Bennie the Book, are you?'' he said suddenly. "I told him I'd have the money by next Tuesday.''

Mallory shook his head. "I'm just looking for someone.''

Kris relaxed visibly. *"That's* a relief! Who are you looking for?''

"A leprechaun named Flypaper Gillespie,'' answered Mallory. "Does he live here?''

"How the hell should *I* know?''

"You're the desk clerk,'' said Mallory. "Look him up.''

"We don't rent to leprechauns,'' said Kris. "What kind of joint do you think we are, anyway?''

"Then he's not here.''

"I didn't say that. I said I didn't know if he lives here or not.''

"But if you don't rent to leprechauns—'' began Mallory.

"Look, Mac,'' said Kris, "there's a big difference between renting to leprechauns and being infested by them. We don't rent to mice, either.''

"You're infested with leprechauns?''

"With one, anyway,'' responded Kris. "I've been laying traps for him for the better part of a year now, but so far it hasn't done any good.''

"What kinds of traps?''

"Oh, the usual—cans of beer, girlie magazines, those little bottles of booze that the airlines give out, stuff like that.'' He paused. "They're always gone in the morning, but he's a clever little son of a bitch. One day I even found his torn tweed jacket in the trap, but no leprechaun." Kris frowned. "I'd like to wring the little bastard's neck. Those were my own magazines!"

"How do you know you don't have more than one?"

"Because I never put out more than one can of beer."

"I don't follow you."

"If there were two of them, I'd find a dead leprechaun next to the trap in the morning. They're not much for sharing."

"I know this is going to seem like a silly question," said Mallory, "but have you seen a unicorn around here this evening?"

Kris shook his head. "What are you looking for— leprechauns or unicorns?"

"One of each," said Mallory. "Do you mind if I take a look around?"

"That's against the hotel's rules," said Kris with a smile of anticipation that Mallory had seen in the course of a hundred previous investigations.

"Just how big a contribution to the Kristem will it take to square things with the hotel?" he asked.

"Oh, fifty bucks ought to do it."

"Don't blow it all on one horse," said Mallory, passing him a bill.

"Not a chance," said Kris. "This baby is earmarked for the Daily Double." He lowered his voice. "My wife's uncle's barber says the fix is in."

"What about the Kristem?"

"The Kristem's perfect, of course," said Kris, pocketing the bill. "But when you get hard information from an absolutely unimpeachable source . . ."

Mallory walked to the door and signaled Felina to bring Filthy McNasty inside.

"Well, I'll be!" exclaimed Kris as the cat-girl entered

the foyer with her burden. "Your partner caught him already!"

"This isn't Gillespie," said Mallory. He turned to the leprechaun. "But he's going to take me to Gillespie's room, isn't he?"

"That wasn't part of the deal!" snapped McNasty.

"The deal was that you'd show me where Gillespie lived," replied Mallory.

"I did! He lives right here!"

"I don't see him."

"This is his building. That was the agreement!"

"This gentleman here," said Mallory, indicating Kris, "has been searching the building for more than a year and hasn't found Gillespie yet."

"That's hardly my fault!"

"No, but it's not your good fortune, either," said Mallory calmly. "It means you're going to have to take me to his room before I release you."

"Beat me, starve me, torture me, pluck out my eyes, drive bamboo splinters under my fingernails, it won't do you any good!" said McNasty defiantly. "I'll never betray a friend!"

"Felina?" said Mallory. "How would you like to beat him, starve him, torture him, pluck out his eyes, and drive splinters under his nails?"

The cat-girl licked her lips and emitted a growl of anticipation.

"On the other hand," said McNasty hastily, "Flypaper's not actually a *friend*. Why should I suffer because *he* stole a goddamned unicorn?"

"A sage decision," agreed Mallory.

"Imagine the nerve of that Gillespie, putting me on the spot like this!" continued McNasty, working himself into a rage. "Me, a sweet, innocent, unworldly, pacifistic, God-fearing leprechaun who never meant anyone any harm!"

"Enough," said Mallory, and McNasty subsided. "Where's his room?"

"On the thirteenth floor," said the leprechaun.

"He's lying," said Kris. "We don't have a thirteenth floor."

"How many floors *do* you have?" asked Mallory.

"Sixteen," replied Kris. "But I don't know of *any* building in New York that has a thirteenth floor. The Kringleman Arms goes right from twelve to fourteen, just like all the others."

Mallory turned to the leprechaun. "McNasty, I'm only going to ask you one more time: where does he live?"

"I already told you: on the thirteenth floor," repeated the leprechaun stubbornly.

"I happen to have fifty dollars that says there's no thirteenth floor in this building," said Kris, pulling out the bill Mallory had just handed him.

"You're on!" said McNasty. "Take me to the elevator!"

"Felina, you come along, too," said Mallory, lifting up the leprechaun. "If Gillespie's actually upstairs, I may need you to spot him."

She joined the two men and McNasty in the elevator.

"Press the button for the fifteenth floor," said the leprechaun.

Mallory did so, the ancient elevator creaked upward at a snail's pace, and a few minutes later the four of them got off, practically bumping into a rotund, white-bearded gentleman who was waiting to go down.

"Happy New Year to all!" said the bearded man, his eyes twinkling. "And to all a good night!"

"I *hate* these old geezers!" muttered Kris as the elevator took the old man down to the lobby. "They're always so damned cheerful! Don't they know Aqueduct is coming up muddy for tomorrow?"

Mallory stopped to survey his surroundings. The rug,

which was actually just a runner that had been laid down along the main corridor, was faded and starting to fray at the edges, the paper was starting to peel away from the walls, and he could hear a steady dripping from a bathroom at the far end of the corridor. Most of the rooms had dusty Christmas wreaths on the doors, and on the wall next to the elevator there was a small blackboard with the message: "Only 358 shopping days until Christmas!"

"What now?" Mallory asked McNasty.

"I could show you much better if you'd untie my feet," said the leprechaun.

"I'm sure you could," agreed Mallory. "What now?"

"The staircase."

Mallory looked around and saw a door with an EXIT sign above it.

"Is that it?" he asked Kris.

The desk clerk nodded, and the detective approached it and opened the door.

"Now climb down two flights."

Mallory led the way, and a few moments later they were facing a door that bore the numeral 12.

"That'll be fifty dollars, please!" said Kris triumphantly.

"Go fuck yourself!" said McNasty. "We're not done yet."

"This had better not be your notion of a joke," said the detective ominously.

"It isn't!" replied McNasty. "Now go up to the fourteenth."

"Why?"

"If you want to see where Gillespie lives, just do what I tell you!" snapped McNasty.

"And if you want to live long enough to see the sunrise, you'd better not be jerking us around," growled Mallory, starting to sweat from his exertion. "You're no goddamned featherweight, you know."

They climbed up one flight to the fourteenth floor.

"Now down a flight, and you're there," promised the leprechaun.

They climbed down again—but when they reached the door, it bore the numeral 13.

"What's going on here?" said Kris, frowning. "We don't have a thirteenth floor!"

"Every building does," said McNasty smugly. "You just have to know how to get to it." He grinned. "That'll be fifty dollars, please."

"I've been up here a thousand times and I never saw this door before!" said Kris.

"That's hardly *my* fault," said the leprechaun. "Okay, tough guy—keep your end of the deal."

"In a couple of minutes," said Mallory, testing the door.

"What's going on here?" demanded McNasty. "A deal's a deal!"

"I'm not going to let you loose inside the building—and if I took you outside and set you free, I don't know for a fact that I could find my way back here."

"But if Gillespie's in there he'll kill me!" protested the leprechaun.

"If you say so," replied Mallory, opening the door.

"Are you sure you don't have any leprechaun blood in you?" muttered McNasty.

Mallory stepped through the doorway and found himself not in a corridor, but in a small, cluttered, windowless room.

"Felina?" whispered the detective. "Is he here?"

The cat-girl shook her head. "No, the room's empty."

Mallory turned on a lamp and looked around.

There was an unmade doll's bed in a corner, with sheets that looked like they hadn't been changed in years. On a tiny table right next to it were Beta, VHS, and Umatic cassettes of *Debbie Does Dallas*, but there were no video decks of any format in the room. The floor was littered with girlie magazines, most of them opened to the centerspreads. There was an ancient dresser with all its drawers missing, a chair with the legs sawed down to half their original length, and a hot plate that was warming a pot of weak coffee. A small table held half a dozen Flash Gordon Big Little Books, perhaps two dozen fishhooks, and a long-overdue library text on the anatomy of unicorns. There were some two hundred balls of string lying around the room and sitting on shelves, each bearing a label scrawled in an unfamiliar language. A large cardboard box at the foot of the bed contained diamonds, marbles, still more fishhooks, and a red golf ball.

"So much for a pot of gold," said Mallory. "He'd need *fifty* pots to hold all this junk."

Felina picked up a ball of string and sat down in the doorway to play with it, while the two men searched the room.

"We didn't miss him by much," said Kris. "He's got half a cup of coffee here that's still warm."

Mallory placed McNasty on the floor and walked over to take a look.

"Son of a bitch!" he exclaimed, examining the mug.

"What is it?" asked Kris.

"The little bastard even robbed *me!* This is my New York Mets mug!"

Kris looked at it and shrugged. "Are you sure? All those sports team cups look alike. You can buy 'em in any supermarket."

"I'm sure," said Mallory. "I broke the handle off a few weeks ago and glued it back on."

"You're not the only guy ever to glue a mug together."

"But it was missing a piece, so I used a section of a cigarette filter to make it fit," said Mallory, pointing to the filter. "I'll be damned! I wonder what else he swiped from me?"

"What have you got that's worth stealing?"

"Not much," admitted Mallory. He began walking around the room. "See if you can find anything like a map of the city, or something with an address scribbled on it."

"Hurry up, you guys!" hollered McNasty. "I've got to get back to Bubbles Malone!"

"Shut up," said Mallory. He stopped in front of an old desk that was covered by mail-order lingerie catalogs and began opening the drawers. One was filled with flashy tie clips, cuff links, and cigarette lighters, some of them quite expensive, all of them obviously stolen; another contained ten more balls of string; a third held two sapphire rings, a hard-boiled egg, and a broken Rubik's cube; and the fourth and final drawer had blank stationery from twenty of Manhattan's finest hotels, plus a pile of canceled three-cent stamps.

Next Mallory opened a small trunk, which contained some fifty hand-knitted argyle socks, no two of them identical. All were far too large for a leprechaun, and it was obvious that he had stolen them from fifty different pairs.

"I've found an address book, if that means anything to you," announced Kris, who had been rummaging under the bed.

"Good!" said Mallory, walking over to him. "Let me see it."

He opened the book and began thumbing through it. There were only six names—Bubbles, Cuddles, Dimples, Freckles, and two Velmas. Each name had some graphic notation scribbled after it; two said "Big boobs!" three more said "Great knockers!" and one of the Velmas had "Fantastic jugs!" leaving Mallory to wonder which description ranked higher on Gillespie's 10-scale. There were no last names, no addresses, and no phone numbers. Mallory went over it again, thumbing through it page by page to make sure he hadn't missed anything, then tossed it onto the bed.

"No good, huh?" asked Kris, looking up from a pile of girlie magazines he was reappropriating. Suddenly he bent down. "What's this?"

"What have you got there?" asked Mallory.

The desk clerk straightened up and held out a leather strap. "Looks like a leather dog leash to me."

Mallory took it from him and examined it, frowning.

"Felina?" he said at last.

The cat-girl looked up from her ball of string. "Yes?"

"Have there been any dogs in here lately?"

She sniffed the air and shook her head.

"Damn!" muttered Mallory.

"You look upset," noted Kris.

"If this is what I think it is, I *am* upset." Mallory put the leash in his pocket and took one last look around the room. "All right," he said. "I've seen everything there is to see here."

He picked McNasty up and walked to the door.

"Just a minute!" said Kris. He picked up his magazines, then walked over to the cardboard box and selected a couple of diamonds. "For the Kristem," he explained with a grin.

"That's fine by me," said Mallory.

They returned to the stairway, climbed down to the twelfth floor, and took the elevator down to the foyer from there.

"Thanks for your help," said Mallory as he walked to the front door.

"What about my fifty bucks?" demanded McNasty.

"We never shook on it," said Kris.

"How could I shake on it? My hands are tied!"

Kris shrugged. "What the hell. Now that I know how to get up to Gillespie's room, what's fifty bucks?" He pulled the bill out and tucked it into the little leprechaun's pocket.

"Are you sure you can find your way back?" asked Mallory.

"Simple," replied the desk clerk. "Fifteen, twelve, fourteen, thirteen." He frowned. "Or was it twelve, fifteen, fourteen, thirteen?"

"It depends on the weather and the day of the week," said McNasty with a gleeful cackle.

Mallory took the leprechaun outside, where he unbound his hands and feet.

"You've got thirty seconds, little man," said the detective.

"To do what?" asked McNasty, hopping around and waving his arms to get some circulation back into his hands and legs.

"To get the hell out of here before I turn Felina loose."

"What are you talking about?" demanded McNasty. "You got what you wanted!"

"I don't like leprechauns."

"Are you some kind of religious maniac or something?" shrieked McNasty, starting to back away. "Everyone knows that leprechauns are God's chosen people!"

"They're also cat-people's chosen appetizers," said Mallory meaningfully.

Filthy McNasty took one last look at Felina and then raced off at high speed, cursing all the way.

"Wait here a minute," said Mallory to Felina. "I've got to make a phone call."

He walked back into the Kringleman Arms and phoned the Morbidium to see if Mürgenstürm had arrived. He hadn't.

"Well," said Mallory, returning to the cat-girl, "I think it's time for us to get over to the Stock Exchange."

"You look puzzled," noted Felina, who was sitting on the sidewalk playing with the ball of string she had brought down from Gillespie's room.

"I am."

"Why?"

"Something very strange is going on," he said, frowning.

"I know. The Grundy stole a unicorn."

He shook his head. "It's more than that. I've got a feeling that I have enough pieces now to start putting things together, but they just don't fit." He paused. "I know *what's* happening, but I don't know *why!*"

"I don't know what you're talking about," said Felina. Suddenly she smiled. "But I do know one thing."

"Oh? What's that?"

"You owe me one of those silver things."

"What silver things?" asked Mallory, thoroughly confused.

"You promised to buy it for me if we found Gillespie's room."

"Oh, that! So I did," he sighed. "All right—we'll walk south on Broadway. If it's cheap and tawdry, it'll be for sale there."

He began to search for a street with which he was familiar. Once he got his bearings it took less than five minutes for him and Felina to reach the shining neon lights of the Great White Way, where he entered a souvenir shop and soon emerged with a silver-sequined G-string, which Felina immediately wrapped around her arm.

"That's not where you're supposed to wear it," he commented.

"I want to be able to see it," she said, holding it up to the light. She displayed it proudly for Mallory, who paid no attention. "You're still frowning," she said.

"I'm still trying to figure things out," he answered distractedly.

"Can I help?"

"I don't think so." He swore softly. "Damn! I'm so goddamned close to putting it together that I can taste it!"

He checked his watch and sighed deeply.

"We'd better get on over to the Stock Exchange and see if Winnifred or Mephisto had any better luck than we did."

But even as he said it, he knew that his companions' quests would have turned out to be fruitless. Deep down in his gut he was absolutely certain that he had learned everything he needed to know, that if he could just find some way to juggle and rearrange the bits of knowledge and information he possessed the entire picture would finally take shape and become clear.

He was still moving the pieces around without any noticeable success when they reached Wall Street.

Chapter
11 ———————————————

2:12 AM–2:38 AM

The rain had stopped by the time Mallory and Felina arrived at the Stock Exchange, and a cold, bone-chilling wind had taken its place. There was no one waiting for them.

The detective looked up and down Wall Street; a few stray pieces of paper were skimming along the ground, and an old dog limped down the center of the sidewalk a block away, but there was no sign of Winnifred or Mephisto.

"Well, we're a couple of minutes early," he said, checking his watch. "You might as well make yourself comfortable. It looks like we're going to have to wait for a while."

Suddenly he heard an eerie wailing.

"What was that?" he asked.

Felina tensed and looked around. "Something's dying," she said with conviction.

He shook his head. "It's probably just the wind."

"Something old and feeble," she purred, her nostrils twitching as she tested the wind for scents.

"Nothing old and feeble could sound that loud," said

Mallory as the wailing sound came to his ears again. It seemed to bespeak an infinite sadness, and terminated in a low, mournful moan.

"Something old and sick and feeble and tasty," crooned the cat-girl.

"I'll settle for it just being feeble," said Mallory devoutly.

A sheet of paper flew by, carried by the wind, and Mallory grabbed it out of the air. It was a newspaper, dated October 29, 1929.

BLACK TUESDAY! proclaimed the headline. STOCK MARKET CRASHES!

Curious, Mallory began reading the lead story, then lost interest, and skimmed an article explaining why talking pictures would drag Hollywood down to financial disaster. Finally he flipped the sheet over and began reading an item about a promising two-year-old named Gallant Fox.

When he was through, he tossed the paper onto the ground and looked down the street again.

"Still no sign of them," he said. He heard another mournful wail. "I wonder what the hell that is?" he asked uneasily.

It was then he discovered that he was alone.

"Felina!" he yelled, but there was no response.

He ran to a corner and looked down the cross street, calling her name again, but couldn't see any sign of her. He then walked back to the front of the building. When he heard the sound of the wind blowing ropes against metal, he checked the various flagpoles that jutted out over the sidewalk, hoping that she might be perched atop one of them. She wasn't.

"Our noble little group seems to keep getting nobler and littler," he muttered, putting his hands in his pockets and pacing up and down in front of the building. After a moment he decided to have a cigarette, and turned his back to the street to shield his lighter from the wind. When

he turned around again he found himself facing the Great
Mephisto, who had his cape wrapped tightly around his
tuxedo.

"Sorry I'm late," said the magician. "Where are
Winnifred and the little horse?"

"They haven't shown up yet."

"And the cat-girl?"

"She was here a minute ago," said Mallory, frowning.

Mephisto stepped into a recessed doorway. "This damned
cape!" he complained. "It's great against snow and rain,
but it doesn't do a damned thing for wind." He grimaced.
"Serves me right for not getting a name brand, I suppose."

"What did you find out?" asked Mallory.

"I still don't know where Larkspur is," replied Mephisto,
"but I do know that the Grundy doesn't have him."

"Where is the Grundy now?"

Mephisto shrugged. "I haven't the slightest idea."

Mallory frowned. "Just a minute. I thought you just
saw him."

"I never said that. I said that he didn't have Larkspur."

"How could you know that if you don't know where he
is?"

Mephisto smiled. "There's more than one way to skin a
cat—with apologies to your feline friend. The Grundy's
too well-protected for anyone, even the world's greatest
magician"—he bowed—"to just walk over to his head-
quarters and see what's going on." He paused. "I gave
serious consideration to using my crystal ball, but it's
rather like a two-way television set: if *I* looked in on him,
he'd be able to see *me*. I didn't like that idea very much; in
fact, I positively *hated* it."

"So what did you do?"

"A number of his flunkies—mostly goblins and trolls—
tend to gather at a little pub not too far from here for
drinks and cards. So I went over there, bought a round of

drinks for the house, sat in for a few hands, and kept my ears open.'' He grinned triumphantly. ''I even won twelve dollars.''

''What did they say?'' asked Mallory, stubbing out his cigarette and trying to light another. The wind kept blowing out his flame, and he finally gave up and put it back in his pocket.

''Well, most of them weren't there,'' said Mephisto, ''but the two who were told me that he's absolutely livid about something.''

Suddenly Mallory chuckled. ''I'll just bet he is.''

''What are you talking about?'' demanded Mephisto.

''The last piece just fell into place,'' Mallory announced.

''What piece?''

''The last piece of the puzzle,'' said Mallory. ''I knew most of it when I left the Kringleman Arms; you just gave me the rest.''

''What's the Kringleman Arms?''

''That's where Gillespie lives.''

''You actually found him?'' exclaimed Mephisto.

''No.''

''But you learned something anyway?'' persisted the magician.

''Just about everything,'' replied Mallory. ''But one thing kept bothering me: if the Grundy is so goddamned powerful, why are Mürgenstürm and I still alive? He may not know about you and Winnifred yet, but it's obvious that—''

''Yet?'' yelped Mephisto, so upset that he let his cape fall open. ''What do you mean—yet?''

''He's bound to find out about you sooner or later,'' said Mallory reasonably.

''Well, he'd damned well better not! That wasn't part of the deal!''

"It doesn't matter," said Mallory. "None of us are in any danger at the moment."

"Why don't you tell me why you think so, and I'll decide whether or not you're right," said Mephisto sulkily. Suddenly the magician noticed that his teeth were chattering, and he wrapped his cape around himself again. The chattering continued.

"All right," said Mallory. "Do you know where the Grundy's flunkies are?"

"Committing crimes, I suppose," said Mephisto. "Or maybe hunting for his enemies," he added morosely.

Mallory shook his head. "They're hunting for Larkspur." He paused for dramatic effect. "I'll tell you something else."

"What?"

"They're not going to find him."

"What makes you say that?" asked Mephisto.

"Because he's dead."

"How do you know?" demanded the magician, startled. "Have you seen his body?"

"No."

"Then what makes you think he's dead?"

Mallory pulled out the leather strap. "The desk clerk found this in Gillespie's room. He thought it was a dog leash." Mallory paused. "But Felina says there haven't been any dogs in the room, and if this thing had been attached to a dog, she'd have smelled it." He tossed it to Mephisto. "It's a lead shank. You attach it to a halter to lead an animal around."

"All that means is that Gillespie stole Larkspur," protested Mephisto. "We already know that."

"It means more than that," replied Mallory. "He'd never have packed it away in his room if he thought he'd be needing it again."

"Unless he already turned Larkspur over to the Grundy," pointed out the magician.

"Then why is the Grundy livid? Where are all his flunkies?"

"He's always in a bad mood," replied Mephisto. "As for his flunkies, New Year's Eve is prime mischief-making time for them. Do you know how many businesses they can loot and how many drunks they can roll before sunrise?"

"He's furious because Gillespie has double-crossed him, and his henchmen are hunting for the unicorn," repeated Mallory confidently.

"How can you be so sure?" said Mephisto dubiously.

"Because we're still alive," replied the detective. "He knows that we're looking for Larkspur. He hasn't had any luck on his own, so why kill someone who might lead him to what he's looking for?"

"Stop saying *we!*" snapped Mephisto nervously. "He doesn't know about *me!*"

"It doesn't make any difference. You're safe as houses until he finds the ruby. *I'm* the one with the problem."

"You?"

Mallory nodded. "How long will that membrane stay open now that Larkspur's dead?"

Mephisto rubbed his chin thoughtfully. "It's difficult to say. It all depends on what time he was killed. I'd guess you have between three and five hours left." He looked up suddenly. "My God, what a tragedy!"

"I thank you for your concern," said Mallory, startled by the magician's earnestness.

"I'm not referring to you," said Mephisto.

"Thanks a heap."

"It's the *city!*" said Mephisto fervently. "Do you know what will happen to it?"

"Nothing," said Mallory.

"You're wrong! Crime will run rampant! There will be

muggings and rapes and murders! The streets won't be safe to walk!''

"What are you talking about?''

"Who do you think commits most of the crimes in your Manhattan?'' said Mephisto. "People from here! Didn't you ever wonder why so few perpetrators of violent crimes ever get caught? It's because they go to your world to commit them, and then come back here to avoid pursuit! And now they're all going to be trapped here! Life will be intolerable—it will be just like *your* Manhattan!''

"You'll adjust,'' said Mallory. *"We* did.''

"How do you adjust to acts of mindless violence?''

Mallory opened his mouth to respond, but suddenly realized that he had no answer. A noise behind him saved him from having to admit that fact to Mephisto.

Mallory and the magician turned to find a uniformed night watchman unlocking the door to the Stock Exchange from the inside.

"You!'' said the man, pointing at Mallory.

"Me?'' asked the detective, startled.

"You came here with a cat-person, didn't you?''

"Yes.''

"I thought so. I saw you through one of the windows.''

"What about it?''

"You'd better come with me,'' said the watchman. "She sneaked in here somehow or other, and I can't get her out.''

"Perhaps I could be of some assistance,'' said Mephisto. "I'm a magician.''

"I don't care who the hell takes her out of here, as long as *someone* does,'' replied the watchman irritably. "I called the cops, but it's New Year's Eve and they're too damned busy.'' He paused. "The bastards actually told me to chase her out myself!'' He turned on his heel. "Follow me.''

Mallory and Mephisto fell into step behind the watchman as he led them across the marble floor of the outer lobby and up to a set of huge double doors that opened onto the trading floor.

"She's in there," said the watchman, backing away.

"You're not coming with us?" asked Mallory.

The watchman shook his head vigorously. "You couldn't get me into that place for a million bucks!"

"Why?" asked Mephisto suspiciously. "It's just the floor of the Exchange, isn't it?"

"Right."

"Then why are you afraid to go there?" persisted the magician. "Thousands of people work there every day."

"If it was daytime I wouldn't have any problem," said the watchman. "But it's different at night."

"Different in what way?" asked Mallory.

"Ghosts!" whispered the watchman.

"Ghosts?"

The watchman nodded. "Every night at midnight they start wailing and moaning, and they don't quit until maybe an hour before sunrise. The whole damned place is haunted."

"If you won't go in there, how do you know that the cat-girl is there?" asked Mephisto.

"I saw her," replied the watchman. "She must have climbed up an outside wall and come in through an open window. Anyway, I saw her climb down the main stairway and sneak onto the floor on my security monitor."

"And she's still in there?" asked Mallory.

"She hasn't come out. Of course, I won't vouch for the fact that she's still alive."

Mallory walked to the door and opened it, while the watchman edged away. "Come on," he said to Mephisto.

"I'm considering possible courses of action," replied the magician hesitantly.

Mallory looked around the trading floor. "There's nothing here."

"Hah!" said the watchman.

"You're sure?" asked Mephisto.

Mallory made no reply, but began walking into the gargantuan room, which was dominated by the overhead ticker-tape screen. Stacked against the sterile walls were literally hundreds of computer terminals and screens and telephones, with still more efficient data and communications stations scattered across the shining, polished floor. He walked down the artificial aisle formed by the technical marvels, and after a moment's hesitation Mephisto followed him.

Suddenly the door slammed shut behind them.

"Felina!" called Mallory.

"Here," said an unhappy voice, and Mallory looked up to see the cat-girl perched atop a huge computer complex.

"What are you doing here?" asked the detective.

"I told you—something was dying."

"And you ate it," concluded Mallory.

"It cheated!" she said, morally outraged.

"Cheated? How?"

She shrugged. "It vanished."

"It dissipated," said a hollow, mournful voice.

"Who's that?" demanded Mallory, spinning around.

"You've nothing to fear," said the voice. "I mean you no harm."

"Where are you?"

A transparent lavender form started to coalesce in the air about fifty feet away, just above a mainframe computer. It disappeared, then took shape again in the middle of an empty aisle, an elongated figure with two dark, empty, staring eyes and a mouth of indeterminate proportions. Its outline was vague and seemed to wither away into nothingness toward the bottom.

"I apologize if my appearance startles or frightens you," said the apparition. "I used to be able to do much better."

"Who are you?" asked Mallory.

"I am a Genie of the Market." It paused. "In fact, I am the very last Genie of the Market."

"Was that you doing all that moaning and wailing?"

The Genie's outline wavered, and some of the color seemed to leave it. "That was my final companion, pouring out his grief and misery before he died," it said mournfully.

"He vanished!" pouted Felina.

"I don't know exactly what a Genie is supposed to look like," said Mallory, "but you don't appear so healthy yourself."

"I am dying," sighed the Genie, turning a pale gray.

"Why?"

"Lack of sustenance. I am starving to death in a world of plenty."

"What do Genies of the Market eat?" asked Mallory.

"Excitement. Suspense. Fear. Triumph." The Genie began vanishing, and pulled itself together with an obvious effort of will. "Ah, you can't know what it was like to live here in the old days! To see billions made and lost in an hour, to live through Black Tuesday, to watch the robber barons make their raids and then claim their just and terrible vengeance!"

"But billions are still made and lost every day," noted Mephisto.

"It's not the same," said the Genie. "Look around you," it continued, forming an arm and pointing to the endless rows of screens and terminals. "Where are the men, where is the activity? Once this place ran through paper by the carload; now can you see so much as a single wastebasket? Everything is done by computers. Orders are taken, trades are made, financial empires rise and fall—but there's no emotion to accompany it, no excitement. Where is the urge to build a personal fortune, the drive to destroy your opponent and trample him into the dust of Wall Street, the thrill of triumph and the despair of defeat? All is gone, dissipated on the wind, just like my companions.''

''Surely there is still *some* emotion left,'' said Mallory. ''Hundreds of people work the computers. *They* must feel elation and depression.''

''It's not the same thing,'' said the Genie with a sigh that echoed through the cold, empty room. ''They have no personal stake in what goes on here; most of the money belongs to pension funds and other institutions. Besides, the machines make the decisions; the men and women are just glorified clerks, carrying out their mechanical masters' orders. Such feeble emotions as they feel constitute nothing more than a starvation diet to us. John D. knew that; that's why he chose to die.''

''John D.?''

''My fallen companion,'' said the Genie. ''I am J. P.''

''For J. P. Morgan?'' asked Mallory.

''Yes,'' said J. P. ''Now *there* was a tyrant, a man of enormous hates and enormous loves!'' The Genie began glowing a bright purple as he spoke of his long-dead namesake. ''The week the market crashed, he spent two hundred million dollars of his own money trying to prop it up single-handedly. He must have given sustenance to fifty Genies all by himself!'' The Genie, glowing ever brighter, was lost in a reverie of recollection. ''And when he used to come in here after battling with Teddy Roosevelt, the air absolutely crackled with energy. You know, we used to have fistfights breaking out on the floor almost every day.''

''Times change,'' said Mallory.

"I know," sighed J. P., his color fading. "And, like the dinosaur before us, we stagger off to extinction, not with a bang but a whimper. I don't even think I'll mind. It's very lonely to be the last of your kind. A day, a week, a month, and I'll be joining my lost companions."

"I'm sorry," said Mallory.

"Don't be," said J. P., a dull gray once again. "It happens to all species—including Man." His outline seemed to become even less substantial. "John D., Cyrus, August—I'll see you soon, my friends!"

And then he was gone.

"Sad," commented Mallory.

"He cheated," sniffed Felina.

"He probably felt that *he* had been cheated," commented Mallory pensively, "even if he never figured out exactly how or why."

"We'd better go," urged Mephisto. "Winnifred ought to be out front by now."

Mallory nodded. "Come on, Felina."

The cat-girl jumped lightly to the floor and raced to the door ahead of the two men.

"Now get her out of here," said the watchman as the three of them left the trading floor.

"We're leaving right now," said Mallory. "And I don't think you'll be bothered much longer by your ghosts."

"Good riddance!" said the man. "The nerve of those damned ghosts—scaring decent men who are just out to make an honest living!"

Mallory made no comment, and a moment later he, Felina, and Mephisto were standing on the sidewalk in front of the Stock Exchange. It had started to slush, a kind of half-rain and half-snow that had the worst features of each.

"What time is it?" asked Mephisto, holding a hand to his forehead in a vain attempt to keep his glasses dry.

Mallory checked his watch. "Two-thirty, give or take a minute."

Mephisto frowned. "Damn! Something's happened to Winnifred!"

"She's not that late," replied Mallory soothingly.

"I've known her for the better part of fifteen years," said the magician, "and she's never once been late for an appointment."

"Why don't you take a look around the corner?" suggested Mallory. "There's an entrance there too. Maybe she's waiting in the wrong place."

Mephisto nodded and walked carefully down the sidewalk, which was decidedly slippery, then turned right at the corner. He returned a few minutes later, holding up his cape so that it wouldn't trail in the slush, then wrapping it around himself again when he reached Mallory.

"No luck," he announced grimly. Suddenly he looked around. "Where's Felina? If she's back in the Exchange again, I say we should just leave her there."

"I sent her back to the Morbidium to wait for Winnifred and Eohippus, just in case they show up there for some reason," answered Mallory.

"Good idea," said the magician. "I never did like cats, anyway."

"Well, that leaves you and me," said Mallory.

"What do you mean?"

"I mean that our next logical step is to find out what happened to Winnifred and Eohippus."

"It's obvious what happened to them," replied Mephisto. "They ran into trouble."

"Then we'd better get them out of it."

"Look," said Mephisto defensively, "I just agreed to do a little fact-finding. I have no intention of going up against the Grundy."

"I thought Winnifred was your friend."

"She is—but I wouldn't take on the Grundy if my own mother's life was at stake!"

"You don't have to," said Mallory. "He may not even know they're on our side."

"*Your* side. Not *our* side."

"I stand corrected," said the detective. "Still, nobody's asking you to fight the Grundy."

"That's *exactly* what you're asking me to do!" said Mephisto, his voice high and whining.

Mallory shook his head. "You're a magician. I'm just asking you to use your powers to find out what's happened to Winnifred and Eohippus." He paused. "You don't even have to leave your home. Just use your crystal ball."

"And if the Grundy has them, he'll know I'm looking for them!" said Mephisto accusingly.

"You'll just be a concerned friend of Winnifred's, not an enemy of the Grundy's," said Mallory persuasively.

"He'll know!" whined Mephisto. "He'll take one look at me and he'll know!"

"Do you have anything else you can use besides a crystal ball?"

Mephisto's brow furrowed in thought. "Well," he said reluctantly, "I've got a magic mirror."

"What does it do?"

"Not much," he said petulantly. "It doesn't like me."

"Could it locate Winnifred and Eohippus?"

"Maybe. It communicates with other mirrors."

"Then can you use the mirror instead of the crystal ball?"

"I don't know . . ."

"You won't have to do anything else," Mallory assured him. "If you can tell me where she is, I'll take it from there."

"You mean that?" asked Mephisto, surprised.

Mallory nodded.

"I call that uncommonly civil of you!" said the magician.

"Thanks. Now, tell me where you live."

"Why?" asked Mephisto suspiciously.

"How else am I going to meet you and find out what you've learned?" asked Mallory irritably, stepping back from the edge of the sidewalk as an enormous yellow elephant turned the corner and began sloshing up the street with its load of partying passengers.

"Well?" persisted Mallory when the elephant had passed by.

"7 Mystic Place." Mephisto looked embarrassed. "Go down a flight. It's the basement apartment." He paused. "I don't see any reason to pay twice as much money for the privilege of wearing myself out climbing endless flights of stairs."

"7 Mystic Place," repeated Mallory. He put his hands on his hips and looked around. "Now, while you're doing that, I suppose I'd better check with the police and the hospitals." He paused. "I might as well start with the cops. If they haven't turned up yet, I can at least report them as missing. Where's the nearest station?"

"It's about half a mile away," said Mephisto. "But they'll just send you to the Missing Persons Bureau. You could save a step by going right there."

"How do I find it?"

"It's two blocks from here," said the magician. "Just turn left at the next corner and then go straight, and you can't miss it."

"Thanks. I'd better be going. I'll check in with you later."

"You know," said Mephisto, "maybe I'll come back with you."

"To the Missing Persons Bureau?" asked Mallory, puzzled.

"To your world," answered the magician.

Mallory stared at him curiously. "You?"

"Vegas is always looking for good magic acts. I might even get on the same bill as Wayne Newton!"

"Let's find out what happened to Winnifred first."

"Of course, of course," said Mephisto, unable to contain his enthusiasm. "But then, look out, Vegas—here I come! Move over, Barbra Streisand! Make way, Rat Pack!"

"The Rat Pack doesn't exist anymore," said Mallory. "They're all old men."

"Then a new Rat Pack will come along. One always does, you know."

"Yeah. Well, until that happy moment occurs, we've got work to do."

"And a time limit to do it in," Mephisto reminded him. "If you're right about Larkspur, the membrane is already starting to harden."

"Then we haven't any time to waste, have we?" said Mallory, walking off across the slush-covered street.

Chapter

12

The Bureau of Missing Persons was a huge building, taking up an entire block. Like most of the other buildings in the vicinity, it was covered with soot and grime, and its windows were badly in need of a washing. Mallory, who had been expecting to find a single room stuck in the midst of a typical bureaucratic jungle, was surprised not only at its size but at the steady flow of people entering and leaving it.

The detective entered the building through the front door and found himself in a reasonably large lobby. Portraits of Jimmy Hoffa, Amelia Earhart, Judge Joseph Crater, and other famous missing persons were prominently displayed on the walls.

Mallory looked around, saw a desk marked INFORMATION, and approached it.

"May I help you, sir?" asked a uniformed man who was standing behind the counter.

"I hope so," replied Mallory. "A friend of mine was late for an appointment; I have reason to believe that she may be in some trouble."

"I see," said the man sympathetically.

"I want to find out if you have any information about her, and if not, I want to report her as being missing."

"Well, that's what we're here for, sir," said the man. "In fact, it's our busiest night of the year." He pulled out a pencil and a small notebook. "Let me just ask you a couple of questions, and I'll send you to the proper department."

"Fine," said Mallory.

"This friend of yours—what's her name?"

"Winnifred Carruthers."

"Any distinguishing features?"

"Not really," said Mallory. "She had a small horse with her, if that helps."

"A small horse, you say?" repeated the man. "Have you tried the S.P.C.A.?"

"No."

"I wouldn't rule it out," said the man, scribbling furiously. "Would you happen to know her eye color?"

"Blue, I think."

"Height?"

"I don't know. Maybe five foot three or four."

"Shoe size?"

"I have no idea," said Mallory impatiently.

"What sign was she born under?" asked the man.

"You mean Zodiac sign?"

"That's right, sir."

"I don't know."

"One last question: was she wanted by anyone?"

"You mean, by the authorities?" asked Mallory.

"By anyone at all."

"Not to my knowledge."

"Right," said the man briskly, putting his pencil and notebook away. "You want the second floor, fourth door on your left when you get out of the elevator. Good luck."

"That's all?" asked Mallory.

"That's all," replied the man cheerfully.

"Thanks, I guess."

Mallory walked to the bank of elevators the man had indicated, waited until a set of doors opened up, stepped inside, and rode up to the second floor. When he got off, he turned to his left and passed a trio of incredibly busy offices, filled with worried parents and desperate husbands and wives and furious collection agents, all pouring out their stories to harassed employees.

Mallory continued walking until he came to a fourth office. There was no frenzied activity here, no piles upon piles of paperwork obscuring the workers from his view, no incessant ringing of telephones, no endless lines of supplicants looking for missing persons. There was only one woman in the office, and she sat at a completely bare desk, reading a paperback romance.

"Hello?" he said tentatively.

She looked up from her book. "Can I help you?"

"I'm looking for a woman named Winnifred Carruthers."

"She's not wanted by anyone?"

"Just by me," replied Mallory.

"Right through there," said the woman, pointing to a door on the far side of the office.

Mallory thanked her, crossed the office, opened the door, and entered a large lounge which was filled with a number of chairs and couches, none of which matched. The wallpaper was an absolutely hideous cacophony of bilious reds and greens, the lamps would have seemed garish even in a New Orleans bordello, and the various throw rugs, three of them light blue and the rest ranging from pink to purple, still had their REMNANT and RE-MAINDER labels attached.

A number of men and women sat in the lounge, some watching a televised New Year's celebration being broadcast from Denver, others reading, a few simply dozing. One man sat at a desk, pen in hand, writing furiously; as quickly as he filled up one sheet of paper he placed it atop a small neat pile and began writing on a fresh one.

Suddenly Mallory became aware of another presence beside him. He turned and found himself facing the strangest human being he had ever seen.

The man stood about six feet tall and had three arms, two on the left side. His face was totally out of balance: he had three eyes, all to the right of his nose, which had only one nostril; his mouth was set into his face at a 45-degree angle; and both his ears were on the left side of his head, one on top of the other. His hair was bright orange, shading to pink at the sides.

"May I help you?" asked the man.

Mallory made no response.

"Sir, may I be of some service to you?" persisted the man.

Suddenly Mallory blinked his eyes. "Excuse me for staring," he said. "You startled me."

"It's all right," said the man wearily. "It happens all the time. Allow me to introduce myself: I am Thelonius Strange."

"John J. Mallory," replied the detective. "I'm looking for a woman named Winnifred Carruthers."

"I regret to inform you that you've come to the wrong place."

"But I was told to come up here," said Mallory.

Strange shook his head sadly. "The mere fact that you're looking for her means that she isn't here. Didn't anyone ask you if she was wanted?"

"I assume they meant by the police?"

"They meant by *anyone*," replied Strange. "We're the Unwanted People."

"What *are* the Unwanted People?"

"Men and women who have outlived their usefuness, or who never had a purpose to begin with." Strange paused. "I, myself, am the Odd Man Out whom you've heard so much about." He sighed. "In school, my teachers could never concentrate on their lectures. They'd start speaking, and then they'd begin to stare at me and forget what they were saying. Whenever I applied for a job, it was the same thing: somewhere in the middle of the interview, the personnel manager would just stop talking in mid-sentence and stare at me. If nineteen people showed up to play baseball, or twenty-three for football, or eleven for basketball, I was always the odd man out. It got to the point where nobody wanted me around at all, so I wound up here."

"I'm sorry," said Mallory.

"One adjusts after a while."

"Some of these people look quite normal," said Mallory, looking around the room. "Why are they here?"

"Each has his own reason."

"Take *him*, for example," said Mallory, pointing to a powerfully built young man who was sitting on a couch, a baseball mitt on his left hand, mechanically tossing a baseball a few inches into the air and catching it. "He looks pretty fit. What's he doing here?"

Strange pulled a pack of small multicolored cards out of his pocket, thumbed through them until he found the one he was looking for, and handed it to Mallory.

"That's him," he said. "Jason McGee."

"It looks like a baseball card," said the detective. "The kind that used to come with a pack of bubble gum."

"It is."

"So he got sent down to the minors," said Mallory. "It happens all the time. How does that qualify him as an Unwanted Person?"

"Read the back of it," said Strange.

Mallory flipped the card over. "Jason McGee," he read. "Seasons played, three. At bats, none. Hits, none. Runs, none. Errors, none." He looked up. "Three years and he never got into a game?"

"That's right."

"How come?"

"Read what his position was," suggested Strange.

Mallory looked at the card again. "Position, fifth baseman." He handed the card back to Strange. "What the hell is a fifth baseman?"

"Me," said McGee, looking over at the detective. "I was the only fifth baseman in the whole damned world, and they never once let me show what I could do."

"Maybe that's because they only have four bases," suggested Mallory.

"But if there'd been five, I could have been the greatest!" said McGee passionately. "I made the team for three seasons in a row, and then they cut me. I bounced around the minors for a couple of seasons, and even went down to the Mexican league." He looked at Mallory with tortured eyes. "Six years as a professional, and I never once got into a ball game! All that training down the drain!" He shook his head sadly. "All those hopes and dreams turned to dust!"

"So you finally wound up here?" asked Mallory.

McGee nodded. "That's right."

"How long have you been here?"

"I don't really know. You tend to lose track of the time in this place."

"Why do you stay?"

"Who needs a fifth baseman?" replied McGee.

"There must be something else you can do."

"Why bother?" said McGee with a sigh. "If they won't let me do what I'm good at, why waste the effort?" He pointed to the man who was writing at the desk. "Now, *there's* a guy who ought to go back into the world."

"Who is he?"

"Sybly Purple," said Strange, as McGee went back to tossing the baseball into the air. "He's a writer."

"What does he write?"

"Mysteries, Westerns, anything at all. He's got a whole shelf full of books he's written."

"He sounds pretty wanted to me," said Mallory. "What's he doing here?"

"Producing his masterwork," said Strange. "Only nobody wants it."

"The Great American Novel?" guessed Mallory.

"With a difference," said Strange. "He's writing the whole thing, all two thousand pages, without putting a single E in it."

Mallory considered Strange's statement for a moment, then nodded his head. "Yeah, I can see where something like that isn't likely to be too high on anyone's want list."

"Neither is the writer," commented Strange sympathetically. "Since he became obsessed with this idea, none of his editors will talk to him anymore. That's why he's here."

"How long has he been working on it?" asked Mallory.

"Six years now."

Suddenly Sybly Purple groaned and ripped up the page on which he'd been writing.

"He must have inadvertently used an E," said Strange. "He tears up fifty pages a day like that."

"He's never going to make it," said Mallory.

"Probably not," agreed Strange.

"Is he writing it under his own name?" asked the detective.

"Of course. It's his masterpiece."

"There's an E in Purple. He's blown it before the reader reaches page one."

Strange's eyes went wide with surprise. "Don't tell him!" he whispered urgently. "The shock just might push him over the edge!"

"It sounds to me like he's over the edge already," replied Mallory dryly.

"Please!" said Strange. "You've no idea what it's like to *be* an Unwanted Person. Don't make it any harder on him!"

"I've no intention of mentioning it to him," Mallory assured him. "I'm just looking for my friend."

"Well, she's not in here. You might go up to the third floor and try the Tank."

"The Tank?"

"It's the holding area for missing persons."

Mallory frowned. "Let me try to assimilate this for a minute," he said. "You're telling me that there are a bunch of missing persons up on the third floor?"

"It's the Missing Persons Bureau, isn't it?" said Strange.

"Where I come from, the Missing Persons Bureau *hunts* for missing persons."

"What a strange idea!" commented Strange. "Here the Bureau collects them and keeps them until they're claimed. If your friend is here, she's almost certainly in the Tank."

"Then I'd better go check," said Mallory. "Thanks for your help."

Strange nodded in acknowledgment, and Mallory went back out through the office. He then returned to the elevators, waited until one arrived, and took it up to the third floor. When he got off he found himself in a very crowded hallway, and simply followed the crowd until he reached the Tank, a huge holding area filled with hundreds of people, some drunk, some crying, a few sleeping, most of them looking totally disoriented.

There was a large reception area with a long counter that reminded Mallory of an airport, except that instead of signs denoting the names of the various air carriers, these signs denoted the lines for those seeking missing persons, those delivering missing persons, and the missing persons themselves.

Mallory stood in the appropriate line, and a moment later a crisply efficient woman dressed in a blue uniform began walking up and down his line.

"You're seeking a missing person?" she asked when she reached him.

"That's right," replied the detective.

"Name of the missing party?"

"Actually, there are two of them," said Mallory. "Winnifred Carruthers, and Eohippus."

"Eohippus who?"

"Just Eohippus."

"Do the parties in question know that they're missing?"

"I don't understand."

"Some people would prefer not to be found," she explained, "and do not, in fact, consider themselves missing. Bank robbers, for example, or eloping couples, or—"

"If they're here, I'm sure they want to be found," Mallory interrupted her.

"Have Carruthers and Eohippus any preference as to who finds them?"

"How the hell do I know?" demanded Mallory irritably.

"I'm only doing my job, sir," she said severely. "I am required to ask these questions."

"Well, it's a damned stupid question!"

"Not necessarily. For example, Winnifred Carruthers may be quite willing to be found by you, but might strongly resist being found by her husband."

"They'll both want to be found by me," said Mallory.

"Then I'll need your name, sir," said the woman.

"Mallory," he replied, "John J. Mallory."

"All right, Mr. Mallory," she said. "If you'll just wait here, I'll see what we can do."

She continued interviewing people in the line, then finally walked up to the Tank and began calling out names over an intercom. Half a dozen men and women walked to the front of the Tank to be reunited with the people who were searching for them, but Winnifred and Eohippus weren't among them.

Mallory stopped the woman as she passed him on her way to the back of the line to interview more searchers.

"They didn't answer," he told her. "What do I do now?"

"Well," she replied, "you could wait and see if they show up."

He shook his head. "I haven't got the time. How do I report them as missing?"

"You tell me."

"I already did."

"Then that's that," she said, starting to walk away.

"Just a minute!"

She turned to face him. "Really, Mr. Mallory, there *are* other people waiting in line."

"Aren't you going to tell the police to look for them?" he demanded.

"The police are rounding up all the missing persons they can find," she replied. "It's standard operating procedure."

"I want to put out an all-points bulletin on them," persisted Mallory. "I think they could be in considerable danger."

"In that case, you want the line for Beleaguered Persons. It's down at the end of the counter."

Mallory glared at her in frustration, then stalked over to the Beleaguered Persons line and left Winnifred's name with a bored receptionist. He checked the time and decided to go to Mephisto's apartment to see if the magician had turned up any information on Winnifred's whereabouts.

He had taken the elevator down to the main floor and was heading for the front door when he almost bumped into Mürgenstürm.

"John Justin!" exclaimed the elf breathlessly. "Thank goodness I've found you!"

"What are you doing here?" demanded Mallory suspiciously.

"Looking for you. We've got a lot to talk about."

"We sure as hell do," said Mallory, grabbing the little elf by an arm and dragging him out into the night.

"What's the matter, John Justin?" asked Mürgenstürm.

"Shut up!"

Mallory looked around, shielding his eyes from the rain with his free hand, saw an all-night coffee shop across the street, and began walking toward it, pulling the elf after him. When he walked in the front door, he spotted an empty table at the back of the room and dragged the elf over to it.

"Sit down," he commanded.

"You're mad at me, aren't you?" asked Mürgenstürm as he climbed up onto a chair.

"How did you guess?" said Mallory.

A female goblin in an apron approached them. "What'll it be, gents?" she asked.

"Peace and quiet," said Mallory, holding out one of the hundred-dollar bills that Mürgenstürm had given him in the clothing store.

She snatched the bill from his hand.

"You got it," she said, ambling off.

"You're becoming a profligate spender, John Justin,"

said the elf disapprovingly. "I worked very hard for that money."

"So did I," Mallory shot back. "Besides, I don't plan to be in this Manhattan long enough to spend all of it." He glared across the table. "All right, you little green bastard— talk!"

"John Justin, I have a feeling that someone has been filling your head with terrible lies about me," said Mürgenstürm.

"Somebody's been lying to me, all right," said Mallory.

"Every word I've told you since we met has been God's own truth!" declared the elf, raising his right hand. "I swear it!"

"Such as not knowing what makes Larkspur so valuable?" asked Mallory.

"Well, *almost* everything," amended Mürgenstürm uneasily. "I may have simplified a few concepts here and there for your convenience."

"You little bastard, you've been lying from the word Go!" snapped Mallory. "You told me that we live in the same Manhattan."

"Well, our Manhattans share many things—buildings, streets, parks—"

"They also share a membrane that's in the process of hardening right now!"

"Then you know that Larkspur is dead?" asked Mürgenstürm, startled.

"Of course I know," said Mallory contemptuously. "Your partner killed him."

"My partner?" asked the elf innocently.

Mallory nodded. "Flypaper Gillespie. He *is* your partner, isn't he—or at least, he was until a few hours ago?"

"Certainly not!"

"We're not going to get anywhere unless you start telling me the truth."

"I may have said a few words to him," said Mürgenstürm indignantly, "but we were never *partners*."

"But he *was* the person you chose to steal the unicorn?" persisted Mallory.

Mürgenstürm nodded unhappily. "He is the most unethical person I've ever come across!"

Mallory stared at him in amusement. "You know, you're almost as incompetent as you pretend to be."

"I resent that!"

"Resent it all you like," said Mallory with a shrug. "The fact remains that you blundered practically every step of the way."

"Hah!" said the elf heatedly. "It was a brilliant plan! Positively brilliant! I'd been honing it to perfection for years!"

"Bullshit."

"Well, days, anyway. Ever since my cousin won the national presidency of our guild."

"What does that have to do with anything?" asked Mallory.

"The guild has been entrusted with protecting Larkspur," explained Mürgenstürm. "The former president lived in Kansas City, and when my cousin won, he transferred Larkspur from Kansas City to New York."

"Why?"

"Larkspur is our most prestigious commission, so naturally the president wants him at his home base."

"So that's how you finagled your way into being allowed to guard him," said Mallory. He pulled out a cigarette and lit it. "And you didn't choose that empty lot by accident, did you?"

"No," admitted the elf. "It's protected by all kinds of spells and charms."

"Including a dandy against the Grundy?" suggested Mallory.

Mürgenstürm nodded. "And a very weak one against leprechauns."

"One that you could somehow counteract or deactivate?"

"Yes."

"So you wanted to steal the ruby," continued Mallory. "But you couldn't do it by yourself, not when Larkspur was in your charge—there'd be too many difficult questions to answer. Besides, there was probably a spell protecting him against elves."

"A real stinker," acknowledged Mürgenstürm bitterly. "There was absolutely no way I could break through it."

"So you contacted Gillespie. You told him that you'd find some way to deactivate the spell against leprechauns, and split the profits with him after he stole the unicorn."

"He didn't even know what Larkspur was worth," said Mürgenstürm. "He was supposed to turn him over to me in exchange for fifty balls of string and a complete run of *Playboy*."

"And when he didn't show up, you realized that he had double-crossed you."

"The filthy little leprechaun!"

"You needed help, but you couldn't go to your guild, and you couldn't use a local detective. They'd have spotted the flaws in your story right away." Mallory stared at him. "So you came to me."

Mürgenstürm nodded unhappily.

"And then we met Felina, and you found out what had happened. Gillespie didn't know what the unicorn was worth, but he knew it had to be pretty valuable for you to put your life on the line, so he went to the one person he was pretty sure *would* know—the Grundy." Mallory paused. "The Grundy wanted Larkspur every bit as badly as you did, but the yard was protected against him, so he made the same arrangement with Gillespie: the leprechaun would steal it, and the Grundy would meet him later." The detective lit another cigarette. "My guess is that Larkspur himself was protected against the Grundy, and that the farther he got from the yard, the less powerful the protection became. That's why the Grundy didn't take him from Gillespie the second he walked out of the yard. Am I right?"

"You're right," admitted the elf.

"And when the Grundy had the chance to kill us in the museum and didn't take it, you realized that Gillespie had double-crossed him as well, and that he was hoping we might lead him to the ruby."

"You really *are* a remarkable detective, John Justin," said Mürgenstürm wearily.

"It's my job," said Mallory with a shrug. "You didn't really visit a ladyfriend when you left me in Central Park, did you?"

"Briefly," confessed the elf.

"But then you went looking for Gillespie at the Kringleman Arms."

Mürgenstürm nodded. "He wasn't there."

"He showed up later."

"You actually saw him?" asked Mürgenstürm.

Mallory shook his head. "I missed him by maybe five minutes."

"How do you know you were that close?"

"The coffee in his cup was still warm." Mallory paused. "That brings us up to the present. Now for the future: when's the auction?"

"How did you know there's going to be an auction?"

"Gillespie doesn't know how to use the stone, and it's too damned dangerous for him to keep with the Grundy and your guild both after it, so I assume he's invited you and the Grundy to bid on it."

"That's why I was looking for you," admitted Mürgenstürm. "I wanted to make sure you hadn't found it before I wasted my money bidding for something that he didn't have any longer." He reached into the air and produced a folded piece of notepaper. "Here," he said, handing it to Mallory.

The detective unfolded it and read it.

AUCTION

The undersigned cordially invites
your participation at an auction for
a gem of rare and wonderful properties.

Time: 3:30 AM

Place: You know where.

—Flypaper Gillespie

Mallory crumpled up the paper and let it roll out of his hand onto the table. Then he looked at his watch.

"Three-thirty," he said. "That's twenty minutes from now." He looked across the table at Mürgenstürm. "Do you know where it is?"

The little elf nodded. "Where I was supposed to pick up Larkspur from him." He looked supplicatingly toward the detective. "I'm afraid to go there alone, John Justin. Will you come with me?"

Mallory smiled grimly.

"I wouldn't miss it for the world," he said.

Chapter
13 ──────────────────────────

Mallory and Mürgenstürm walked along the deserted dock area as a lonely foghorn sounded in the distance. A thick blanket of fog had rolled in off the East River, embracing the local waterfront dives and hiding them from view.

"We'd better be getting close," remarked Mallory, peering through the fog at a cargo ship from Lemuria being pulled by two tiny tugboats. "You've only got about seven minutes left."

"We are," Mürgenstürm assured him. "It's just a block away." He looked up at Mallory. "I want you to know how much I appreciate this, John Justin."

"I'm not doing it for *you*," replied Mallory.

"But I thought we were friends," said the little elf.

"Come off it, you little green wart," said Mallory. "You've been lying to me and trying to use me from the first minute we met. Hell, the only reason you want me along now is because you're afraid to face the Grundy by yourself."

"That's not true!" protested Mürgenstürm.

"Isn't it?"

"Well, not entirely. I also cherish your companionship." Mürgenstürm paused and stared up at Mallory. "If you're not doing it for me, why *are* you here?"

"Two of my friends are missing," answered Mallory. "I've got a feeling that they'll turn up here."

"Who are they?"

"You wouldn't know them."

"I might," said the elf. "I know a lot of people."

"Yeah," said Mallory, "but these two tell the truth. You probably move in different social circles."

"That was unkind, John Justin," said Mürgenstürm.

"Probably," agreed the detective with no hint of an apology.

One of the tugboats sounded its foghorn, and a ship of Graustarkian registry, which had loomed up out of the mist, turned hard to starboard to avoid the Lemurian vessel.

"Aren't you frightened?" asked Mürgenstürm.

"Of what?"

"The Grundy, of course!" said the elf incredulously.

"He's not going to kill anyone until he gets his hands on the ruby," replied Mallory.

"If he wins the auction, he'll *have* the ruby!"

"I didn't say he wouldn't discourage you from bidding," noted Mallory dryly. "As for having the ruby, buying it is one thing; getting his hands on it is another."

"What do you mean?"

"You don't think Gillespie will be stupid enough to bring it to the auction, do you? He's going to want to protect himself."

"I suppose so," said Mürgenstürm. Suddenly his face lit up. "What would you say to a pooling of resources?"

"All but a couple of hundred dollars of my money is worthless here," Mallory reminded him. "I don't *have* any resources."

"He won't want money," explained the elf. "I told you what our original deal was."

"I don't have any string or dirty magazines."

"But you can help me collect them!" urged Mürgenstürm.

Mallory laughed contemptuously. "Do you seriously believe that he's going to let you buy the ruby on credit while the Grundy is sitting right there?"

"Probably not," admitted Mürgenstürm. His expression hardened. "But I've got to try! At least one thing I told you *is* true: my guild will kill me for losing Larkspur. I've got to get my hands on that ruby so I can escape to your Manhattan."

"Why not just go now, before the membrane hardens?"

"Because if the Grundy gets it, he'll come after me because of all the trouble I've caused him."

"I can't say that I blame him," replied Mallory. "You've been a pain in the ass to a lot of people."

"I know," said Mürgenstürm. "But you don't know what it's like to be an elf!" he added plaintively. "You can rise just so high in the guild, and no higher."

"Like your cousin?" said the detective with a touch of sarcasm.

"That's unfair!"

"But true. Why don't you simply admit that you were looking for a shortcut?"

"I was just trying to improve my station in life!"

"Stupid," said Mallory, shaking his head. "Just plain stupid."

"I resent that!"

"You think not?" said Mallory. "What the hell would you have done with the stone if this scheme had gone off like clockwork? Use it to move between your Manhattan and mine? You can already do that."

"Sell it," said Mürgenstürm promptly.

"To the Grundy? You may get your wish."

"To a jeweler in *your* world. It's the most perfect gem I've ever seen. It's worth millions, John Justin!"

"Jesus!" said Mallory disgustedly. "You were going to take Larkspur's ruby and let some fat New York matron wind up wearing it around her neck without ever knowing what it was?"

A sickly smile spread across Mürgenstürm's face. "You make it sound so . . . so crass and unfeeling."

"And what about all the people you've stranded forever?" continued Mallory. "And not just people, either. How many Gnomes of the Subway are going to starve to death because the supply of tokens from my Manhattan is going to dry up?"

"Don't say things like that," whined the elf. "I was just trying to secure a better life for myself!"

"Well, you seem to have secured a briefer one, anyway," replied the detective. "I hope you think it was worth it."

They walked another fifty yards in silence. Then Mürgenstürm stopped before a large building that looked out over the docks.

"Well, I'll be damned!" said Mallory, an amused smile on his face. "A genuine old abandoned warehouse!"

"You've heard of it before?" asked Mürgenstürm.

"Heard of what?"

"The Old Abandoned Warehouse," replied the elf. "That's where we are."

Mallory put his hands on his hips and looked at The Old Abandoned Warehouse. It took up almost a block, and seemed to be made entirely of gray aluminum siding. He could discern only one door, though he assumed that there were numerous truck docks around the corner. There were five windows scattered across the front of the building; four were dark, but there was a diffused yellow light piercing the fog from the fifth.

"You're right on time, Mürgenstürm," said a deep voice, and Mallory turned to find himself facing a huge, blue-skinned man in a purple sharkskin suit, light blue shirt, violet tie, and navy blue shoes and socks. He stood just under seven feet tall, and weighed in the vicinity of 500 pounds. "Who's this guy with you?"

"His name's Mallory," said the elf. "He's okay. I vouch for him."

"Who's your friend?" Mallory asked Mürgenstürm.

"The Prince of Whales. He owns the warehouse."

"I thought you were supposed to come alone," said the Prince of Whales.

"He's my bodyguard," replied the little elf.

The Prince of Whales glared at Mallory for a moment, then shrugged. "He ain't gonna do you much good against the Grundy. But what the hell—it's no skin off my ass. Go on in."

"Thank you," said Mürgenstürm.

The elf walked up to the door and opened it, and Mallory followed him into the interior of The Old Abandoned Warehouse. The place was filled with row upon row of free-standing shelving units, each holding treasures stolen from the detective's Manhattan: costume jewelry, old pulp magazines in plastic bags, kitchen appliances, rubber tires, canned dog and cat food, stereo and videotape equipment, furs, and even some stoneware. Where the shelves stopped, the area was cluttered with huge packing cases containing everything from television sets to self-propelled lawn mowers.

Mürgenstürm turned to his right and walked up to the building's office. The blinds were drawn, but Mallory could tell that the light was on, and he assumed it was the same one he had seen from outside.

The little elf opened the door cautiously.

"Hi, partner!" said a high-pitched, smirking voice. "I'm so glad you could make it."

Mallory stepped through the doorway and found himself in a large office, some twenty feet on a side. A number of chairs lined one wall, facing a desk that dominated the other side of the room. Seated behind the desk was a leprechaun.

"Mr. Mallory, I presume?" he said with an unpleasant grin.

"And you must be Flypaper Gillespie," said Mallory.

Gillespie nodded. "We meet at last."

"Where are my friends?" demanded Mallory.

"I don't know who you're talking about."

"Eohippus and Winnifred Carruthers."

"Never heard of them," said Gillespie, still grinning.

Mallory walked to the office door.

"Where are you going, Mr. Mallory?" demanded the leprechaun.

"To take a look around."

"For your friends?"

"Possibly you overlooked them," said Mallory with a grim smile.

"I wouldn't do that if I were you."

"Why not?"

"Because it would make me unhappy," said Gillespie. "I do bad things when I'm unhappy."

"You're breaking my heart," said Mallory, reaching for the doorknob.

"I meant what I said, Mr. Mallory," said Gillespie, opening a drawer. He pulled out something familiar and set it atop the desk.

Mallory stared at the tiny figure for a moment.

"Eohippus?" he said at last.

The horse whinnied a weak acknowledgment.

"But you're two inches smaller than you were!" exclaimed Mallory.

"That's because I keep doing *this* to him," giggled Gillespie, whacking the horse sharply in the middle of the back with a plastic ruler. "Now get away from the door—or I'll beat your little pet here until he's so small that he vanishes right in front of your eyes."

Mallory glared at the leprechaun, then slowly walked back to the opposite side of the office.

"Where is Colonel Carruthers?" he demanded.

"I don't believe I'm going to tell you," said Gillespie happily. "When I get tired of whipping the horse, I'm going to start on *her*."

"Unless I start on *you*," said Mallory ominously.

"Lay a finger on me and you'll never see Carruthers again—and *nobody* will ever see the ruby," said Gillespie with a confident laugh. He turned to Mürgenstürm. "Well, little green partner, how's life been treating you today?"

"You are a despicable creature!" said Mürgenstürm.

"You ain't seen nothing yet," said the leprechaun. "Sit down."

"I'd rather stand," said the elf.

"But *I'd* rather you didn't," said Gillespie.

Mürgenstürm sighed and climbed onto a chair.

"You, too," snapped Gillespie to Mallory.

"No, thanks," said Mallory, leaning against a wall.

"We'll see about that!" said Gillespie, picking up the plastic ruler again.

"You touch the horse and I'll tear your arm right off your body," said Mallory softly.

"Hah!" said Gillespie. "You're hardly in a position to tell *anyone* what to do! You need the ruby worse than any of them!"

"That's true," agreed Mallory. "But if you lay a finger on Eohippus, you're going to be a one-armed auctioneer."

Gillespie stared at him for a long moment, then put the tiny horse back into the desk drawer.

"You're going to regret talking like that to me!" he hissed. "I promise you that."

"Cut the bullshit and start the auction," said Mallory. "You're not scaring anyone."

"When the Grundy gets here."

Mallory checked his wristwatch. "It's three-thirty-two. Obviously the Grundy isn't interested in what you have to sell."

"*I'll* be the judge of that, if you don't mind," said a deep, rich voice to his right.

Mürgenstürm whimpered in terror, and Mallory turned to see a strange being standing a few feet away from him. He was tall, a few inches over six feet, with two prominent horns protruding from his hairless head. Hie eyes were a burning yellow, his nose sharp and aquiline, his teeth white and gleaming, his skin a bright red. His shirt and pants were of crushed velvet, his cloak satin, his collar and cuffs made from the fur of some white polar animal. He wore gleaming black gloves and boots, and he had two rubies suspended from his neck on a golden necklace. When he exhaled, small clouds of vapor emanated from his mouth and nostrils.

"Well," said Gillespie, breaking the silence, "I believe all the interested parties are present. Mallory, have you met the Grundy?"

"Indirectly," said Mallory, recalling his confrontation with the gorilla in the museum.

The Grundy gazed at him. "You've made a serious error in judgment coming here, Mr. Mallory. You are involving yourself in matters that are none of your concern."

"I'm a non-participant," said Mallory. "If you want to get mad at someone, get mad at the guy who double-crossed you," he added, jerking a thumb in Gillespie's direction.

"His turn will come, never fear," promised the Grundy with conviction.

"But not until you get the ruby," grinned Gillespie. "And you ain't getting nothing until I'm long gone and safely hidden."

The Grundy paid him no attention, but turned to Mürgenstürm. "And after *his* turn, *yours*."

Mürgenstürm opened his mouth to reply, but he was shaking so badly that no words came forth.

The Grundy returned his attention to Gillespie. "I sense another presence."

Gillespie took Eohippus out of the drawer, held him up for the Grundy to see, and then put him back.

"All present and accounted for," he grinned. "And now, gents, I think we'll start the auction."

"Two hundred balls of string!" shouted Mürgenstürm.

"That's not even a nice floor for the bidding," said Gillespie. "It's more like a sub-basement."

"Three hundred balls, and complete runs of *Playboy* and *Penthouse*!" replied the elf.

"Grundy, you're being awfully quiet," said the leprechaun. "Did you come all this way not to bid?"

The Grundy stared at Gillespie, two thin streams of vapor drifting out of his nostrils and obscuring almost all of his face, except for his luminous yellow eyes.

"I offer you a swift, painless death for your transgressions," he said at last.

"That's not much of an offer," said Gillespie, obviously unfrightened.

"You are selling something that doesn't belong to you."

Gillespie chuckled. "If it belonged to anyone, it belonged to the unicorn, and he's past caring about it now." He stared directly into the Grundy's eyes. "And you can stop threatening me. You're not going to touch a perfect hair of my beautiful head until you've got your hands on the ruby.'' He looked over at the detective. ''Mallory, how about you? You want to make a bid?''

Mallory shook his head.

''Well, Grundy, how about it? Or do I turn the ruby over to the elf here?''

''To my initial bid, I will add the sum of one million dollars, and allow you a reasonable amount of time to enjoy it before I kill you.''

''How much is that in beer and ice cream cones?''

''You figure it out,'' said the Grundy coldly.

''Mürgenstürm?''

''Five hundred balls of string, and I'll throw in a run of *Hustler*.''

''And a giraffe,'' said Gillespie.

''A giraffe?'' asked Mürgenstürm. ''Why?''

''I've always wanted one.''

''And a giraffe,'' said the elf with a sigh.

''That still doesn't come to a million bucks,'' said Gillespie. ''What can we add to it?'' Suddenly he smiled. ''I have it! Kill Mallory for me.''

''I can't!'' protested Mürgenstürm.

''Do you want the ruby or not?'' said the leprechaun.

''But—''

''That's my new minimum bid!'' screamed Gillespie. ''You don't make it and you're out of the running!''

''Right now?''

''That would be premature,'' grinned Gillespie. ''You only have to kill him if you win.''

Mürgenstürm turned to Mallory. ''I'm sorry, John Justin,'' he said, ''but I've *got* to have that ruby!'' He turned back to Gillespie and nodded.

''Well, now we're getting somewhere!'' said the leprechaun happily. "Have I encouraged you to enter the bidding, Mallory?"

"Not even a little bit," replied the detective.

"Maybe you'd change your mind if I took another inch or two off your pet."

"I wouldn't do that if I were you," said Mallory.

"My oh my!" smirked Gillespie. "All of these people threatening to kill poor little old me!" His smirk changed instantly into a contemptuous frown. "And not a one of you with the guts to do it! What a delightful situation!"

"You heard me," said Mallory.

"Don't forget who has the ruby, asshole!" snarled the leprechaun. He took Eohippus out of the drawer and picked up the ruler.

"Quick!" shouted Mallory. "Is she in the building?"

"Yes!" said Eohippus, as Gillespie began to bring the ruler down across his back.

"That's all I wanted to know."

Before anyone could stop him, Mallory pulled out his pistol, aimed it at Gillespie, and pulled the trigger. The leprechaun flew backward off the desk, a bullet lodged between his eyes.

"NO!" screamed the Grundy.

"My God, John Justin!" cried Mürgenstürm. "What have you done?"

"I've eliminated some vermin," replied Mallory calmly, as he put the pistol back in his pocket. "Nothing more."

"Fool!" screamed the Grundy, flames leaping from his mouth. He pointed an arrow-sharp finger at Mallory. "You meddling fool! It was within my grasp, and now I've lost it!"

He uttered a mystic word, and suddenly a huge fireball appeared in his hand. "Prepare yourself for the smell of burning flesh, the melting of teeth and bones, the excruciating agony of the inferno!"

"Throw that at me and you'll never see the ruby again," said Mallory.

The demon froze. "Speak quickly!" he commanded.

"Gillespie didn't have it." Mallory tapped his chest with his thumb. "*I* do."

"He's lying!" said Mürgenstürm. "I know where he's been every minute since he got here!"

The Grundy glared at Mallory. "Answer his charge."

"Gladly," said the detective. "Since Gillespie didn't know what the ruby could do, it stood to reason that he killed Larkspur because it was easier to hide a stone than a unicorn. He knew that all of us were turning the city upside down looking for him, so he hit upon the one place where it would be safe until after the auction."

"Where?" demanded the Grundy.

"My office," replied Mallory. "As long as I was here, in this Manhattan, that was the perfect place for it." He paused. "I finally figured it out when I found my coffee mug in his room. I'd been drinking from it just before I came here—which meant that Gillespie had paid a visit to my office *after* I'd left it. He could only have had one reason for that: to hide the ruby."

"It makes sense," admitted Mürgenstürm.

"Silence, worm!" snapped the Grundy, and Mürgenstürm looked like he was about to faint.

"Of course," added Mallory, pulling out a cigarette and lighting it, "it's not there any longer. I had Felina get it while I was at the Missing Persons Bureau." He looked at the Grundy. "And, believe me, if with all your powers you couldn't find Gillespie, you sure as hell aren't going to be able to find *her*."

"You are a shrewd man, Mallory," admitted the Grundy. "Where is it now?"

"In a safe place," Mallory assured him. "And now, gentlemen," he concluded with a smile, "if you still want the stone, you're going to have to deal with *me*."

Chapter
14 ——————————————————

"What do you want for it?" asked Mürgenstürm.

"My needs are a little different from Flypaper Gillespie's," replied Mallory. "For starters, I want my friends freed and safely away from here before we even start talking."

"Done," said the Grundy. He vanished for perhaps twenty seconds, then reappeared. "If you will step outside the office, you will find the woman waiting for you."

Mallory picked up Eohippus and walked out into the warehouse. As the Grundy had promised, Winnifred was waiting for him nearby, a bewildered expression on her face.

"Are you all right?" he asked.

"Yes," replied Winnifred. "But it was most disconcerting! One minute I was bound and gagged in a storage closet, and then the Grundy himself set me free!" She looked up at Mallory. "That was *your* doing, wasn't it?"

He nodded. "What happened to the two of you?"

"I bribed some leprechauns to tell us where Gillespie was," said Winnifred ruefully. "Evidently they immediately raced ahead and warned him, because he was waiting for us." She shook her head. "I must be getting old, Mallory. I would never have made that mistake twenty years ago."

"Don't worry about it," said Mallory. "You're all right now, and that's all that matters." He paused. "I want you to take Eohippus back to the Morbidium and wait there."

"You're not coming with us?" she said, frowning.

He shook his head. "I've still got business to conduct in there," he said, gesturing toward the office.

"With the Grundy?" she demanded.

"Yes."

"Then we're staying too!" said Eohippus adamantly.

"No, you're not," replied Mallory. "The first piece of business I transacted was a guarantee of your freedom. Besides," he added, running a hand gently over the tiny horse's battered body, "you can't be six inches tall. I don't want you taking any more chances."

"But he'll kill you!" protested Eohippus.

"Not while I know how to find the stone, he won't."

"He'll torture the location out of you," said Winnifred.

"I've taken precautions."

"You're a remarkable man, John Justin Mallory," she said earnestly. "How soon should we expect you at the Morbidium?"

"You're not waiting for *me*," said Mallory. "Felina's got orders to show up there if I don't check in with her by a specified time."

"Has she got the ruby?"

"Not anymore."

"What should we do if she shows up?"

"You'll figure it out," said Mallory, handing Eohippus to her. "Patch him up and take good care of him."

"I will," she promised. "Good luck, Mallory."

"Thanks," he said, accompanying her to the front door. "Now, get going."

He waited until they had left, watching through one of the windows to make sure that the Prince of Whales had let them pass. Then he turned and went back to the office.

"Thanks for letting them go, Grundy," said Mallory.

"They are merely spear carriers in this little drama," replied the demon with a condescending shrug. "I have no interest in them."

"He'll kill them as soon as he gets the ruby!" said Mürgenstürm.

"I give you my word that I will not," said the Grundy.

"He's lying, John Justin!"

Mallory turned to Mürgenstürm. "There's only one person in this office who's lied to me," he said harshly. "And only one who's volunteered to kill me."

"I wouldn't have done it!" swore the elf. "I had to say it, or Gillespie would have given the ruby to the Grundy!"

"You know, you're such a smooth liar that you probably even believe what you're saying," remarked Mallory disgustedly.

"You know it's the truth!"

"I don't know any such thing," snapped the detective. "Mürgenstürm, you're as charming as anyone I've met in this Manhattan—but charm has nothing to do with worth."

"You're a very perceptive man, Mallory," said the Grundy, walking over to the desk and sitting on the edge of it. "You have no intention of turning the ruby over to him, do you?"

"No," said Mallory.

"John Justin!" shrieked Mürgenstürm.

"Sooner or later every man has to face the consequences of his actions," said Mallory. "Now it's your turn."

"But it's not fair!"

"Was it fair to slaughter Larkspur and strand thousands of people in the wrong Manhattan?"

"But that was never my intention!" wailed the elf.

"Someday I'm going to have to tell you what the road to hell is paved with," said Mallory. He turned to the Grundy. "We have no use for him. Let him go."

"He must die for what he's done," said the Grundy sternly.

"He will," Mallory assured the demon. "His own guild will kill him at sunrise."

"And if he escapes them?" demanded the Grundy.

"Then he can spend the rest of his life peering into shadows to see if they're lying in wait for him."

A savage smile crossed the Grundy's face. "I *like* that."

"I thought you might."

The demon turned to Mürgenstürm. "Begone!"

"But—"

"If you are still within my domain at sunrise, I will come after you myself," promised the Grundy.

Mürgenstürm glared at Mallory.

"Thanks a lot, *friend!*" he said bitterly.

"Friends don't do what you did," said Mallory. "Now, get the hell out of here. Sunrise isn't that far off."

Mürgenstürm walked to the door, seemed about to say something, thought better of it, and left.

"Wait," said the Grundy. He closed his eyes for a moment, then opened them. "All right. He's left the building." He turned to Mallory. "All that remains is to settle upon a price. I seem to be the only interested party left."

"Wrong," said Mallory.

The demon growled deep in his throat, and the smoke issuing from his nostrils turned a bright blue.

"Who else is there?" he demanded.

"There's me."

"You?"

Mallory nodded. "That stone is my ticket home."

"I've tested the membrane," said the Grundy. "It will remain permeable for two or three more hours. We can conclude our transaction and you can still go home after you turn the ruby over to me."

"But I don't know if I'm going to turn it over to you," replied Mallory.

"*What?*" growled the demon, his eyes glowing even brighter.

"You're the Grundy," said Mallory. "You kill things. You cause plagues. You slaughter unicorns for these damned jewels. You've even made *my* Manhattan unsafe. Why should I give you the key to additional power?"

"Fool!" raged the Grundy, leaping to his feet. "You don't begin to understand!" He stared at Mallory, his eyes mere slits in his horned head. "Do you think I *wanted* to kill Larkspur?"

"You sure as hell didn't try to talk Gillespie into returning him," said Mallory.

"Gillespie was never supposed to kill the unicorn!" snapped the Grundy. "He was only supposed to deliver it to me!"

"And you, of course, would have returned it to Mürgenstürm's guild," said Mallory sardonically.

"Never!" bellowed the Grundy. "I would have kept possession of the animal, and eventually, when it died of old age, I would have appropriated the ruby, as is my right. But I didn't want Larkspur to die yet! Closing the membrane will make my work all the harder!"

"Your work consists of doing terrible things," said Mallory. "How the hell does a dead unicorn make it harder?"

The Grundy shook his head savagely. "Fool! My work

is to be a balance point, a fulcrum against the worst tendencies of worlds."

Mallory stared at him. "What are you talking about?"

"I'm talking about why I need the ruby!"

"What's all this crap about fulcrums and balance points?"

"It is my duty to act as a balance against the worst tendencies of a world. In *this* Manhattan, where anarchy reigns and cause is not always followed by effect, I am a force for order."

"You impose order by killing and looting?" said Mallory incredulously.

"I am a demon. My nature restricts the ways in which I can function. I *must* maim and kill and pillage! It is what I was born to do!"

"All of which constitutes as poor a justification for evil as I've ever heard."

"Don't you understand? This society is without direction! It *needs* a common enemy to give it a sense of purpose." The Grundy paused. "*I* am that enemy."

"And much against his will, the noble demon takes the onerous burden upon himself, is that it?" said Mallory sardonically.

"I can take it upon myself precisely because I *am* a demon!" thundered the Grundy. "I take nourishment from death, I revel in grief and injustice!" His face glowed with an unholy ecstasy. "There is an exquisite mathematical precision to the creation of suffering, a geometric beauty in the state of hopelessness, a fierce primal joy in the creation of terror. *You* could no more fulfill my function in this universe than I could fulfill *yours*."

"So you become the common enemy. What about all the other would-be enemies of the state?"

"That's why I wanted Larkspur to live. I cannot by my very nature reform a lawbreaker; nor will I permit the existence of competitors—but I can impose order on this world by letting my would-be competitors commit their crimes in *your* Manhattan."

"For which my Manhattan thanks you," said Mallory dryly.

"Your Manhattan *should* thank me. An overly regulated society needs lawbreakers, just as *this* society needs a sense of order." The Grundy stared at Mallory. "Do you even begin to comprehend what I am saying to you?"

"I'm working on it," said Mallory. "Just out of curiosity, what about the other two worlds?"

"What other two worlds?"

"The worlds those rubies give you access to," said Mallory, pointing to the Grundy's necklace.

"I was very young when I acquired my first ruby," replied the demon. "My powers were immature, and I didn't know how to control them."

"You destroyed the whole world?"

"I gained considerable knowledge from the experience."

"Well, I'm glad *somebody* did. What about the other one?"

"It was a rational world, dedicated to all that is best in Man," said the Grundy. "It was approaching a state of utopia when I obtained the ruby."

"And now?"

"I visited it with chaos, I introduced hatred and bigotry and jealousy into its soul, I destroyed their monuments to Reason and forced them to erect pagan statues to me."

"For their own good?" said Mallory dryly.

"Certainly," replied the Grundy. "One cannot appreciate a utopia without having experienced a dystopia, any more than one can appreciate the concept of Good without having experienced Evil."

"You keep talking about balance, and good and evil, and your sense of purpose," said Mallory. "But all I hear is how you bring ruin to everything you touch."

"Humanists will tell you that Good and Evil are relative concepts, that there are no absolutes in the universe," said the Grundy. He growled contemptuously. "Humanists are fools! There is absolute Good and absolute Evil. The universe requires not just one, but both. I represent the one, and my job is to oppose the other."

"Who represents Good?" asked Mallory.

"Just as I do not exist in all times and places, neither does my counterpart. In some universes he is Jesus, in some Mohammed; in some he is nothing more than an abstract ideal, a concept embedded in a thought or a word."

"And you try to kill off the Good?"

The Grundy shook his head. "The universe would be as out of balance if I killed my Opponent as it would be if he killed me. I may try to subdue him, just as he tries to subdue me, but neither of us can ever win. I destroy a man, and he creates a child; he plants a flower, and my breath withers it; I enslave a race, and he imparts to them a vision of freedom; he creates a monument, and I gnaw at its foundations."

"If you've achieved a balance, why do you need another ruby?" asked Mallory.

"To maintain balance in yet another world," answered the Grundy. *"Your* world."

"If by balance you mean murder and rape and war, then my world's already got a little more balance than it knows what to do with," replied Mallory dryly.

"I will bring confusion out of order, hate out of love, pollution out of sterility—and from my strength my Opponent will drink deep and increase his own."

Mallory stared at him for a long moment.

"You've caused enough misery for one lifetime," he said at last. "I don't intend to let you bring any more to my world."

"You will not turn the ruby over to me?" demanded the Grundy.

Mallory shook his head. "My world's got enough problems without you adding to them."

"But I already *have!*" laughed the Grundy. "Larkspur lived for more than fifty years. Who do you think whispered dreams of empire into the ear of a frustrated Austrian housepainter? Who placed the machinery of execution in Stalin's hands? I was at My Lai and Auschwitz, at Phnom Penh and Hiroshima. It was I who told Idi Amin how to exercise his power, who designed the dungeons of Paraguay, who convinced Neville Chamberlain to trust his fellow man." He paused and stared directly into Mallory's eyes. "And yet you survived, and you grew, and you prospered, for my Opponent never rests. I blow polio upon the winds, and he guides Jonas Salk's hand; I walk the battlefields and ravage the wounded, and he transmutes bread mold into a magical elixir. I slaughter the satiated, and he feeds the starving. The balance still exists—but for it to continue, I *must* have the ruby."

"No."

"But *why?*" demanded the Grundy, slamming his fist against the wall in frustration and leaving burn marks on the shattered plaster. "I have explained the situation to you! Surely you see the necessity of it!"

"Consider it a social experiment," said Mallory. "I think one world deserves a chance to survive without your particular notion of balance."

The Grundy sighed and shook his head. "Then some other entity will come along to take my place."

"Perhaps," acknowledged Mallory. "But I can't worry about that. All I can do is concentrate on what I can control—and I control the ruby."

"I have ways of extracting it from you," said the Grundy ominously.

"I'm sure you have," said Mallory. "But they won't do you any good. If I don't report to Felina at four-thirty and every hour thereafter, neither you nor I will ever see the stone again."

"You would forfeit your life to deny me the ruby?"

Mallory stared levelly at the demon. "You're not going to kill me as long as you have a chance of getting your hands on it, so why don't you stop threatening me?"

"I have no desire to kill you at all," answered the Grundy. "It would not aid my efforts to achieve a balance here. In a world dedicated to disorder, you alone seem able to make sense of the disparate pieces." He smiled ironically. "In truth, Mallory, my needs and your character are such that, in this world at least, we should be allies." The smile vanished as suddenly as it had appeared. "But I am compelled by my nature to seek the stone, and if you stand in my way I will crush you."

"Well," answered Mallory, "you seem to like paradoxes, so consider this one: as long as I stand in your way, there's a chance that you may wind up with the ruby—and the second you knock me down, it's lost to you forever."

"Then I will watch you every minute of every day," promised the Grundy. "Power possesses an insidious, fatal attraction to all beings, and that ruby is power incarnate. Sooner or later you will be drawn to it, and then I shall strike."

"Don't pursue me *too* closely," said Mallory wryly. "Give temptation a chance."

"You have proven to be a worthy antagonist," said the demon sincerely. "I shall be sorry to kill you."

"Then don't."

"Give me the ruby, and leave in safety."

"If my world is going straight to hell, it's going to do it without your help," said Mallory firmly. "Besides," he added, "if I gave you the stone, you'd hunt me down and kill me in my Manhattan for the same reasons that you admire me here."

The Grundy grinned, displaying a set of truly impressive canines. "You are a very wise man, Mallory. I salute you!"

"How do I compare with your Opponent on this world?" asked Mallory, returning his grin.

"It is not given to me to know the identity of my Opponent, or else I would kill him." Suddenly he stared intently at the detective. "It might even be you."

"That's not very likely," replied Mallory. "I just got here."

"But my Opponent works in strange ways. He could be using you just as I use the rubies."

"I wouldn't count on it. I'm a free man, possessed of free will, and if I defeat you I plan on taking all the credit for it myself."

"Then the battle lines are drawn," announced the Grundy, "and you and I shall wage war over the Yin and Yang of it."

He made a quick gesture in the air, which was followed by a puff of reddish smoke and a popping sound, and suddenly Mallory was alone in the office.

Mallory stepped out into the warehouse, looked around, lit a cigarette, and opened the front door. The Prince of Whales was waiting for him.

"You done with your business?" he demanded gruffly.

"Actually, I have a feeling that we're just beginning," answered Mallory, walking out into the cold Manhattan morning.

Chapter
15

4:11 AM–4:48 AM

Mallory began shivering as he walked along the water-front, and suddenly realized that he hadn't activated his robe. He quickly adjusted the belt, and a moment later he could feel the heat spreading through the fabric.

After he had walked for perhaps half a mile, he turned to his left, leaving the river behind him. Before long he came to an all-night drugstore. It seemed to be frequented solely by goblins and Gnomes of the Subway, and the moment he entered it he became aware that he was the recipient of several sullen glares.

"I wouldn't hang around if I was you, buddy," said the goblin behind the cash register. "This place is strictly off-limits to humans, you know what I mean?"

"I won't be here long," Mallory assured him. "I just need a map of the city."

The goblin pulled one out from behind the counter. "Here you go," he said. "Take it home and study it, and see if you can learn not to come where you're not wanted."

"What do I owe you?"

"Fifty cents."

Mallory reached into his pocket and pulled out two of Mürgenstürm's quarters, laid them on the counter, and turned toward the door.

A large apelike creature, so covered with hair that its facial features were hidden, blocked his way.

"You're a long way from home, ain't you?" said the ape in a guttural voice.

Mallory took a quick glance behind him to see if there was another exit. There was—but half a dozen goblins stood between it and him, each of them grinning in anticipation of the bloodletting to come.

"I'm not looking for any trouble," said the detective.

"You don't have to *look* for it!" snarled the ape. "It's right here waiting for you!"

"Okay," said Mallory with a shrug. "But when I'm late for my appointment with the Grundy, he's going to know who to blame."

Suddenly the ape looked very unsure of himself. "The Grundy?"

"I'm Mallory. Don't you ever read a newspaper?"

"I don't believe you," said the ape.

"That's up to you," replied the detective. "Just don't ever say that you weren't warned."

The ape began pacing back and forth in front of Mallory, slapping his chest and trying to work himself into a killing rage—but his eyes kept darting to the shadows, looking for a sign of the demon.

"Get out of here!" he growled at last. "It's more bother to rip you apart than it's worth."

Mallory quickly walked out the door.

"And don't show your face in here again!" yelled the ape, his belligerence returning as Mallory widened the distance between them.

Mallory put a couple of blocks between himself and the drugstore and then stopped beneath a flickering streetlamp, where he unfolded the map. When he found the location he wanted, he memorized the shortest route, then put the map into his pocket and began walking.

Ten minutes later he came to Mystic Place, turned the corner, and walked up to Number 7. Just before he climbed down the stairs to the basement apartment, he saw a flash of green out of the corner of his eye.

Then he was knocking at the door, and the Great Mephisto peeked through the curtains.

"It's me," said Mallory. "Let me in."

"Are you alone?" demanded Mephisto.

"More or less."

"What the hell does that mean?"

"Just open the goddamned door," said Mallory.

The magician opened his door, pulled the detective inside, and slammed it shut.

"Any luck?" asked Mephisto.

"Haven't you been watching in your crystal ball?"

"I've been trying to find Winnifred."

"Get yourself a new crystal," said Mallory. "She's already been rescued."

"By you?"

Mallory nodded.

"That's wonderful news!" said Mephisto enthusiastically. "Don't just stand there. Come on in!"

Mallory followed the magician from the small foyer into the living room. There was a crystal ball on a cherrywood coffee table and an oddly shaped mirror on the wall, but beyond that the room seemed unexceptional. There were a number of chairs and couches, all done in a hideous Danish modern with mauve slipcovers, a shelf of books that were so neat and dust-free that they seemed more decorative than functional, a color television with two video decks hooked up for dubbing, and a handful of paintings of big-eyed elfin children on black velvet.

"It's not exactly a palace," said Mephisto apologetically, "but the rent is reasonable, and the utilities are free."

"I had envisioned something with a little more atmosphere," replied Mallory.

"Atmosphere?"

"Illuminated manuscripts, boiling caldrons, bats hovering overhead, that sort of thing."

Mephisto laughed. "That's the Grundy's place you're describing, not mine."

"Somehow I thought all magicians' lairs would look that way," commented Mallory, walking over to the mirror and staring at his reflection.

"Well, I'm not really so much a magician as an illusionist," replied Mephisto.

"What's the difference?"

"A magician practices magic, of course."

"What does an illusionist do?"

"Card tricks, sleight of hand, pulls rabbits out of hats—you know the routine."

"But you've got a crystal ball and a magic mirror."

"Well, along with being an illusionist, I'm also an opportunist," replied Mephisto easily. "I bought the mirror at a bazaar in Marrakesh, and I stole the crystal ball from a magician in Tulsa."

"Then you're not a magician at all."

"Oh, I can do *some* magic," answered Mephisto. "Enough to get by. But what I'm really good at is card tricks." He reached into the air and pulled out a nine of hearts, waved his hand over it, and then displayed it again. All the hearts had vanished. "You look unimpressed," he noted. "It's just an audience warmer-upper. I've got much better ones."

"It's a hell of a card trick," said Mallory. "I just don't think it will do much good against the Grundy."

"The Grundy?" asked Mephisto nervously.

Mallory nodded. "He knows I'm here."

"You led him to my apartment!" said Mephisto accusingly.

"He already knows where you live," replied Mallory. "Hell, you're probably in the telephone book."

"But he didn't know that I had anything to do with you!"

"Believe me, he doesn't give a damn about you," said Mallory. "It's me he wants."

"If he wanted you, you'd be dead by now."

"He's waiting for me to lead him to the ruby."

"You know where it is?" asked Mephisto intently.

"Yes."

"Where?"

"You'll live longer if you don't know," said Mallory. He looked around the room. "How can I get in touch with him from here?"

"With the Grundy?"

"That's right."

"You'll tell him I've got nothing to do with all this?"

"I promise."

Mephisto sighed deeply. "I suppose the best way is to try using Periwinkle," he said at last.

"Who or what is Periwinkle?" asked Mallory.

"My magic mirror," explained Mephisto.

"How does it work?"

"You just tell it what you want, and hope that it's in a good mood." He grimaced. "It's rather spoiled."

"Well, I like that!" said a high-pitched, whining voice.

Mallory turned to the mirror, and saw that it had suddenly developed strangely human facial features: a broad, expressive mouth, a narrow, angular nose, and large, round, bloodshot eyes. "I stay here all day long in this cold, drafty apartment, I lie to your creditors, I help you cheat at cards, and this is the thanks I get. Rather spoiled, indeed!"

Mallory approached the mirror.

"I need to speak to the Grundy," he said.

"Oh, you do, do you?" snapped Periwinkle. "Well, *I* need an owner who has some knowledge of interior decorating, who cleans his carpets every now and then, who shows a little compassion for a mirror that has hopes and fears and desires just like anyone else!"

Mallory stared at the mirror, unable to produce an answer.

"I think it's his lack of consideration that bothers me the most," confided Periwinkle. "Do you know that he picks his toenails while he sits there drinking beer and watching wrestling matches on television?"

"Now, just a minute!" said Mephisto.

"Look!" screamed the mirror. "Now he's going to hit me!"

"I am *not* going to hit you!" said the magician wearily.

"I was *happy* in Marrakesh," whined Periwinkle. "I had respect and position, I was treated like a member of the family, I wasn't locked in a room and forgotten for days at a time." It rolled its bloodshot eyes plaintively. "Father, father," it intoned, "why hast thou forsaken me?"

"I'm sorry," said Mephisto to Mallory. "It's just going to be one of those nights."

"You think I can't do it, don't you?" said the mirror accusingly. "You think I can't contact the Grundy whenever I want!"

"Can you?" asked Mallory.

"There's no limit to what I can do," said Periwinkle. "Watch!"

Suddenly its facial features vanished and its surface became momentarily cloudy. Then it cleared, to reveal a baseball diamond.

"What the hell is that?" asked Mallory.

"The fifth game of the 1959 World Series," said Periwinkle proudly. "That's Luis Aparicio leading off first base, and Nelson Fox about to lay down a bunt."

"Impressive," admitted Mallory.

"That's nothing!" said Periwinkle enthusiastically. "Feast your eyes on this!"

The ballgame faded, to be replaced by a scene showing Humphrey Bogart and Clark Gable leading a ragtag army of Afghans into battle.

"The Man Who Would Be King," announced the mirror.

"You must be mistaken," said Mallory. "I saw that movie—it had Sean Connery and Michael Caine."

"Ah," said Periwinkle. "But this is the version John Huston *wanted* to make twenty years earlier and couldn't get funding for."

"Really?" said Mallory. "I'd like to see it someday."

"I can tell you're a man of taste and perception," said Periwinkle approvingly. "Not like the cardsharp over there. All *he* ever asks me to show are Russ Meyer movies."

"Not everybody likes artsy-fartsy movies," said Mephisto defensively. "Some of us just like a good story."

"With no clothes and lots of forty-eight-inch bosoms," said the mirror sarcastically.

"Well, it makes more sense than all those morbid Swedish films you keep asking me to watch."

"I'm just trying to broaden your horizons," explained the mirror. "We're stuck with each other for better or worse, so we might as well try to find some common ground for conversation. But no, not you. You can't take it when a mirror tries to rise above its station, to acquire a little culture, to upgrade its standard of living!" Periwinkle's face reappeared, and it rolled its eyes toward Mallory. "Do you see what I have to put up with? Is it any wonder that sometimes I get a little moody?"

"What'll it take to put you in a good enough mood to contact the Grundy?" asked Mallory.

"A little kindness, a little consideration, that's all." It paused. "By the way, did you know that you were followed here?"

"By Mürgenstürm," said Mallory, nodding his head. "I caught a glimpse of him just before I climbed down the stairs."

"What does he want?" asked Mephisto.

"What does *everyone* want?" replied Mallory ironically. "If he had half a brain, he'd get the hell out of town while the getting is good. The Grundy and his guild are both going to be hunting him at sunrise." He turned to the mirror. "I don't want to be rude, but I've still got things to do tonight. Are you going to put me through or not?"

"And I thought you were different!" sniffed Periwinkle. "I thought you were thoughtful and sensitive. I should have known better! You're all alike!" It paused. "I'll connect you," it continued petulantly. "I'll let him know exactly where you are, and I hope he does something awful to you."

Suddenly the mirror fogged over, and then the Grundy's visage appeared.

"Why have you contacted me?" asked the demon.

"I thought I'd let you know that I've already made my first checkpoint."

"You are lying. The cat-girl isn't there."

"I'm not going to give you a chance to get your hands on her," said Mallory. "I told her to make sure I was standing in front of this building at four-thirty. I don't know where she was hiding, and I don't know where she is now." He paused. "But I know where she's going to be in an hour, and if she doesn't see me, the game's over."

"I have infinite patience," said the Grundy grimly. "I can wait."

"I just wanted to make sure you don't jump the gun when I leave here. I still don't have the stone, and I'm still making my rendezvous points, so it would be self-defeating to kill me now."

The Grundy looked past Mallory to Mephisto. "You have allied yourself with the enemy," he said ominously.

"No, sir!" said Mephisto. "Not me! I just met him tonight. I swear it, Grundy!"

"*He* is a worthy adversary," continued the Grundy. "*You* are a cowardly, whimpering, incompetent, second-rate illusionist, fit to amuse guests at cocktail parties and nothing more. You thought you could oppose my goals with no risk to yourself. You were wrong!"

"No!" whined Mephisto.

"I will attend to you later," promised the Grundy. "Not for what you have done, but for what you are."

His image vanished, and suddenly Periwinkle was just an ordinary mirror again.

"See?" shrilled Mephisto. "See what you've done?"

"I didn't do anything," replied Mallory. "You joined us of your own free will."

"But I didn't know it would come to this!"

"That's a chance you took," said the detective with a shrug. "You don't go up against someone like the Grundy without taking risks. You knew that, and if you didn't know it then you should have."

"Platitudes!" screamed Mephisto. "The Grundy is going to kill me, and all I hear are platitudes!"

"He was probably bluffing," said Mallory. "After all, he let Winnifred and Eohippus go."

"What do I care about a fat old woman and an animal? It's *me* I'm worried about!"

"They're worth ten of you!" said Mallory heatedly. "They went out and faced the enemy. You hid in your apartment and talked about how brave you are."

"Well, I'm not talking now!" said Mephisto suddenly, reaching into the air and producing a wand. He pointed it at Mallory. "You've got a gun in your pocket. Take it out *very* carefully."

Mallory stared at him without moving.

"I'm not kidding, Mallory!" snapped Mephisto. He pointed the wand at a lamp, and suddenly the lamp—shade, bulb, and base—disappeared with a loud popping noise. "This isn't a toy. Now, take the gun out and drop it on the floor."

Mallory groped in his pocket for the gun and withdrew it gingerly by the barrel.

"On the floor!" repeated Mephisto.

Mallory placed the gun on the floor.

"Now slide it over to me with your foot."

Mallory did so.

"Now what?" asked the detective.

"Mürgenstürm must have given you a retainer," said the magician. "Let's have it."

The detective pulled the thick wad of bills out of his pocket and dropped them on the floor.

"You're wasting an awful lot of effort," said Mallory. "There's no way that I'm going to tell you where the ruby is."

Mephisto grinned. "I don't give a damn where it is!"

Mallory looked puzzled.

"You haven't figured it out, have you?" said Mephisto. "If I stay here the Grundy is going to kill me sooner or later, so I'm going to *your* Manhattan. The membrane will stay permeable long enough for me to get through it." He smiled triumphantly. "The Grundy won't follow me as long as the ruby's here—after all, it means a hell of a lot more to him than *I* do—and the best way to keep it here is to kill you before the Grundy can find some way to make you reveal its location to him."

"If I die, that ruby will be back in my Manhattan within an hour."

"Perhaps," said Mephisto. "But whoever takes it there won't know that I'm the one who killed you. They'll assume the Grundy did it, and they won't have any reason to come hunting for me." He paused. "I hate to do this to you, but it's your own fault for getting me involved in the first place." Suddenly he smiled. "You know, I think I may really get myself a job as a magician in Vegas after all."

"I don't know how to lay this on you," said Mallory, "but card tricks aren't exactly in demand these days."

"Then I'll work on sawing a lady in half."

"Good idea," said Mallory. "You shouldn't run through more than two or three dozen ladies before you get it right."

"I hope you enjoyed that joke," said Mephisto seriously, "because it was your last."

Chapter 16

Mallory looked desperately around the living room for some means of defending himself, but it was useless: there was nothing within his reach that he could throw at Mephisto, no loose rug that he could pull out from under the magician's feet, no piece of furniture close enough to hide behind.

"Shit!" he muttered under his breath.

"You look unhappy," gloated Mephisto.

"I am," said Mallory.

"I don't blame you. Nobody wants to die."

"It's not that," said Mallory. "Everyone dies sooner or later." He looked into Mephisto's eyes. "But I feel cheated. I was thrust into a strange world, and in six hours I solved one hell of a mystery, recovered the jewel, and found a way to hold the Grundy at bay." He shook his head. "To accomplish all that, only to be wiped out by an asshole like you . . ."

"That's it!" snarled Mephisto, pointing the wand between Mallory's eyes. "You're dead!"

"You're not making *me* a party to murder!" snapped Periwinkle.

And then, suddenly, the magician screamed in agony as an unbearably bright light struck his eyes. He reeled backward and careened off a wall, then crashed into a couch and fell heavily to the floor as his wand flew halfway across the room.

Mallory, too, was temporarily blinded. He felt his way across the living room floor until he came to Mephisto, wrapped his left hand in the magician's hair to hold his head steady, and delivered a right to the chin. He couldn't see the reaction, but he felt Mephisto's body go limp.

As his vision began returning he saw the wand lying on the floor and picked it up, then took back his money and began looking for the pistol.

"What is it, Mallory?" asked Periwinkle.

"The gun," he replied. "I can't find it. I must have kicked it under a piece of furniture when I was groping around for him."

"Don't worry about it," urged the mirror. "Just leave."

"I can't leave the gun here! He'll come right after me."

Mephisto groaned and rolled onto his side.

"If he wakes up and you're still here, he won't need the gun," said Periwinkle. "You don't know how to use the wand, and he does. He can order it to kill you."

Mephisto groaned again.

"He's coming to," said Periwinkle urgently. "Leave quickly—and hide the wand!"

"How about just breaking it?" asked Mallory, snapping the wand in half as he spoke.

"It still has potency. Take it with you, and hide it when you get the chance."

"All right," said Mallory, hurrying to the door. "And thanks."

"If you *really* want to thank me, arrange for me to be moved to a more respectable setting."

"I'll see what I can do," Mallory promised.

"Don't forget now!" yelled Periwinkle as Mallory slammed the door behind him. "You *owe* me!"

Mallory thought he could see Mürgenstürm darting into a doorway as he ran down the street, but he didn't have time to look more closely, for Mephisto, bellowing and cursing, emerged from his apartment with the pistol in his hand and fired off a couple of shots in the detective's direction.

Mallory ducked between two buildings, found that his path was open to the alley that ran behind them, crossed it, tossed the broken wand onto the roof of a garage as he raced by, and soon emerged on the next block. He could still hear the sound of gunfire, but it was a little farther away now, and he slowed his pace to a trot.

Two more blocks brought him to the end of the residential area, and he momentarily debated whether to double back to where the streets were darker or take his chances in the commercial section, where he might at least be able to find some means of defending himself.

He was still considering his options when he saw two uniformed military men entering a bar. Hoping that he might be able to beg, borrow or steal a weapon from them, he sprinted across the bright avenue and entered the bar a moment later.

As he paused, panting, just inside the doorway, he surveyed his surroundings. The walls were covered with scenes of battle, covering every American war from the Revolution right up to Vietnam. Several grim generals stared out from framed, autographed photographs, and there was also a snapshot of Teddy Roosevelt and his Rough Riders. A long bar dominated one side of the room, opposite a number of plain wooden tables and armless chairs. A jukebox played an endless series of military marches.

There were perhaps ten patrons standing at the bar, and another fifteen sitting at tables around the room. All were decked out in full military regalia, though their uniforms seemed more in keeping with an elaborate costume ball than with any army unit Mallory had ever seen.

The longer Mallory looked at them, the more he realized that something was wrong. Their heads were too round, their bodies too trim, their bearing too perfect. Finally, as one of the soldiers turned and offered him a friendly smile, he knew what had bothered him: their facial features had been painted on. There were no jutting jaws or angular noses, no ears that stuck out from the sides of the head, no hair in need of cutting—just black dots for eyes and nostrils, red lines for mouths, circles for ears, and varnished black hair that seemed to fit their heads like skin.

He looked at their hands, half-expecting to see wooden joints instead of knuckles, but all of them were wearing white gloves. Their uniforms practically glowed with epaulettes and sashes, medals and brass buttons, silver sabres and shining pistols.

"Welcome to Pinnochio's," said the bartender, who seemed as human as Mallory. "What can I give you to start the New Year off on the right foot?"

Mallory approached the end of the bar. "Whiskey'll do just fine," he said.

"You got it," said the bartender pleasantly, pouring him a glass.

"And one for yourself," added Mallory, slapping some coins down on the counter.

"Why, thank you, sir," said the bartender. "I call that mighty Christian of you!"

"Are you Pinnochio?" asked Mallory, as the bartender poured his own drink.

"Goodness, no, sir," laughed the bartender. "In point of fact, there isn't any Pinnochio. It's just a name." He paused. "I find that it makes my clientele feel more at home."

"Tell me about them," said Mallory.

"Well, as you can see for yourself, sir, they're all military men."

"They look like they're all toy soldiers."

"That, too," agreed the bartender. "They tend to stop by after midnight. I suppose that's why they're all officers; the enlisted men probably have to be back in their barracks by now." He took a sip of his drink and emitted a satisfied *"Ah!"* "Anyway," he continued, "they sit around and talk about the war until the wee small hours, and then go back to their regiments."

"What war?" asked Mallory.

The bartender shrugged. "Whichever one they're fighting."

"Do their weapons work?"

"You can't fight a war with nonfunctioning weapons," replied the bartender. "In fact, more than once I've seen a pair of them wager on who could dismantle and rebuild one of their weapons faster while blindfolded. Of course," he added, "that's strictly done with their pistols. It's pretty hard to dismantle a sword."

"I can imagine," said Mallory, wondering how to broach the subject of borrowing a pistol.

The sound of gunfire came to his ears, and a couple of the officers farther down the bar began peering out into the street.

"New Year's Eve!" complained one of the officers, a tall man with a thick gray moustache. "You'd think the bastards would have the decency to wait until sunrise!"

"Excuse me," said Mallory, moving down the bar. "But who, exactly, are you at war with?"

"That's the damndest thing about it!" complained the officer. "We don't know."

"An unknown enemy?" asked Mallory.

"He's damned well known to *someone*," replied the officer. "But nobody tells us anything." He looked at Mallory. "You're new here, aren't you?"

Mallory nodded. "My name's Mallory."

"MacMasters, sir—*Major* MacMasters," said the officer, extending his hand. "Always pleased to meet the local citizenry."

"How much action have you seen in Manhattan?" asked Mallory curiously.

"None," replied Major MacMasters. "I'm just here until my transfer request is approved and I'm sent to the front."

"Wherever that may be," said Mallory dryly.

"Not knowing who the enemy is doesn't mean that we can't harass and harry him!" said Major MacMasters defensively.

"How?"

"We know he's infiltrated our forces, so we've taken countermeasures to discourage him."

"Such as?"

"Have you ever heard of the Department of Redundancy Department?" asked Major MacMasters.

"I can't say that I have," replied Mallory. "It sounds fascinating."

"It's more than fascinating. It's damned effective!"

"What does it do?" asked Mallory.

"Maybe you should talk to the head of it." Major MacMasters gestured toward one of his companions. "Mallory," he said, as a tall, trim man approached them, "allow me to introduce you to Captain Peter Anthony Captain."

Mallory extended his hand. "Captain Captain?"

"Right," said Captain Captain, taking his hand and shaking it vigorously. "What can I do for you?"

"Tell him about the Department," said Major Mac-Masters.

"There's not all that much to tell," answered Captain Captain. He turned to Mallory. "We're in charge of all the army's red tape."

"How does that help you harass the enemy?" asked Mallory.

"You'd be surprised what you can do with a little red tape," replied Captain Captain with a smile. "Take the case of Grobinsky, for example."

"Who is Grobinksy?"

"We don't know," admitted Captain Captain. "But we know that he's not one of *us*. He's an enemy infiltrator who somehow rose to the rank of Lieutenant Colonel."

"So what did you do to him?" asked Mallory.

"We began by transferring him to Manhattan, just to see where he wanted to be reassigned. But he was a tricky son of a bitch: all he requested was a transfer to the front." He lit a small cigar. "Next, we had him fill out fifty-seven identical forms, which he then had to take to fifty-seven separate governmental offices around the city. Finally, after he had made the rounds, we tentatively approved his transfer, pending a physical examination."

"Let me guess," said Mallory. "He had to take fifty-seven of them."

"Right," said Captain Captain. "And we found that his weight varied by two pounds between the first and last of them." He smiled. "Naturally, we accused Grobinsky of being an enemy spy—six of him, anyway. The other fifty-one Grobinskys were cleared for transfer."

"So what happened?" asked the detective.

"He took six more physical exams, and since his weight

was the same on all six, the charges were dropped—but all six of him were denied transfers."

"What about the other fifty-one?"

"Each and every one of them was transferred from Manhattan to Manhattan."

"Isn't it diabolical?" grinned Major MacMasters. "The poor bastard has been locked away with acute schizophrenia for almost half a year now!"

More gunfire came to their ears.

"They're getting closer," remarked Captain Captain.

"Good!" said Major MacMasters. "All this inactivity was beginning to pall."

"Are you guys really looking for a battle?" asked Mallory.

"Absolutely!" said Major MacMasters. "When all is said and done, battling is our function in life."

"I might be able to help you out," said Mallory.

"Oh? How?"

"Well, since it's obvious that you're not going to be sent to the front, how would you feel if the front came in here?"

"You mean into Pinnochio's?" asked Captain Captain uncomprehendingly.

"Right," said Mallory. "I think there's an excellent chance that the guy doing the shooting out there is one of the enemy's most accomplished spies."

"There is?" asked Major MacMasters, his little black eyes shining with excitement.

Mallory nodded. "I have reason to believe that he's on a reconnaissance mission." He paused. "I think I can lure him in here."

"Capital!" cried Major MacMasters. Suddenly his eyes narrowed. "Why would he follow *you* in here?"

"Because he's trying to kill me."

"But you're a civilian," interjected Captain Captain. "What does he have against you?"

"I'm fighting a private little war against the Grundy," answered Mallory.

"Let me think this out," said Major MacMasters. "If you're *against* the Grundy, and this man is out to kill you . . ."

"Then he must be *with* the Grundy!" concluded Captain Captain triumphantly. "Of course we'll help you, Mallory! We may not know who the enemy is, but we know that he must be in league with the Grundy!"

"I'd prefer that you just detained this guy for a while, rather than killing him," said Mallory.

"We'll be the best judge of whether he deserves killing or not," said Major MacMasters firmly.

"Well, before you put him to the sword, you ought to know that he's got some possessions that might prove very useful to you," said Mallory.

"Such as?"

"Well, for starters, he's got a magic mirror that can give you direct access to the Grundy."

"Oh, Tactical would give a pretty penny to get their hands on something like *that!*" exclaimed Captain Captain happily. "Thanks for the information, Mallory."

"I want you to do me a favor in exchange for it," said Mallory.

"We're already saving your life," complained Major MacMasters. "What else do you want?"

"Give the mirror a nice setting," said Mallory. "Something classy. Maybe a wall of the War Room in the Pentagon."

"What difference does it make?"

"I promised it."

"You made a promise to a mirror?" asked Major MacMasters. "That's most irregular!"

"It's not a normal mirror," said Mallory, feeling distinctly foolish.

"Obviously not," agreed Major MacMasters. He considered the proposition. "All right, Mallory—we'll agree to your terms."

"And don't worry," added Captain Captain. "By the time the Department of Redundancy Department gets through with him, he won't be *worth* killing!"

"All right," said Mallory. "Get your men ready."

He took a deep breath and walked back out onto the street. There was no sign of Mephisto, and since he didn't want to get too far from Pinnochio's front door, he decided against walking up and down the street to attract the magician's attention, but instead leaned against the nearest streetlamp.

After five uneventful minutes Mallory put a cigarette in his mouth and pulled out his lighter. Then a shot rang out, and the cigarette was cut in half.

"I've got you now!" cried Mephisto, stepping out from around a corner. "Hands over your head, Mallory!"

Mallory raised his hands and started backing away from the magician.

"It was a nice try," continued Mephisto, "but you've got to get up pretty early in the morning to pull the wool over my eyes!"

"That's the stupidest metaphor I ever heard," said Mallory, still backing up toward Pinnochio's door.

"If you're so goddamned smart, how come *I've* got the gun?" laughed Mephisto.

"Dumb luck," replied Mallory.

"The world is divided into winners and losers," said Mephisto. "And the winners *make* their luck."

"If you say so," said Mallory, diving through the open door of the tavern.

"You're not getting away from me twice!" yelled Mephisto, breaking into a run.

Mallory ducked down behind a table and watched as the magician burst through the doorway, only to be instantly subdued and disarmed by Major MacMasters and his fellow officers.

"What's going on here?" bellowed Mephisto. "Let me go!"

"Looks decidedly like a Russkie to me," remarked Major MacMasters, staring at him while two men held him motionless.

"I don't know," said another. "I think he might have a trace of Arab blood."

"Definitely Slavic," offered a third. "Note the beady eyes and weak chin. Definitely an untrustworthy type."

"We'll find out soon enough," said Captain Captain, shouldering his way through the crowd. "What's your name, fella?"

"The Great Mephisto!"

"Do you capitalize the *G* in Great?"

"What the hell difference does it make?" demanded the magician.

"We need to know these things for our records," replied Captain Captain.

"I never thought about it," admitted Mephisto.

"We'll come back to that," said Captain Captain. "I'm a patient man. Now, how do you spell Mephisto in English, German, French, Italian, Spanish, Arabic, Swahili, and Serbo-Croatian?"

Mallory stood up and walked to the door.

"You'll keep him on ice for a few hours?" he asked.

"Mallory!" screamed Mephisto. "I'll kill you!"

"Shut up, you!" said Captain Captain. He turned to the detective. "I'd say it's going to take the Department at least a week just to get his name, rank, and serial number right. He'll be filling out forms for the next six months before we can even begin to process him.''

Mallory grinned, saluted him, and went back out into the street. He could still hear Mephisto's threats and curses when he was two blocks away.

Chapter
17 ————————————————————

Mallory turned north on Fifth Avenue. The street was almost deserted except for a few elephants carrying passengers and a number of street-cleaners riding rhinoceroses which pushed the slush from the broad thoroughfare with metal plows that were attached to sturdy leather harnesses.

He stopped at an all-night newsstand and purchased a paper to see if there were any coverage of Flypaper Gillespie's death, and was relieved to find that there was absolutely no mention of the leprechaun. The lead story was devoted to the capture of a foreign spy by off-duty military officers in a local tavern, but no details had been released.

He tossed the paper in a trashcan, checked his watch to make sure he was on schedule for his next checkpoint, and began walking north again.

At 38th Street he came to a huge crowd that had gathered around a trio of breakdancing gremlins, and had to step into the street to circle around them. Before he could make it back to the sidewalk he had been joined by a tall, somber-looking, bearded man in a turban and a flowing white robe.

"I'm pleased to see that such vulgar displays don't interest you, Sahib," said the man, falling into step beside him. "You strike me as a man of rare perception."

"What are you selling?" asked Mallory wearily.

"Eternal peace."

"Let me guess," said the detective. "You're an undertaker?"

The man smiled patronizingly. "I am a mystic, who has divined the answers to the great mysteries of the ages."

"Which you dispense for a small honorarium?" suggested Mallory.

"I take no money for myself!" replied the man with great dignity.

"You give these answers away for free?" said Mallory skeptically.

"Absolutely! All I ask is a small donation to cover my overhead."

"Your overhead consists of a turban," said Mallory, increasing his pace.

"Not so, Sahib!" the man corrected him. "I am the proprietor of Abdullah's Mystic Emporium."

"Never heard of it."

"It's on the next block. Perhaps you would care to stop in and join your fellow seekers after Ultimate Truth?"

"I don't think so," said Mallory.

"Have you never felt a desire to probe the eternal mysteries?" said the man persuasively.

"Like life and death?"

The man wrinkled his nose contemptuously. "We have gone beyond such simplistic questions."

"Then what the hell mysteries *do* you answer?" asked Mallory.

"Those that affect our daily lives, of course."

"Such as?"

"Why can't adults open childproof bottles?" said the

man meaningfully. "Why do elevators all arrive at the same time?" He paused to assess Mallory's reaction, then continued. "Why can you never find a taxi when it's raining?"

"They're fascinating questions," agreed Mallory. "But I think I'd rather let them remain great unsolved mysteries."

"We're also having a sale on transistor radios."

"Not interested."

"Ah, Sahib, my heart bleeds for you! You are making such a mistake!"

"Do you really want some business?" asked Mallory suddenly.

"Most certainly," the man assured him.

"There's an ugly little elf about half a block behind me."

The man looked back down the street. "I do not see him."

"He's hiding," said Mallory. "It's kind of a game we're playing. Anyway, collecting radios is one of his hobbies."

"It is?" asked the man eagerly.

Mallory nodded.

"I also happen to have some stereo headphones marked down to cost."

"Right up his alley," Mallory assured him.

The man stopped walking, bowed low, and made a gesture with his hand. "A thousand blessings upon you, Sahib!"

"My pleasure," replied Mallory with a smile.

The detective continued walking north. After another six blocks he stopped and looked behind him, and saw a green shape dart into a recessed doorway some two blocks away.

"One side, buddy!" cried a voice, and Mallory turned to see a pair of elephants plodding up the middle of Fifth Avenue, towing what looked for all the world like a basketball court. Half a dozen wildly exuberant young men sat atop each elephant, swigging beer and singing their college fight song. The elephants were turning onto a cross street, and Mallory found his way blocked as the court slowly began edging around the corner.

"What the hell is going on?" asked Mallory.

"We came, we saw, and we conquered!" yelled one of the young men triumphantly.

"What are you talking about?"

"The big game! We won 55–54 in overtime!" replied the student.

"*Anyone* can cut down the basketball net for a trophy!" cried another. "*We're* taking home the whole goddamned court!"

"Where are you guys from?" asked Mallory.

"Florida!" they chorused proudly.

"And you're going to pull the court all the way home?"

"That's right!"

"I hate to tell you this," said Mallory, "but you're going the wrong way."

"We're stopping off in St. Louis first to visit my girl friend," explained one of the young men.

"Lots of luck," said Mallory.

"Keep out of the way, or you'll need luck more than we do!"

The elephants kept pulling, and Mallory stepped into a store to wait until his path was clear again.

He found himself in a gallery which displayed some 200 very large paintings, most of them landscapes and city scenes. The quality of the work was unexceptional, and he wondered how the proprietor managed to sell enough of them to cover the overhead of a Fifth Avenue location.

"Welcome to the Reverie Travel Agency," said a friendly voice, and Mallory turned to find a well-dressed middle-aged woman approaching him. "How may I help you?"

"Travel agency?" he said, surprised. "It looks like an art gallery to me."

"A popular misconception," she agreed. "Actually, I wouldn't care to have any of these paintings hanging in *my* house. They're really not very good."

"Then why display them?" asked Mallory.

"How else would you know where you were going?" she replied.

"I don't quite follow you."

"These are our travel posters," she said.

"You should have chosen a better artist," said Mallory.

"Oh, there are better artists around, to be sure," she answered. "But there is only one Adonis Zeus."

"He's the painter?"

She nodded. "A Greek gentleman. I don't know very much about him—he doesn't like to talk about himself, although he did mention once that he didn't come from Athens. I got the distinct impression that his people were mountaineers." She paused. "Anyway, he tried to sell his paintings all over Manhattan, but every art gallery in the city turned him down. Then, about four years ago, he approached us, and we've been very happy with him."

"I can't imagine why," said Mallory honestly.

"Then let me show you," she said, walking over to a painting of a wooded landscape. "What do you think of this?"

Mallory studied the painting. "Nothing special," he said at last.

She smiled. "Then watch."

She reached into the painting and pulled her hand out a moment later holding a small dried leaf.

"Do that again," said Mallory, staring incredulously at the leaf.

"Gladly."

She reached in once more, and pulled out a small woodland flower.

"That's amazing!" exclaimed Mallory. "And anyone can just reach into one of these paintings?"

She looked amused. "You still don't understand. Anyone can take a vacation in one of these paintings."

"Really?"

She nodded, and led him past a number of paintings. "What's your fondest desire, Mr. . . . ah?"

"Mallory."

"What's your fondest desire, Mr. Mallory—Mallorca, the Greek Isles, Jamaica?" She pointed to each painting in turn. "A trip up the Amazon? A pastoral woodland? You no longer have to worry about passports and airline connections. You simply rent the painting for the length of your proposed trip, and make easy regular payments."

"And you can go anywhere?"

"Anywhere that Adonis Zeus has painted."

"Even if the place he painted never existed?" asked Mallory curiously.

She smiled. "Come with me into our Fantasy Showroom, Mr. Mallory."

He followed her through a narrow doorway.

"Not everyone is as imaginative as yourself," she said, "so we tend to display only the more popular vacation spots out front. This room is for our more adventurous clients."

She led him to a painting of a nearly naked man killing a lion with a knife. "Tarzan's Africa," she explained. She pointed to another. "Alice's Wonderland." She walked a few feet away and pointed to a painting of a cluttered Victorian room, filled with books, chemicals, and an odd assortment of trophies.

"221-B Baker Street," she announced. "A romantic

chamber of the heart, a nostalgic country of the mind, where it is always 1895."

She led him past another row of paintings. "Would you like to be lost in a harem? Have you a desire to re-animate dead tissue in your laboratory? Shoot it out with Rooster Cogburn? Raft down the Mississippi with Huck Finn and Tom Sawyer? Serve on the *Pequod* as it hunts for the White Whale? All of these trips we can arrange, and more."

"How does it work?" asked Mallory.

"Well, you can open an account if you plan to use us a minimum of three times a year. Otherwise, we'll require some form of identification for our records, and you can either pay us the full rental fee or make a deposit and subscribe to one of our payment plans."

"I meant, how does the painting work?"

"All you have to do is choose your vacation and tell us how long you plan to be away, and we'll wrap the painting and turn it over to you." She smiled. "Then you simply take the painting home, hang it on a wall, and step into it."

"How do I get out?"

"The very same way. If you plan to extend your vacation, do step out long enough to give us a call, though; we levy quite a large daily fine for overdue paintings."

"What if I wanted to take a permanent vacation?" asked Mallory.

"You mean a retirement rather than an excursion?" she asked.

He nodded. "Exactly."

"There's no problem at all, Mr. Mallory," she said. "Any of our paintings can be purchased as well as rented." She paused. "May I ask what type of retirement you had in mind?"

"I'm not sure yet," he said. "Do you mind if I look around a bit?"

"Not at all," she said pleasantly. "I'll be in the next room. When you've chosen what you want, simply bring it up to the sales desk."

"Thank you," said Mallory.

He began walking up and down the rows of paintings, passing representations of the gods carousing on Mount Olympus, Ichabod Crane fleeing from the Headless Horseman, King Arthur leading his Knights of the Round Table into battle, the Gray Lensman firing his blasters at the agents of Boskone, Winnie-the-Pooh and Piglet on a heffalump hunt, Pogo Possum and Albert the Alligator fishing in the Okefenokee Swamp, and Humphrey Bogart, Sydney Greenstreet, Peter Lorre, and Mary Astor examining the Maltese Falcon.

When he came to a painting of Captain Hook engaged in mortal combat with Peter Pan, he stopped and stared at it intently. When he found the item he was searching for aboard Hook's ship, he took the painting off the wall and carried it to the sales desk.

"An excellent choice, Mr. Mallory," said the saleswoman approvingly. "Second star to the right and straight on until morning."

"How much will it be?" he asked.

"Is this a rental or a purchase?"

"A purchase."

"The price is only two hundred dollars," she replied. "We're having a sale on children's stories this week. You've made a most fortuitous selection." She paused. "However, since you plan to retire into it, I'm afraid that payment will have to be made in full."

"I'm from out of town," he said hesitantly. "I don't know if my identification will be valid here."

"There's no problem," she assured him. "Identification

is really only necessary for rentals, not for outright purchases.''

Mallory pulled out his last two hundred-dollar bills and handed them to her.

''I'm sure you'll enjoy joining the Lost Boys, and staying young forever,'' she said with a smile. ''And, of course, you'll be meeting Princess Tiger Lily, and Tinker Bell, and Wendy and Michael and John.''

''I'm looking forward to it,'' said Mallory. ''Can you wrap it? It's still drizzling out, and I wouldn't want anything to damage it.''

''Of course,'' she said. She pulled a sheet of brown paper out from under the desk, wrapped it around the painting, and taped it together. When she was done she handed it to him. ''Thank you for your patronage, Mr. Mallory—and *do* enjoy your painting.''

''I intend to,'' he promised her.

He paused by the door and pulled his street map out of his pocket, studied it for a moment, took out a pen, circled a location, and then replaced both the pen and the map in his robe's spacious pocket. He looked out the window and, seeing that the basketball court had finally turned the corner and was on its way to St. Louis, tucked the painting under his arm and went out.

He couldn't see any sign of Mürgenstürm, so he made a production of lighting a cigarette and tying his shoelace until he finally spied the little elf half a block away. Once he was sure that Mürgenstürm had spotted him, he began walking again.

He proceeded north for a few more blocks, then turned west and began winding in and out of narrow side streets, making it difficult but not impossible for Mürgenstürm to keep shadowing him.

Finally, after leading the little elf on an incredibly intricate route for the better part of twenty minutes, he came to the Kringleman Arms, climbed the front stairs, and entered the foyer.

"Hello again," said Kris, looking up from the center-spread of a girlie magazine. "Did you ever find Flypaper Gillespie?"

Mallory nodded. "He won't be back again."

"How about the unicorn? Did you find it too?"

"Yes."

"You've been a busy boy tonight, haven't you?" said Kris with a grin.

"And I'm not through yet," replied Mallory. "How's the Kristem coming?"

Kris shrugged. "They haven't run any races since you left, so it's doing pretty much the same."

"It's still got some bugs in it?"

"A few," said the desk clerk defensively.

"You know," said Mallory thoughtfully, "what you really need is a sponsor."

"A sponsor?" repeated Kris.

Mallory nodded. "Someone who's willing to put some venture capital into a legitimate field-test of the Kristem."

"I agree," said Kris. "But where am I going to find someone like that?"

"He may be standing right in front of you," said the detective.

"You?"

"It's a possibility," replied Mallory. "But there's a condition."

"There always is," muttered Kris unhappily.

"You may not mind this one."

"Okay. What is it?"

"I'm just visiting this Manhattan. I want to know if the Kristem works in *my* Manhattan."

"So you want me to field-test it there, is that it?" asked Kris.

"Right."

"No problem," said the desk clerk happily. "Hell, the seats are more comfortable at your Aqueduct anyway." Suddenly he stared intently at Mallory. "How much money are we talking about?"

"Lots," said Mallory.

"You've got yourself a deal! When do you want me to start?"

"Soon," said the detective. "But first let's go up to Gillespie's room for a moment."

"Okay—but you're not going to find anything up there. I kind of cleaned him out after you left." He frowned. "I could kill the little bastard!"

"Oh? Why?"

"Most of the jewelry was imitation!"

"Well, no one ever said he was smart—just dishonest." Mallory saw a flash of green out of the corner of his eye. "Do you remember the way to Gillespie's room?"

"Fifteen, twelve, fourteen, thirteen," replied Kris. "Easy as pie."

"Fifteen, twelve, fourteen, thirteen," repeated Mallory. "You're sure about that?"

"I've been up there three times since you left," Kris assured him.

"All right," said the detective. "Let's go."

They took the elevator to the fifteenth floor, then climbed down to the twelfth, ascended to the fourteenth, and finally went back down to the thirteenth.

"Here we are," said Kris, opening the door.

"You really *did* clean him out, didn't you?" remarked Mallory, inspecting the nearly barren room. The magazines, videotapes, and almost all of the booty had been removed. Very little remained except for Gillespie's broken-down furniture, his doll's bed, his cooking utensils, fifty unmatched argyle socks, and a few hundred balls of string.

"I figured that I was just taking his overdue rent out in trade," replied Kris with a smile.

"And you're doubtless holding it in trust until Nick the Saint asks for it," said Mallory dryly.

"You got it," acknowledged Kris.

Mallory began unwrapping the painting.

"What's that?" asked the desk clerk.

"What does it look like?"

"Like some no-talent kid traced a comic book onto a piece of canvas," said Kris.

Mallory held the painting up to the light. "It does, doesn't it?" he agreed.

"Now, if you *really* want to see some art," said Kris confidentially, "come back down to the lobby and I'll show you some of the magazines I confiscated from up here."

"Perhaps later," said Mallory, searching the walls until he found a nail protruding from the plaster. "This looks like the perfect place for it," he announced, hanging the painting on the nail.

"If you say so," replied Kris. "I still don't know what you see in it, though."

"It has hidden qualities," said Mallory. "Maybe it'll grow on you."

"Like a fungus," said Kris with conviction. He looked at the detective curiously. "Is this all you came up here for—to hang that painting on the wall?"

"And to wait," replied Mallory.

"For who?"

"For whoever comes in the door next," said Mallory. He walked over to the coffeepot. "Would you care for some coffee?"

"No, thanks. I live on that stuff all night."

"Well, if you've no objections, I'll have some," he said, picking up the pot and filling his New York Mets mug. "After all, it's my goddamned cup." He was just preparing to take a sip when the door opened and Mürgenstürm, a huge revolver in his hands, entered the room.

"All right, John Justin!" he said. "Where is it?"

"Where is what?" asked Mallory innocently.

"You know what I want! Where's the ruby?"

"Ruby?" said Mallory. "I haven't seen any ruby around here." He turned to Kris. "Have you seen one?"

"I don't know what you're talking about," said Kris, backing away from the elf.

"It will be daylight in less than an hour!" snapped Mürgenstürm. "If I don't get my hands on it, I'll die!"

"That's hardly my fault," replied Mallory. "You had ample time to get out of town."

"They would have found me," said the elf with conviction. "If I have to die, I won't die alone—I promise you that, John Justin!" He took a step forward. "Now, where is it?"

"You'd really kill me, wouldn't you?" said Mallory.

"I have no choice."

Mallory sighed. "All right," he said. "I'll show you."

"I'm glad we understand each other," said Mürgenstürm. "Where is it?"

"In there," said Mallory, pointing to the painting.

"In *there?*" repeated Mürgenstürm incredulously.

"In Captain Hook's treasure chest," explained Mallory. "I thought it would be safe until I decided to come back for it."

Mürgenstürm's eyes narrowed. "Smart, John Justin— very smart." He smiled triumphantly. "But I guess I'm just a little bit smarter!"

"Maybe so," agreed Mallory. "And maybe not."

"What are you talking about?"

"The Grundy's probably been watching every move

either of us have made since we left the warehouse," said Mallory. "You don't really think he's going to let you enter the painting, do you?"

Mürgenstürm closed his eyes in intense concentration for a moment, then opened them. "I've frozen Time for him again. He'll be no threat for at least ninety seconds."

"He's going to be one mad demon when he snaps out of it," said Mallory.

"By then I'll be in your Manhattan with the ruby," said Mürgenstürm. "Stand over by the wall there, next to your friend."

Mallory moved where the elf indicated.

"I'm taking my gun with me," said Mürgenstürm. "If you try to follow me, I won't hesitate to use it."

"I believe you," said Mallory.

"You'd better," said Mürgenstürm. He dragged a chair over to the painting, climbed up on it, and entered the world of Peter Pan.

Mallory immediately walked along the wall to the corner of the room, approached the painting cautiously, and, when he reached it, quickly turned it to the wall.

"Charm's no substitute for brains, either," he said with a grim smile.

"What the hell is going on?" demanded Kris.

"I haven't got time to explain," said Mallory. "We've got less than a minute before the Grundy snaps out of it and starts watching me again. Do you still want to field-test the Kristem?"

"Hell, yes."

"All right," said the detective, pulling his street map out of his pocket. "Take Fourth Avenue until you come to this little side street—I've marked it on the map."

"And then what?"

"You'll find two guys sitting outside playing chess."

"In this weather, at six in the morning?" said Kris dubiously.

"That game seems to be the one constant in an ever-changing universe," said Mallory. "That's why I chose it." He stared intently at the desk clerk. "Now, listen carefully, because I haven't got time to repeat it. There will be a saltshaker on white's queen's bishop five. Open it up and empty the salt out. Assuming that a friend named Felina followed my orders, at the bottom of it you'll find the biggest ruby you ever saw. Take it to my Manhattan immediately, pawn it or sell it, and you'll have sufficient operating capital for the Kristem. Do you understand?"

"Yes, but—"

"No buts," said Mallory, checking his watch. "Wait until I've been gone for a few minutes before you go after it—and if you want to live long enough to test the Kristem, don't mention the ruby to *anyone!*"

"Whatever you say."

"That's what I say. Now, let's go. He'll be awake in another ten seconds."

They walked to the door, climbed down the stairs to the twelfth floor, and took the ancient elevator down to the first floor.

"By the way," asked Kris as Mallory was about to leave, "what'll happen to the elf?"

"I guess he'll have to learn how to get along with Captain Hook and Mister Smee until someone flips the painting over," said Mallory with a smile.

"But no one has any reason ever to go up there again," the desk clerk pointed out.

"Well," replied Mallory, "that's the chance you take when you become a pirate."

Kris laughed. "Care for a drink before you leave?"

"No, thanks," said Mallory. "I've still got a couple of things to do before sunrise."

"Thanks for stopping by," said Kris. "It's been an interesting night."

"My pleasure," said Mallory. Then, for the Grundy's benefit, he added, "We'll talk more about my funding the Kristem the next time I stop by."

Before Kris could answer, Mallory walked out the door and began strolling down the wet pavement, feeling very pleased with himself as the early morning sky began changing from black to gray.

Chapter
18 ————————————————————

Since he had no intention of arriving at his destination before Kris had time to retrieve the ruby, Mallory walked at a leisurely pace, stopping to look into the more interesting store windows he passed, purchasing a fresh pack of cigarettes, browsing over the paperback rack in front of a newsstand. When he reached the Broadway area he stopped at a pastry shop and selected a dozen doughnuts of various shapes and flavors, then went next door and bought a pound of ground coffee.

He checked his watch again, decided that he had given Kris more than enough time to pick up the precious stone and make his way through the membrane, and increased his pace. Eight minutes later he reached Mystic Place, and a moment later he descended the stairs to Mephisto's front door.

It was locked, but he had little difficulty jimmying it with a credit card. He checked the wall, and discovered that Captain Captain hadn't wasted any time sending a crew over for Periwinkle.

Mallory went into the kitchen, put the doughnuts in the

refrigerator, and made up a pot of coffee. Then he returned to the living room, sat down on an uncomfortable Danish modern couch, picked up a telephone from an equally ugly end table, and dialed Information. They gave him the number of the Morbidium, and a moment later he was speaking to Winnifred Carruthers.

"Mallory!" she exclaimed. "Are you all right?"

"I'm just fine," he assured her. "How about you?"

"We made it home without any trouble."

"Good," said Mallory. "How's Eohippus?"

"His wounds are healing. We've made a stall for him out of a children's casket that we filled with straw. He says he likes it here, and we've invited him to stay."

"I'm glad to hear it."

"I'm just bursting with questions," she continued. "What happened to the ruby, and how did you escape from that terrible place?"

"Tell you what," said Mallory. "I'm about half an hour's walk from the Morbidium. Why don't you come by and I'll tell you all about it over coffee and doughnuts?"

"I'd love to," said Winnifred. "Where are you?"

"7 Mystic Place. I'll leave the door unlocked."

"Isn't that Mephisto's address?"

"I've sublet the apartment from him," said Mallory.

"Oh?" said Winnifred. "What's happened to him?"

"He was called away rather suddenly on official government business," said Mallory with a smile. "I don't think he'll be needing the apartment for the next couple of years."

"Well, I'd best hang up and start on over," said Winnifred. "I'll see you in ten minutes."

"I said half an hour."

"I thought I'd catch a horse-drawn carriage," she explained. "They tend to line up at the end of my street; it should be no trouble to get one at this time of night."

"Then get it twenty minutes from now," said Mallory.

"Is something wrong?"

"No," he answered. "But there's one last thing I have to do, and I don't want you around for it."

"Will you be all right?"

"Probably."

"It's got something to do with the Grundy, hasn't it?" she said.

"Yes."

"Be careful, Mallory."

"I'll do my best," he replied. "See you in half an hour."

He hung up the phone, then looked around the room again, searching for some way of contacting the Grundy. His gaze came to rest on the crystal ball, and finally he picked it up and examined it. As he turned it over, searching in vain for some sort of control, snow seemed to fall out of the sky onto a pastoral setting, and when he set it back down it seemed intent on showing him an old Marx Brothers movie.

Finally he sighed, picked up the phone, and asked Information for the Grundy's number. After an initial shriek of horror, he was informed that the Grundy's number was unlisted.

"What the hell," he muttered to himself, staring at the dial. "You don't hit the moon if you don't shoot for it." Then, carefully, he dialed G-R-U-N-D-Y.

Instantly there was a puff of reddish smoke, and the Grundy stood before Mallory in all his demonic glory.

"Son of a bitch!" said Mallory. "It actually worked."

"I saw you trying to make contact with me, and decided to accommodate you," said the Grundy. He stared at the detective, his eyes glowing balefully. "The membrane has hardened, Mallory. You have lost your last chance to escape."

"You've lost even more than that," said Mallory, leaning back on the couch. "The war's over, Grundy."

"What are you talking about?" demanded the demon ominously.

"The stone's in *my* Manhattan, where neither you nor I can get at it."

"I don't believe you."

"Believe whatever you want," said Mallory with a shrug. "But you'll never see the ruby again. You're going to have to be satisfied with *this* world."

"Nobody would willingly relinquish an object of such power," said the Grundy with conviction. "You still have it, Mallory, and this attempt to convince me that a man of your qualities would give it up is unworthy of you."

"If you say so."

"I do," said the Grundy. "But you have still blundered. You had the opportunity to walk away in safety, and you ignored it. Now I shall watch and wait, and when you reach for the ruby I shall strike. However brief the remainder of your life may be, you will spend it here.'"

"There are worse places to be," replied Mallory. "Hell, in one night I learned the ground rules, found the ruby, and managed to keep it from you. Who knows? In a week's time, I could own this place."

"This Manhattan is not the utopia you think it is, Mallory," said the demon.

"Perhaps not," acknowledged Mallory. "But on the other hand, it's no worse than the one I left."

"You think not?" thundered the Grundy. "Then keep your eyes on the crystal!"

He made a gesture with his hand, and suddenly Mallory could see the intersection of Fifth Avenue and 57th Street in Mephisto's crystal ball. A number of pedestrians were standing at the corner, waiting for the light to change.

"The policeman, I think," said the Grundy, pointing an

arrow-shaped finger toward a cop who was directing traffic. Suddenly the policeman clutched his chest and collapsed. "And the old woman," added the Grundy. He pointed again, and an elderly lady was jostled and fell into the street, right in front of a passing carriage.

The Grundy turned to Mallory, a malevolent smile on his thin lips. "Do you know what I have done this night in your world and mine—the grief I have caused, the lives I have taken, the terrible toll I have extracted in pain and misery?"

"I can imagine," said the detective.

"I doubt it," said the Grundy contemptuously. "Watch again, Mallory."

A large office building appeared in the crystal ball. The Grundy snapped his fingers, and suddenly a flame shot up from his forefinger. He lowered his head to it and blew gently—and the office building immediately turned into a fiery inferno.

"What have you in your arsenal to match such power, Mallory?" demanded the Grundy.

"Nothing yet," admitted Mallory. "But in one night I've cut your domain in half." He paused. "Who knows? Someday I may find a way to do the same to you."

"Then perhaps I should kill you now."

"Perhaps," agreed Mallory. "But you won't, not as long as you think I've got the ruby."

"True," said the Grundy. "But I shall vent my anger upon the city. It will be visited with death and decay, and you will be the cause of it."

"I thought your function was to bring order to it, not chaos."

"There is an almost perfect order in destruction."

Mallory shook his head. "Why? Because you destroy things in a pleasing pattern? We've got pattern killers where I come from, too—and when we catch them we lock them away, not in jails, but in insane asylums.''

The Grundy laughed. "In point of fact, you lock them away for a period of weeks or months, and then turn them back out on the streets to kill again.'' He stared at Mallory. "If you truly wish your actions to be meaningful, come over to my side and join me in my unending battle against the Opponent.''

"I'll choose my own enemies, if it's all the same to you.''

"There is a difference between an enemy and an irritant,'' said the demon. "You are an irritant, nothing more.''

"Don't bet on it,'' said Mallory. "Every world's got ground rules, even this one. And someday, when I learn enough of them, I may come after you.''

"Are you threatening me?'' roared the Grundy.

"I would never presume to threaten the most powerful demon around,'' said Mallory. "Let's just say that I'm using this crystal ball to predict the future.''

"Then look deeply into it and tell me what you see!''

And suddenly Mallory could see his own image in the ball, his skin corrupted by some hideous disease, his body broken and mangled, his eyes filled with pain and defeat.

"That is what the future holds for you, and nothing else!'' promised the demon.

Mallory looked up from the crystal ball and forced himself to smile nonchalantly. "That's even more impressive than one of Mephisto's card tricks.''

Suddenly the Grundy grinned. "The Opponent has picked an excellent tool!'' he said approvingly. "I knew it the first time I saw you!''

"Then I passed the exam?''

"The *first* one,'' acknowledged the Grundy. "Each succeeding one will be harder.''

"Tell me something," said Mallory. "Did you really kill those people and set that building on fire?"

The Grundy nodded. "Certainly. I draw my sustenance from pain and misery."

"I'll have to do my best to stop you."

"I expect no less of you, Mallory—but you will lose in the end, as everybody loses to Death in the end."

"Then I'll have to try to win the battles, and let the war take care of itself," replied Mallory.

"And *I* shall watch you day and night," promised the Grundy, "and when you finally attempt to retrieve the ruby, as sooner or later you must, I shall strike."

"I told you—the stone is gone."

"And *I* told *you* that no one would ever willingly let it out of his possession—especially not a man like you."

"Your nature has given you tunnel vision, Grundy," said Mallory. "You can't imagine yourself ever giving it away, so you can't conceive of anyone else doing it either, not even to save an entire world."

"And no one would."

Mallory shrugged. "If you say so."

"Let me leave you with this thought, Mallory," said the Grundy. "Larkspur lived for less than seven decades."

"So?"

"So war and slavery, repression and torture, bigotry and hatred, the Crusades, the Inquisition, the prison at Andersonville, and the Black Hole of Calcutta—all were invented by *your* race, not *mine*." He paused. "Do you really think that denying me the ruby will turn your world into Nirvana?"

"Maybe you're right," said Mallory. "Maybe there are no Nirvanas. But I think they deserve the right to fail without your help."

"Be grateful that I know you're lying, Mallory," said the Grundy. "If you ever convinced me that you were

telling the truth, I would have no reason to let you live."
He paused. "My patience, like my age, is infinite. Eventually you will make your move, and then the image you
saw in the crystal will become your reality."

The demon made a gesture with his hand, and suddenly
there was another puff of reddish smoke and a popping
sound as the air rushed into the place he had just vacated.

Mallory sat motionless for several moments, then sighed,
got to his feet, and went into the kitchen to check on the
coffee.

Chapter
19 ————————————————————

Dawn

"Mallory!" shouted Winnifred from the apartment doorway. "Are you all right?"

Mallory came out of the kitchen to greet her. "Couldn't be better," he replied. "Come on in and have a doughnut."

She entered the apartment cautiously. "Has the Grundy been here?"

"Been and gone," said Mallory. He led her to the kitchen table and pulled out a chair for her. "What do you like in your coffee?"

"Just cream." She stirred restlessly. "Damn it, man—tell me what happened!"

Mallory smiled. "We agreed to disagree."

"And the ruby?"

"It's back in my world."

Suddenly she looked around apprehensively. "Perhaps we shouldn't discuss it. He might be listening."

"It's all right," said Mallory. "He doesn't believe me anyway." He handed her a cup of coffee, then poured one for himself. "Damn, but I miss my New York Mets mug!"

"Is it in your Manhattan?" she asked.

"As a matter of fact, it's in Flypaper Gillespie's room," he replied.

"Then why not go get it if you like it so much?"

"I suppose I will, in three or four years or so," answered Mallory.

He brought the doughnuts over to the table and offered one to Winnifred.

"Thank you, Mallory," she said, taking it from him and dunking it in her coffee.

"I'm afraid I've eaten about half of them already," he apologized. "But I haven't had a meal since Mürgenstürm brought me here."

"Which brings up an interesting question," said Winnifred. "Now that you seem to be here permanently, what do you plan to do with your life?"

"The same thing I've been doing."

She shook her head. "Things are different here. You've got the Grundy to contend with, and no end of leprechauns, elves, goblins, and the like. Your methods may not work."

Mallory smiled. "They've worked pretty well so far. And the criminals I find here can't be any worse than the deadbeats and pushers and wife-beaters I used to deal with."

"Perhaps," she admitted. "But even our system of jurisprudence is different."

"In a way, it's better," he replied thoughtfully. "At least Gillespie isn't going to commit any more crimes, and my friend Mürgenstürm isn't in a position to plea-bargain himself back onto the street before sunrise." He nodded approvingly. "Yeah, I think I can function here just fine."

"I hope you're right," said Winnifred.

"There's one thing I *do* need, though," he said tentatively.

"Oh? And what is that?"

"A partner."

"You're looking at me in a very odd way, Mallory," she said.

"You want to get out of the Morbidium, don't you?" he replied. "How does the Mallory and Carruthers Detective Agency sound to you?"

"Do you mean it?" she said, her eyes alight with excitement.

"Discreet Confidential Investigations," he continued. "A Subsidiary of Grundy and Opponent, Limited."

"What was that?" she asked abruptly.

He smiled. "A private joke." He leaned forward. "Well, how about it? Are you in?"

"Of course I'm in!" she replied. "Last night was the first time I've felt really alive in fifteen years!"

"Good," said Mallory. "That's settled." He paused. "We might as well work right out of the apartment. There's no sense renting an office until we stockpile a little money."

"It sounds good to me," said Winnifred, finishing her coffee. "Don't be so stingy with those doughnuts, Mallory."

"Where's your little horse?" purred a familiar voice, and they turned to see Felina standing in the kitchen doorway.

"What are you doing here?" asked Mallory.

"I'm hungry," she said, walking over and rubbing her hip against him. She turned to Winnifred with an innocent smile. "Where's Eohippus?"

"He's at home," Winnifred said coldly. "Have a doughnut."

Felina leaped easily to the top of the refrigerator. "I'd rather have milk," she said, licking her forearm.

Mallory stared at her for a moment, then sighed, opened the refrigerator, and poured her a tall glass of milk.

"What the hell," he said, taking his seat again. "I suppose every business ought to have an office cat."

"What we really ought to have are clients, now that we're in business," said Winnifred, casting a single glance of distaste at Felina and then ignoring her.

"Oh, I don't think there will be any great shortage of work in the days to come," said Mallory.

"I can't tell you how glad I am to get back into harness," said Winnifred enthusiastically. "After all those years of inactivity, it feels like heaven."

"Well," replied Mallory with a contented sigh as the first rays of sunlight peeked in through a kitchen window, "it'll have to do until Nirvana comes along."

APPENDIX A

Complete racing record of Eohippus

Age	Starts	1st	2nd	3rd	Earnings
2	8	0	0	2	$1,310.00
3	14	0	1	0	900.00
4	7	0	0	0	———
5	19	0	0	1	550.00
6	10	0	0	0	———
	58	0	1	3	$2,760.00

APPENDIX B

Stalking the Unicorn with Gun and Camera

*Monograph by Colonel Winnifred Carruthers,
published by The Blood Sports Club, Ltd.*

When she got to within 200 yards of the herd of Southern Savannah unicorns she had been tracking for four days, Rheela of the Seven Stars made her obeisance to Quatr Mane, God of the Hunt, then donned the Amulet of Kobassen, tested the breeze to make sure that she was still downwind of the herd, and began approaching them, camera in hand.

But Rheela of the Seven Stars had made one mistake—a mistake of *carelessness*—and thirty seconds later she was dead, brutally impaled upon the horn of a bull unicorn.

Hotack the Beastslayer cautiously made his way up the lower slopes of the Mountain of the Nameless One. He was a skilled tracker, a fearless hunter, and a crack shot.

He picked out the trophy he wanted, got the beast within his sights, and hurled his killing club. It flew straight and true to its mark.

And yet, less than a minute later, Hotack, his left leg badly gored, was barely able to pull himself to safety in the branches of a nearby Rainbow Tree. He, too, had made a mistake—a mistake of *ignorance*.

Bort the Pure had had a successful safari. He had taken three chimeras, a gorgon, and a beautifully matched pair of gryphons. While his trolls were skinning the gorgon he spotted a unicorn sporting what looked like a record horn and, weapon in hand, he began pursuing it. The terrain gradually changed, and suddenly Bort found himself in shoulder-high kraken grass. Undaunted, he followed the trail into the dense vegetation.

But Bort the Pure, too, had made a mistake—a mistake of *foolishness*. His trolls found what very little remained of him some six hours later.

Carelessness, ignorance, foolishness—together they account for more deaths among unicorn hunters than all other factors combined.

Take our examples, for instance. All three hunters—Rheela, Hotack, and Bort—were experienced safari hands. They were used to extremes of temperature and terrain; they didn't object to finding insects in their ale or banshees in their tents; they knew they were going after deadly game and took all reasonable precautions before setting out.

And yet two of them died, and the third was badly maimed.

Let's examine their mistakes, and see what we can learn from them.

Rheela of the Seven Stars assimilated everything her

personal wizard could tell her about unicorns, purchased the very finest photographic equipment, hired a native guide who had been on many unicorn hunts, and had a local witch doctor bless her Amulet of Kobassen. And yet, when the charge came, the amulet was of no use to her, for she had failed to properly identify the particular sub-species of unicorn before her—and as I am continually pointing out during my lecture tours, the Amulet of Kobassen is potent only against the rare and almost-extinct Forest unicorn. Against the Southern Savannah unicorn, the *only* effective charm is the Talisman of Triconis. *Carelessness.*

Hotack the Beastslayer, on the other hand, disdained all forms of supernatural protection. To him, the essence of the hunt was to pit himself in physical combat against his chosen prey. His killing club, a beautifully wrought and finely balanced instrument of destruction, had brought down simurghs, humbabas, and even a dreaded wooly hydra. He elected to go for a head shot, and the club flew to within a millimeter of where he had aimed it. But he hadn't counted on the unicorn's phenomenal sense of smell, nor the speed with which these surly brutes can move. Alerted to Hotack's presence, the unicorn turned its head to seek out its predator—and the killing club bounced harmlessly off its horn. Had Hotack spoken to almost any old-time unicorn hunter, he would have known that head shots are almost impossible, and would have gone for a crippling knee shot instead. *Ignorance.*

Bort the Pure was aware of the unique advantages accruing to a virgin who hunts the wild unicorn, and so had practiced sexual abstinence since he was old enough to know what the term meant. And yet he naively believed that because his virginity allowed him to approach the unicorn more easily than other hunters, the unicorn would somehow become placid and make no attempt to defend itself—and so he followed a vicious animal that was compelled to let him approach it, and entered a patch of high grass that allowed him no maneuvering room during the inevitable charge. *Foolishness*.

Every year hundreds of hopeful hunters go out in search of the unicorn, and every year all but a handful come back empty-handed—if they come back at all. And yet the unicorn *can* be safely stalked and successfully hunted, if only the stalkers and hunters will take the time to study their quarry.

When all is said and done, the unicorn is a relatively docile beast (except when enraged). It is a creature of habit, and once those habits have been learned by the hopeful photographer or trophy hunter, bringing home that picture or that horn is really no more dangerous than, say, slaying an Eight-Forked Dragon—and it's certainly easier than lassoing wild minotaurs, a sport that has become all the rage these days among the smart set on the Platinum Plains.

However, before you can photograph or kill a unicorn, you have to find it—and by far the easiest way to make contact with a unicorn herd is to follow the families of smerps that track the great game migrations. The smerps, of course, have no natural enemies except for the rafsheen and the zumakim, and consequently will allow a human (or preternatural) being to approach them quite closely.

A word of warning about the smerp: with its long ears and cute, fuzzy body, it resembles nothing more than an oversized rabbit—but calling a smerp a rabbit doesn't make it one, and you would be ill-advised to underestimate the strength of these nasty little scavengers. Although they generally hunt in packs of from ten to twenty, I have more than once seen a single smerp, its aura glowing with savage strength, pull down a half-grown unicorn. Smerps are poor eating, their pelts are worthless because of the difficulty of curing and tanning the auras, and they make pretty unimpressive trophies unless you can come up with one possessing a truly magnificent set of ears—in fact, in many areas they're still classified as vermin—but the wise unicorn hunter can save himself a lot of time and effort by simply letting the smerps lead him to his prey.

With the onset of poaching, the legendary unicorn herds numbering upward of a thousand members no longer exist, and you'll find that the typical herd today consists of from fifty to seventy-five individuals. The days when a photographer, safe and secure in a blind by a waterhole, could preserve on film an endless stream of the brutes coming down to drink are gone forever—and it is absolutely shocking to contemplate the number of unicorns that have died simply so their horns could be sold on the black market. In fact, I find it appalling that anyone in this enlightened day and age still believes that a powdered unicorn horn can act as an aphrodisiac.

(Indeed, as any magus can tell you, you treat the unicorn horn with essence of gracch and then boil it slowly in a solution of sphinx blood. Now, *that's* an aphrodisiac!)

But I digress.

The unicorn, being a non-discriminating browser that is equally content to feed upon grasses, leaves, fruits, and an occasional small fern tree, occurs in a wide variety of habitats, often in the company of grazers such as centaurs and ~~pégásúsés~~ pégásíṁ the pegasus.

Once you have spotted the unicorn herd, it must be approached with great care and caution. The unicorn may have poor eyesight, and its sense of hearing may not be much better, but it has an excellent sense of smell and an absolutely awesome sense of *grimsch*, about which so much has been written that there is no point in my belaboring the subject yet again.

If you are on a camera safari, I would strongly advise against trying to get closer than 100 yards to even a solitary beast—that sense of *grimsch* again—and most of the photographers I know swear by an 85/350mm automatic-focus zoom lens, providing, of course, that it has been blessed by a Warlock of the Third Order. If you haven't got the shots you want by sunset, my best advice is to pack it in for the day and return the next morning. Flash photography is possible, of course, but it does tend to attract golem and other even more bothersome nocturnal predators.

One final note to the camera buff: for reasons our alchemists have not yet determined, no unicorn has ever been photographed with normal emulsified film of any speed, so make absolutely sure that you use one of the more popular infrared brands. It would be a shame to spend weeks on safari, paying for your guide, cook, and trolls, only to come away with a series of photos of the forest that you thought was merely the background to your pictures.

As for hunting the brutes, the main thing to remember is that they are as close to you as you are to them. For this reason, while I don't disdain blood sacrifices, amulets, talismans, and blessings, all of which have their proper places, I for one always feel more confident with a .550 Nitro Express in my hands. A little extra stopping power can give a hunter quite a feeling of security.

You'll want a bull unicorn, of course; they tend to have more spectacular horns than the cows—and by the time a bull's horn is long enough to be worth taking, he's probably too old to be in the herd's breeding program anyway.

The head shot, for reasons explained earlier, is never a wise option. And unless your wizard teaches you the Rune of Mamhotet, thus enabling you to approach close enough to pour salt on the beast's tail and thereby pin him to the spot where he's standing, I recommend the heart shot (either heart will do—and if you have a double-barreled gun, you might try to hit both of them, just to be on the safe side).

If you have the bad fortune to merely wound the beast, he'll immediately make off for the trees or the high grass, which puts you at an enormous disadvantage. Some hunters, faced with such a situation, simply stand back and allow the smerps to finish the job for them—after all, smerps rarely devour the horns unless they're completely famished—but this is hardly sporting. The decent, honorable hunter, well aware of the unwritten rules of blood sports, will go after the unicorn himself.

The trick, of course, is to meet him on fairly open terrain. Once the unicorn lowers his head to charge, he's virtually blind, and all you need do is dance nimbly out of his way and take another shot at him—or, if you are not in possession of the Rune of Mamhotet, this would be an ideal time to get out that salt and try to sprinkle some on his tail as he races by.

When the unicorn dictates the rules of the game, you've got a much more serious situation. He'll usually double back and lie in the tall grasses beside his spoor, waiting for you to pass by, and then attempt to gore you from behind.

It is at this time that the hunter must have all his wits about him. Probably the best sign to look for is the presence of Fire-Breathing Dragonflies. These noxious little insects frequently live in symbiosis with the unicorn, cleansing his ears of parasites, and their presence usually means that the unicorn isn't far off. Yet another sign that your prey is nearby will be the flocks of hungry harpies circling overhead, waiting to swoop down and feed upon the remains of your kill; and, of course, the surest sign of all is when you hear a grunt of rage and find yourself staring into the bloodshot, beady little eyes of a wounded bull unicorn from a distance of ten feet or less. It's moments like this that make you feel truly alive, especially when you suddenly realize that it isn't necessarily a permanent condition.

All right. Let us assume that your hunt is successful. What then?

Well, your trolls will skin the beast, of course, and take special care in removing and preserving the horn. If they've been properly trained they'll also turn the pelt into a rug, the hooves into ashtrays, the teeth into a necklace, the tail into a flyswatter, and the scrotum into a tobacco pouch. My own feeling is that you should settle for nothing less, since it goes a long way toward showing the bleeding-heart preservationists that a unicorn can supply the hunter with a lot more than just a few minutes of pleasurable sport and a horn.

And while I'm on the subject of what the unicorn can supply, let me strongly suggest that you would be missing a truly memorable experience if you were to come home from safari without having eaten unicorn meat at least once. There's nothing quite like unicorn cooked over an open campfire to top off a successful hunt. (And do remember to leave something out for the smerps, or they might well decide that hunter is every bit as tasty as unicorn.)

So get out those amulets and talismans, visit those wizards and warlocks, pack those cameras and weapons— and good hunting to you!

APPENDIX C

Report from the Bureau of Beleaguered Persons

NAME OF PRESUMED BELEAGUERED PERSON: Winnifred Carruthers

REPORTED BY: John Justin Mallory

DATE OF REPORT: January 1

ACTION TAKEN: Due to understaffing, search procedures were not instituted until January 5, at which time inquiries were made at Harry's Bar and Grill (see attached) and Crazy Willie's Neighborhood Tavern (see attached). Since this was done on consecutive lunch hours, voucher for overtime pay is appended, as is invoice for expenses incurred ($82.75). None of our regular informants at either location has any knowledge of the subject.

RECOMMENDATION: It is this department's considered opinion that if Winnifred Carruthers is still alive, she is in all likelihood no longer Beleaguered, and we have accordingly passed her file on to the Bureau of Missing Persons.

APPENDIX D

Formal Inquiry into the Activities of the Great Mephisto

The Great Mephisto was taken into custody for questioning at Pinnochio's in the early morning hours of January 1. The fifty-seven preliminary seventy-two-page forms that he filled out during the ensuing two months were rejected, as he had not capitalized the *G* in "Great," and it took him nine more weeks to fill them out properly. Three more months were spent on his basic physical exam, as his pulse rate differed by as much as two percent from one reading to the next. He was then required to sign his name 20,000 times, as our handwriting experts noticed certain slight variations in his signature on the preliminary forms.

At present he has been in custody for 287 days, and formal questioning is expected to begin sometime within the next six to eight months.

I am pleased to report that the inquiry is progressing smoothly, and that we are actually seventeen days ahead of schedule.

Respectfully submitted by
Captain P. Captain,
Department of Redundancy Department

APPENDIX E

The Game (1937 to present)

White:	Black:
1. P—Q4	1. P—KB4
2. P—K4	2. P × P
3. Kt—QB3	3. Kt—KB3
4. P—KB3	4. P × P
5. Kt × P	5. P—KKt3
6. B—KB4	6. B—Kt2
7. Q—Q2	7. O—O

8.	B—R6	8.	P—Q4
9.	B × B	9.	K × B
10.	O—O—O	10.	B—B4
11.	B—Q3	11.	B × B
12.	Q × B	12.	Kt—B3
13.	QR—K1	13.	Q—Q3
14.	K—Kt1	14.	P—QR3
15.	R—K2	15.	QR—K1
16.	KR—K1	16.	P—K3
17.	Kt—K5	17.	Kt—Q2
18.	Q—Next Table (!)	18.	Saltshaker—QB5

APPENDIX F

Results of the Kristem's Initial Field-Test

January 1: Ruby sold for $225,000 to dealer in "estate jewelry" who wishes to remain anonymous.

January 2: $30,000 wagered on Can't Miss at 17-to-1. Ran ninth. Remaining bankroll: $195,000.

January 3: $25,000 wagered on Alltheway at 25-to-1. Ran fourth. Remaining bankroll: $170,000.

January 3: $50,000 wagered on Sure Shot at 9-to-5. Won, disqualified, and placed second. Remaining bankroll: $120,000.

January 4: $50,000 wagered on Daily Double combination of Safe As Houses and Big Price. Ran eighth and fifth, respectively. Remaining bankroll: $70,000.

January 5: $40,000 wagered on Victory Lane at 6-to-1. Broke leg, did not finish. Remaining bankroll: $30,000.

January 8: $30,000 wagered on Flyaway at 70-to-1. Still running. Remaining bankroll: Zero.